I0563680

# THE MERRY PAST

THE *PROMENADE* AT *CARLISLE HOUSE.*

*(After a Mezzotint by J. R. Smith, published by him 24th Jany. 1781, to represent the Fashions derived from Foreign.)*

# THE MERRY PAST

BY

RALPH NEVILL

LONDON

DUCKWORTH & CO.

3 HENRIETTA STREET, COVENT GARDEN

1909

*All Rights Reserved*

Le temps qui change tout, change aussi nos humeurs :
Chaque age a ses plaisirs, son esprit et ses mœurs.

# THE MERRY PAST

## I

HE who studies the records of the eighteenth
century, and contrasts the life of the past with
that of to-day, is of necessity impressed with the vast
changes that have, within the last hundred and fifty
years, entirely transformed England in its life, habits,
appearance, and, above all, in its traditional characteristics.

There was much about the old order of things
which it is impossible to condone, but, on the other
hand, in some respects England can hardly be said
to have changed for the better. A comparison of
the characteristics of other days with those of the
present time almost conveys the impression that this
country was formerly inhabited by a totally different
race, which vanished, leaving scarcely a descendant
to perpetuate the tradition of its ideas and ways.

Thoroughly to realise the transformation which
has taken place, it is necessary not only to master
the great historical events of history, but also
to investigate the lighter phases of life, many of
which are only chronicled in the letters or ephemeral
publications of the time. These are of necessity often

frivolous enough reading, which the serious historian is somewhat prone to despise.

Nevertheless, there is a good deal that is of interest to be gleaned from the accounts of that robust country life which is now so entirely a thing of the past. Nor are the records of the hunting squires to be despised—hardy, healthy, jolly men, none too clever, perhaps, but as a class vastly superior to the town-bred buck, whose main occupation in life was to gamble, drink, and dally with the facile beauties, many of whom loved not wisely but too well. Few people then led a strenuous life, but it was more natural than that which the vast majority leads to-day. The Englishman thought he was the finest fellow in the world, and as such, provided he had means, did pretty much as he liked. In the eighteenth century his salient characteristic was a love of pleasure and of sport, combined with a tenacious determination to defend personal liberty as regards his amusements.

The day of the faddist was not yet, and there was little indulgence for Paul Prys, even when such individuals had some appearance of being animated by excellent motives.

Personal liberty was highly prized by Englishmen, every one of whom prided himself on a man's house being his castle.

One of the Georges, it is said, being out hunting pursued the track of the game over a gentleman's fence, into his enclosure or park, where he chanced to be then walking. The gentleman at once accosted

the King with, " Stop, sir, this is not a patent path."
The Royal sportsman, unaccustomed to such freedom
of address, replied with some heat, " Sir, do you
know whom you address ? " " Yes," rejoined the
gentleman, " I know that I have the King of Great
Britain talking to me, but I, too, am a king when upon
my own property." Upon this the King, clapping
his hand on the pommel of the saddle, astutely exclaimed, with an air of exultation and pleasure, " Now
I see that I am the greatest King on earth, for while
other monarchs rule over slaves, I reign over princes."

Whilst in a vast number of ways our manners and
customs have undergone a decided change for the
better, there has been a marked weakening in certain
ancient and admirable features of the national character. Responsibility in serious matters is too often
shirked, glossed over, or shifted on to other shoulders.
Sturdiness of mind is rare, and no one dares to speak
out, whilst every effort is made to compromise with
the ideas advocated by the class of individual whom
a new and clever writer has so aptly called " the
superior person from the gutter."

Though much is heard of improvements in the
general well-being of the masses in great towns,
little is ever done to render the lot of the rural
population more agreeable.

In old days the hay-harvest, sheep-shearing, and
the wheat-harvest were always occasions for special
festivity, where master and men jointly celebrated
the fruits of their toil in the fields. Of all such
celebrations the Hock-cart or Harvest-home, when

the last sheaf of wheat had been garnered, was the
most prolific of feasting and merrymaking. Much
good feeling prevailed between the landlord who
resided on his estates and a robust tenantry who on
such occasions came into touch with one another—
village life was more enlivening than it is to-day.

Owing to various causes the pleasures of the humblest
class of the population have been considerably curtailed
within the last hundred years, during which time many
social diversions, that used to be so characteristic and
illustrative of " merrie England," as regards sports and
pastimes, have been gradually disappearing, until they
will soon cease to be anything but matter of tale and
story. This has already taken place as regards not a
few of the hardy and enlivening games and revels of
the lower classes ; and that the same spirit which has
consigned them to oblivion will not be tardy in interfering with and finally upsetting those of the upper,
is well within the bounds of possibility.

The enlightened public opinion which has within
a space of time a little less than a century swept away
a number of brutal sports and pastimes has, at the
same time, greatly augmented the flow of sturdy
countrymen into the large towns, for whilst sup-
pressing the somewhat uncivilised amusements of a
less sensitive age it has put nothing in their place
except board schools, which of necessity inculcate
contempt for the somewhat primitive joys of rural
existence.

The rustic of the present day has not that feeling
for sport which animated his ancestors, and incident-

ally produced the poacher. More often than not he has come to regard it merely as an amusement for the city gentleman from London, who has taken the " big house," and some who draw their ideas from the more hysterical portion of the Press have become openly hostile.

At the present time even the more reputable forms of sport which survive are a constant object of attack from many a quarter, and without doubt the House of Lords alone prevents a few of them from being suppressed under the maudlin pretext of enforcing that peculiar form of sentimentalism which dubs itself Humanitarian.

The puling cant of overweening morality, with which the present day so much abounds, would, if given a free rein, prohibit all sport which humanitarians have the effrontery to declare tends towards the unnecessary destruction of animal life, and is therefore contrary to Nature! She, as every observer of wild life knows, is absolutely ruthless with regard to her children. Instead, then, of inveighing against sportsmen who are generally humane men, let these same humanitarians arraign the wisdom by which such things are permitted to be, and send forth their whining complaints that the lion was not born to feed on grass, and the tiger on wild herbs.

The occasionally tolerated brutality of the eighteenth century has, of late years, become transformed into a supersensitive sentimentality, which is without doubt a very significant and dangerous symptom of the (let it be hoped) temporary decay of vitality which causes the popularity of so many fads. Complete ignorance of the ways of the world is not seldom an appanage of sentimentalism. Mr. George Love, of the Royal Society for Prevention of Cruelty to Animals, told a meeting in the early part of the present year that an old lady had written protesting against the horribly cruel practice of scratching horses before a race. One poor animal, she had read with grief, had even been " scratched " on the very day of the race. There is no limit to the absurdities of our national faddism which is constantly seeking to exert its enervating influence, and to dragoon the population at large into an existence of doleful flaccidity.

In the dark ages of ignorance and superstition, mankind were unfortunately taught to believe that they were never so acceptable to their Maker, as when they not only abstracted themselves from all the pleasures of life, but inflicted upon themselves severe and unnecessary tortures. Human nature was represented as the sink of depravity and wretchedness ; and misery and sorrow the unavoidable lot of humanity. This disposition to view the dark side of life is not altogether obsolete, there being still in England numbers who advocate solemnity and gloom. The advocates of strict Sunday observance, for instance, in reality foster the most painful feelings, if not the worst passions of the human heart.

With the introduction of universal education it might have been thought that a more tolerant view of Sabbath observance would have triumphed, and that, as in the Merrie England of Pre-Reformation days, cricket and other harmless games would have been generally recognised as a legitimate Sunday amusement on our village greens, around which the elders might sit quaffing their pots of ale. The very contrary, however, is the case, for hardly a year goes by without some tyrannical attempt at making that dismal institution, the English Sunday, more dismal still by means of Sunday closing. It is, indeed, almost impossible to conceive how, in the present age of civilisation, such measures can be seriously discussed.

Pleasure is the gift of Nature ; it is the first good thing that she points out to us from the moment we appear in the world, and every man surely should have the right of enjoying himself upon a day which, no matter what canting hypocritical Judases may say, was designed as much for recreation as for repose.

If ever there can be any justification for raising the cry of one law for the rich and another for the poor, it is in such a case as this. While the rich are luxuriously sipping their wines, and pampering their appetites with every luxury which the art of the cook can supply, upon what principle is it that the poor man, after a hard week's work, is to be denied the draught to which his labours have given such a relish ?

Surely the workers require some relaxation on one day of the week to enable them to return to the same unvaried round of life. The rich fly from town to country, and from country to town. As fancy prompts them they rush across England in their motors, or across the Channel for a continental tour. But the poor have no change of situation or of place :

to them the scene is always the same : and though their conditions of existence have been improved, few of the amenities of social life are within their reach.

The affectation of superhuman benevolence and fine feeling has become a profession—numbers of people make a good living out of " Social Reform." Many of these no doubt are sincere, but others exactly resemble the Puritan who administered the celebrated rebuke to Charles II. When that monarch had been guilty of some gross breach of decorum and decency with a loose woman, which attracted the notice of the clergy, it was resolved to reprove him for his incontinence and public transgression. The body of the clergy having appeared in the Audience Room ; one of them, of the name of Douglas, persuaded the others to let him go up alone to the King, in order that he might rebuke him with greater asperity. He accordingly walked up to Charles, but instead of the expected admonition, gravely, and in a low tone of voice, advised his Majesty when he did such a thing again, to be sure and shut the shutters !

Within the last sixty or seventy years an insidious spirit of almost frankly tolerated hypocrisy has insinuated itself into English life; as a result public men are practically forced to be perpetually indulging in one form or other of cant, which in some cases turns their whole existence into a carefully acted lie.

The difference which so often exists between a man's public utterances and his doings in private life is well shown by the following incident, which occurred in France during the preliminary discussions on the Concordat, under Napoleon. At that time everything was going well when an ecclesiastic of high rank, who gave his assent to all the other clauses, opposed himself most sternly to that which sanctioned the marriage of those priests who, during the Revolution, had presented themselves before the altar of Hymen. In vain did the First Consul remonstrate in the strongest possible manner—the invariable answer was, " that a priest should never forget his vow of *chastity*, and that nothing on earth could either excuse or absolve its violation " ! At last considerable tension having begun to prevail, the inexorable advocate of celibacy quitted the Palace of the Tuileries in an abrupt manner, leaving Bonaparte a good deal ruffled by his seemingly unconquerable opposition.

Just at this moment, however, Fouché, then Minister of the Police, chanced to appear upon the scene, and being informed as to what had happened, immediately said, " Leave the matter to me, and I engage that ' our man ' shall sign the clause within three days."

As likely as not this minister, a man of consummate address, was perhaps spurred forward on such an occasion by his own personal feelings, for he himself had been a married priest ! Knowing, from experienced sagacity, the haunts and foibles of every man of note in Paris, Fouché immediately instructed agents to watch the recalcitrant ecclesiastic, and at dusk, on the evening of the same day, the stern church-

man was seen to leave his hotel, wrapped up in a grey
riding-coat, and throw himself into a sorry *fiacre*.
This vehicle wended its way for about a league from
Paris to the country house of Madame Visconti, a
lady of notorious character. At one o'clock in the
morning two of the *mouchards*, having previously
gained over a servant of the house, entered the lady's
bed-chamber ; and, as an apology for their rudeness,
stated that they were in quest of a forger of *Billets de
Banque*, whom they knew to be there concealed. In
the course of a careful search, the ecclesiastic was
drawn from under the bed, and was immediately
addressed by his title with a thousand excuses for
the impoliteness offered to a man of his rank. " Whoever you are," said he, with the utmost perturbation,
" you are in possession of my secret, and I will give
you 10,000 francs each, if you will promise not to
divulge it." " Secrecy, monsieur," said the chief
searcher, " is the duty of our profession. We cannot
take your money, but we promise not to mention
what has occurred to any one but the Minister of the
Police, to whom we owe a faithful account." " I
will triple the sum, if you will promise not to divulge
it to any person." " That is impossible, monsieur.
We must give an account of our mission to our em-
ployer" ; and with this the spies disappeared.

On their departure, the startled priest immediately
perceived the political trick which Fouché had so
adroitly played him, and realised that nothing
was left to him but to comply with what was demanded. He repaired early the next morning to the

Tuileries, and signed, without discussion or observation, the clause which but the preceding day he had so strenuously opposed. Bonaparte, who knew nothing of the transactions of the intervening night, was completely astonished at this sudden change, and, though aware of the subtlety of Fouché, could not divine by what means he had thus instantaneously attained his end. The latter thought it expedient to let his master into the secret, for the trick was too clever to be buried in oblivion.

Modern Puritanism is in some respects a feeble echo from the days of those joyless stalwarts the Roundheads, though the modern Barebones hardly possesses the solidity of character of Cromwell's men. Love of Social Reform is in all probability, in the case of a large number of its latter-day advocates, merely a pose, with others a not unlucrative profession, and with yet others a pastime.

Meanwhile, according to the printed reports of the innumerable societies which exist for the purpose of dragooning humanity into sobriety and virtue, England would seem capable of being made into an earthly paradise by coercion.

The reports in question are certainly very creditable to the talents of the honorary or stipendiary secretaries who compose quarterly or annual reports and other documents, to satisfy the great army of faddists that its subscription money is well employed, but from a serious scientific point of view most of them are absolutely undeserving of attention.

As has previously been said, the triumph of

# The Merry Past

Puritanism in England has occurred within the last sixty or seventy years. As long ago as 1824 its unreasoning forces were gathering strength.

A writer of that day, commenting upon this, said : " It requires no vote of the House of Commons to tell us that the power of cant has increased, is still increasing, and ought to be put down. The modern Pharisee, not content with his Bible, tract, and missionary societies, is never happy unless he interferes with the pleasures and amusements of others : if he does make an exception, it is in favour of the rich, not the poor.

> ' Raise not your scythes, suppressors of our vice—
> Reforming Saints, too delicately nice !
> By whose decree, our sinful souls to save,
> No Sunday tankards foam, no barbers shave.
> And beer undrawn, and beard unmown, display
> *Your* holy reverence for the Sabbath day ! '

" Such is their zeal nowadays that the Londoner, in his Sunday's walk, dares no longer munch an apple or crack a nut. The whole stock of a wretched old woman was lately seized on a Sunday by some of these Pharisees, when they knew it was not during Divine service, and were depriving the poor woman of putting a bit of bread in her own and her children's mouths."

As an American writer * has very happily said, in all probability the nearest approach to the Puritan hell

---

* Mr. Price Collier in his admirable book, " England and the English."

would be a place where " everyone was obliged to mind his own business."

From time to time Puritanism suddenly lashes itself into a frenzy about some matter which in reality is perfectly immaterial as regards morality. Nude statues, which perhaps of all things in the world are least calculated to excite the passions, would seem to be a constantly recurring source of irritation.

When the Achilles statue was erected in Hyde Park in 1822, the want of drapery was declared to be extremely shocking. Ex-Sheriff Parkins, indeed, informed the public, through the columns of the " Morning Herald," that if his mother, who was a Newcastle woman, had caught any of her children looking at such an object, she would have soundly whipped them.

This was recently parallelled in the case of a supersensitive individual, who during the controversy as to the alleged indecency of certain statues about to be erected on the new building of the British Medical Association at the corner of Agar Street, Strand, proudly informed a representative of the Press that he had pasted paper across the windows of his office in order to guard against any risk of contamination !

The House of Commons is largely to blame for the unhealthy atmosphere of cant which pervades the country. Members too often speak in favour of and vote for measures, of the injustice and futility of which they are perfectly aware.

Few of either party possess the slightest moral

courage. Many members, for instance, who publicly favour measures of the type of the last Licensing Bill (which amongst other arbitrary provisions appointed inspectors for clubs), will privately admit the dubious benefits to be derived from such interference with the liberty of the subject.

Not a few of those members who voted for the Bill which has just been mentioned were, as a matter of common knowledge, delighted at its rejection by the Lords, though they themselves had lacked the moral courage or independence to vote against it.

Amongst the various changes nothing is more striking than the parochial tone which has crept into parliamentary life, and also the shameless cynicism of certain politicians who change sides for quite obvious reasons, their political convictions being, as it were, always up for sale.

A famous wit once said that fiction was a good resource for the newspapers, as one lie made two paragraphs. Many have taken this hint to heart, and the speech of to-day is too often employed in explaining away the assertions of yesterday.

In old days the House of Commons was composed of a singularly unemotional body of men, most of whom had a considerable knowledge of the world and of the limitations of human nature.

To-day a large proportion of members would seem to hold the belief that legislative interference with the life and habits of the people is capable of producing a sort of earthly paradise. Laws, which for no good reason impose irritating restrictions upon individuals, are discussed as being great measures of national regeneration by politicians who do not hesitate to borrow from the phraseology so dear to dissenting ministers.

There seems to be no finality about their legislation, for in spite of the increase of restrictions, more are constantly being proposed—a doubtful tribute to the success of the system in general.

Human nature is the same in all ages, states, and stages ; and however we may attempt to alter its essential characteristics by injudicious coercion, so surely will this all-powerful law overreach us in the end. We may, indeed, proceed for a time on our maddened way, like unto an impetuous and hot horse, without immediately being pulled up ; yet as surely as the steed in question shall we experience the effects of our headlong course, and be eventually brought to a standstill.

Whenever or wherever ill-considered laws, out of harmony with the general trend of human nature, stop up one source of public demoralisation, they never fail to open many others, which rush with redoubled violence through all the walks of life upon the community. If we could by Act of Parliament begin the world anew, remodel society, and alter the present nature and propensities of man, lawgivers might in one week do as much good as they have since the world was created done mischief. If we wish to augment the sum of national vice (and thereby misery), we must drive it to take refuge in holes and corners, where it will ensconce itself, make nests, and fence itself round with its own votaries, each species of man's vicious nature forming so many republics in the body corporate. And this, in sober fact, is all that the law has hitherto done for society, in regard to its moral effect. When the streets of London are cleared, and all the houses of entertainment are closed upon a Sabbath day, where do our Solons imagine the people will be ? Do they think they will be at prayers or asleep ? There are few members of the legislature who attach much importance to the study of human nature ; each member, therefore, like an unskilful surgeon, applies a healing plaster to the sore which comes under his own notice, without enquiring into the general state of the patient's constitution.

A great cause for the multiplication of laws is without doubt the fact that in one way or another such an increase is popular with lawyers, a class which in reality rules the country. Nothing can be done without these men, a large number of whom always sit in the House of Commons.

Modern government all over Europe is largely in the hands of those connected with the profession of the law, and though formerly some protests were made against such a state of affairs, it has now come to be regarded as an almost inevitable consequence of the modern parliamentary system. In England also lawyers have in some degree lived down the dubious reputation which caused so many of the smaller fry of the profession to be held in detestation by a large section of the population. It was the nefarious practices of such pettifoggers which brought that kind of stigma on the honourable majority of the profession, which vulgar prejudice most uncharitably did not disassociate from the black sheep. Many a limb of the law in other days was like the fox among poultry, ravenous and destructive, sparing neither young nor old, while the cries of the helpless but served to improve the keenness of his appetite, and augment the wrongs of the unfortunate.

In connection with this subject, the following historical reminiscence may not be out of place.

For ages the inhabitants of the Isle of Wight were notorious for their aversion to every process of the law. Whenever a misunderstanding arose between any two of them it was the local custom to submit it to a jury of neighbours, no professional lawyer being allowed to interfere on any pretence whatever—a state of affairs which gained the islanders much commendation from their less fortunate neighbours on the mainland.

In the reign of Queen Elizabeth, however, when Sir George Carey was appointed Captain General and Governor of the island, an attorney-at-law came to settle at Newport, having perceived the favourable opportunities for making a fortune. His little tricks and mercenary insinuations soon set the once happy and peaceable inhabitants at great strife, insomuch that a formal petition was presented to the Governor, praying that they who had so long lived in amity with each other, might be fairly quit of this nuisance, and once more restored to order and good neighbourhood.

# The Merry Past

Sir George Carey, after maturely deliberating on the subject, came to Newport, and, finding their complaints to be justly founded, caused the lawyer to be brought to open trial; and, upon evidence of his guilt, sentenced him to undergo the "*Burning Shame*," and be banished the island. The punishment of the "Burning Shame" was as follows:—

A barrel was taken, with one of the bottoms out, and, through the other, a hole made just big enough to admit the head of the culprit. This barrel was put over him, so as to bear on his shoulders and confine his arms, but not so low as to impede the progress of his limbs.

On the outer side of the barrel was screwed a great number of iron sockets, and in each socket a lighted candle, with which the condemned was led, by two conductors, to the North Bridge, amidst the rude acclamations of the people, mingled with rough music; that is to say, the pig cutter's horn, the horseshoe and brass kettle, marrow-bones and cleavers, together with the frying-pan and the salt box.

The lawyer was taken to the market-place of Newport, in his "Burning Shame," and fixed in the most conspicuous station; there one of the elders of the corporation called to the people to look upon him, and then recapitulated the evils brought upon them by his cunning. The exordium over the sentence of banishment was read; and, in the illuminated tub, with bells at his knees, the lawyer was conducted to the outer bridge that led to Cowes, and upon the signal given by the horn-blowers, the hunt began, the culprit making all the speed he could, while men, women, children, and even decrepitude joined in the chase, hooting the poor devil till he had fairly entered the passage-hoy prepared to convey him from that paradise which his low cunning endeavoured to convert to a pandemonium.

It was the business of his two conductors to stop their charge whenever a light expired till it was restored again, which, happening as often as the lawyer went too fast, made the procession of the " Burning Shame " of near half a day's length.

Modern lawyers, of course, are generally scarcely qualified by their misdeeds for the " Burning Shame " —numbers of them are honourable men—nevertheless, as a class, they may be called the croupiers of national life, for it is they who conduct the game, receiving very substantial remuneration whoever wins or whoever loses.

The amount of Bills which are annually drafted has become simply prodigious; many of these happily never get beyond an initial stage.

Of late years the House of Commons, satiated it would seem with ordinary legislation, has begun to manifest a tendency towards the insertion of humorous provisions in certain Bills.

Good specimens of this were the clauses in the Children's Bill (which most appropriately came into force on the 1st of April) prohibiting little boys from smoking, and fining parents ten pounds for not providing a fireguard, even if destitute of the few shillings necessary to buy one!

# The Merry Past

With respect to personal liberty Scotland (apparently to the delight of its inhabitants, as the Scotch members are always in favour of restriction) has fared even worse than England. Even in the great towns of Scotland all restaurants are shut at ten, after which no alcoholic refreshment can be obtained. It does not, however, appear that any striking increase of sobriety has been the result. In all probability the very pharisaical observance of the Sabbath, at first imposed upon the Scotch people against their natures, has since grown into a sullen, sulky habit, which incapacitates them from much natural enjoyment.

Though the Scotch are endowed with excellent brains and are by no means devoid of a sense of humour, the national life is somewhat blighted by a stern Puritanism which looks askance at pleasure.

In former days, however, the Scotch would not appear to have been so Puritanical. Lord Lovat was fond of pleasure and luxurious. He used, for instance, to send eight miles every day for the water he drank. He was exceedingly fond of highly-seasoned minced veal, and probably on most occasions ate rather more than prudence dictated— on the plea that it was difficult to persuade the stomach, because it had no ears—as he never could gratify his taste and appetite for his pet dish without suffering from the indiscretion. When confined in the Tower, only two hours previously to his execution, he thought he might, with perfect impunity, make a hearty meal of his favourite fare : and, as the story goes, he actually did consume a large mess of the said minced veal, saying that he should be gone before the customary unpleasant effects of his over-indulgence.

Previous to the Rebellion, it is said Lord Lovat had remained for two years in bed in a state of despondency, but when the news of Prince Charlie's landing was communicated to him, he started up, and cried, "Lassie, bring me my brogues—I'll rise noo!"

The accession of the middle class to power, whilst producing a vast amount of parochial and grandmotherly legislation, has in many respects modified and changed public life.

Up to the year 1770 the exercise of public speaking was confined to M.P.'s, men of the law, and a few stragglers of divinity. But now the case is altered; and the wonder is, not to find a man who can speak, but to find one who cannot. There is, at present, scarcely a village that does not produce its orators.

In old days the House of Commons was undoubtedly the best school in the world for eloquence, which has had its effect, too, upon the nation in no slight degree, notwithstanding the generally received opinion that the English are indifferent to the pleasures of imagination and passion. Burke, Pitt, Fox, Bright, Gladstone, and many others, proved to what an extent fine oratory was able to move men's minds.

It moves no one now. The art of public chatter has made vast strides in popularity within the last hundred years or so, with the result that a less importance is attached to oratory than was formerly the case.

At the present day the speeches of the great majority

of public men arouse but very languid interest; so much, indeed, is this the case that they are seldom reported at any length. A conspicuous exception, however, is the case of Lord Rosebery, whose brilliant and interesting utterances are ever welcomed by all who possess the slightest claim to culture and common sense.

Elections are now far more decorous than in old days, when candidates did not fawn upon the electors in any great degree—bluffness was their prevailing characteristic.

A gallant general, being elected a representative for one of the eastern counties, gave a public entertainment to the electors after the fatigue of the contest, and, on his health being drunk, addressed his constituents in the following laconic speech :— "Gentlemen, I am no orator, and therefore you must not expect from me a fine speech. That I can fight, I believe none of you can doubt; that I can drink, you shall all be assured of before we part. So God bless you all, and leave me to defend your rights."

Another gentleman, proposing a candidate for a southern borough, terminated his harangue with the following words : "Gentlemen, it is of the utmost importance that we select men of tried and approved political abilities; that so, whilst the other nations of the earth are writhing beneath the lash of an unfeeling tyrant, we and our posteriors may haply escape the strokes of his afflicting rod."

At the present day, the speeches of public men are

generally more remarkable for their concealment of the real feelings of the speaker than anything else. It was not so in the eighteenth century, when not a few spoke their thoughts out with unbridled freedom. Such a one was old Lord Coningsby, a staunch opponent of the Pretender. This nobleman had distinguished himself at the Battle of the Boyne, and a handkerchief with which he stanched a wound received there by King William the Third was formerly (and perhaps still is) preserved at Cashiobury Park. In 1718, having reason to believe that the Jacobites were plotting at Hereford, he addressed the Mayor and Corporation as follows :—

"Mr. Mayor, your servant—Gentlemen, yours : d—n you all ! I'll have you to know, by G—d, that I am Lord Lieutenant and Custos Rotulorum of this county, and Lord High Steward of this city (and that for life) ; and, G—d d—n you, I'll do what I please with you and your city.

"I hear some of you are for that Pretender ; by G—d, a fellow whom his own mother has disowned ; and I am informed that a lady, of the strictest virtue and best reputation, would have deposed before you upon oath, by G—d, that that impudent rascal, that sits there, said that this fellow was the rightful heir to the crown : you refused to take her oath ! by G—d, her deposition ! G—d d—n you, I speak to you, Mr. Mayor—and you, Mr. Taylor, who are a Jacobite, and a fellow without a soul, G—d d—n you. I am also informed that a pack of wretches, one of whom is an exciseman, and another of 'em a fellow who eats the

King's bread, meeting in the market-house on the 10th of June, drank the Pretender's health, and proclaimed him King. And I hear you had your oaken boughs and white roses, G—d d—n you. There are but three honest men in the town, by G—d; which are, Tom Bailey, Dr. Lewis, and Mr. Biron."

In those days the aristocracy, in a great measure, dominated the country, nevertheless there would appear to have been less class hatred than to-day, when a directly opposite state of affairs exists.

The great land-owning class, which then lived much upon their estates, were, as a rule, popular, unlike the *noblesse* across the Channel, which was in many instances despised and loathed.

In the early part of the eighteenth century gentlemen of rank and fortune lived mostly upon their own estates in the country; they had little intercourse with the capital, but drew whatever supplies they wanted from tradesmen who lived in the nearest city or market town. This intercourse carried the tradesmen frequently to the houses of the great, where, when their business was done, they received the hospitality of the steward's room, or other part of the establishment that was consistent with their own rank. In this way a certain degree of intimacy was kept up between inhabitants in the towns and residents in the country.

Most of the old French nobility before the Revolution saw little of their tenantry, and made but intermittent visits to their châteaux. These houses, generally in a ruinous state and badly furnished, were occasionally visited by their owners, accompanied probably by a party of guests, and a numerous tribe of domestics. Such visits were generally the result of a passing caprice; often of necessity, in order to recover fresh vigour for the excesses of Paris—rarely for the true enjoyment of the country. Their appearance was not welcomed by their tenants, from whom certain extra services were then required, whilst provisions of all kinds, grain, fish, flesh, fowl, were all in requisition. The servants brought from Paris were plundering and insolent. From all these causes the gentry, who spent their time at cards or billiards, or promenading in their formal gardens in stiff Parisian dresses, were only known on their estates to be hated and despised.

The French *noblesse* was ruined by the Revolution, their estates being now, almost without exception, broken up, or in other hands.

The same fate now threatens many a fine old property in this country, various forces conspiring to impoverish those who own land upon which Radical rapacity has cast its predatory eye. The present tendency of English democracy, indeed, in this respect would seem to incline to what is little less than confiscation, and the prospects of landowners in general are gloomy in the extreme. The influence and power of the old aristocracy is gone, and the proletariat rules, not only from below, but from above, no inconsiderable portion of the more recently created members of the House of Lords being distinctly plebeian in origin, though this is not unnaturally glossed over as much as possible.

There are many recently ennobled families which might have very appropriately adopted some simple instrument or article of domestic utility as their badge.

"Who sent this ?" demanded a widowed Peeress, with anger depicted upon her sorrowing countenance, as she pointed to a somewhat peculiarly shaped floral tribute, amongst the wreaths sent by friends of her departed lord, who had once known that dignity which manual labour imparts.

"Beg your pardon, my lady," was the family butler's reply, "it ain't a 'pickaxe,' it's an 'hanchor.'"

A great brewery at one time was considered an almost certain passport to the House of Lords, but of recent years, owing to various causes, many an individual engaged in this industry has come to be considered very "small beer" indeed.

Careful enquiry into the origin of the families of a good many peers, who have been created within the last fifty years, would reveal some amusing results. Most of our modern patricians have not the frankness of that Duke of Leeds who lived at the beginning of the nineteenth century.

"My family," said the Duke, "deduces its origin from Jack Osborne, the shop-boy of a pin maker on London Bridge, in the reign of one of the Henrys. The only daughter of his master fell from a window into the Thames : the lad saw her danger, and rescued her. Some years after the young lady had many noble suitors ; but ' Jack won her,' said the old citizen, ' and he shall wear her.' "

Another nobleman, noted for his independent character, whose father had been connected with some ironworks, being twitted one day by a duke on the obscurity of his birth, very coolly answered : " It is true I am the son of a blacksmith ; but if your Grace's father had chanced to be one, you would have been a blacksmith too ! "

## II

THE Englishman of the past was essentially a sturdy individual in mind as well as body, whilst possessed of much sound common sense, which was once an essentially British characteristic.

The influx of the population into the towns is probably largely responsible for the anæmic mentality of latter days.

The robust and sturdy yeomen, a class which was a national asset of the highest worth, have almost ceased to exist, engulfed in the maelstrom of agricultural depression, in which "the squires" have also disappeared. The latter, in spite of their faults, were very often good and kindly men, who were popular with their tenants and kept alight that flame of local life which has now practically flickered out. In the middle of the eighteenth century, it is true, there were a number of useless squires, men who "belted" their three bottles of port after dinner, and for the latter portion of their lives seldom knew how to find their way to bed. These, however, were comparatively few in number. Whatever may have been his faults, the jolly squire who lived in the country more or less all the year round looking after his dependents and estate was a thoroughly English product, imbued with all the virtues and prejudices of the type, occasionally leavened by a spice of originality which added to his popularity about the countryside.

From his house flowed a constant stream of unostentatious charity. He knew most of the villagers by name and was a prominent figure at the merry-makings, which were such a feature of old English country life. Not infrequently he had seen a good deal of the Continent before marrying and settling down, and whilst thoroughly contemptuous of foreigners and foreign ways could tell many a queer tale of amorous adventure in Spain, or of wild nights amidst the delights of the Palais Royal.

The fine old English squire was a man whose own happiness was closely connected with that of his domestic dependents, the general prosperity of his tenants, who surrounded his mansion, and the hospitable association with his numerous neighbouring friends. His hounds were kept from an instinctive attachment to the sport itself as well as to perpetuate the traditions of his ancestors, and not from the least desire of having his name blazoned forth in every part of the county, for keeping what he had neither property to support nor spirit to enjoy.

His religion, whilst of a simple kind, was thoroughly sincere, whilst his relations with the parson were generally of a pleasant and intimate kind.

His hospitality, though plain, was good and profuse, whilst he was ever ready to come to the aid of his humbler neighbours did misfortune overtake them.

# The Merry Past

The amusements and recreations of the old-fashioned squire were summed up in one word, "sport," which to him was the main end and object of earthly existence. Whilst it is possible that he contributed little to the so-called progress of the world, he contributed much to the general happiness of those amongst whom he lived, and for this reason most of these old squires were sincerely lamented by the crowd of friends and retainers who respectfully followed them to their last home.

The race of men who made field sports the sole aim and end of their existence was the product of the immediate era in which it lived.

The Squire Westerns, who dined in scarlet and buckskins, drank ale in preference to wine, and smoked clay pipes, acquired such habits as the natural result of their environment and of an existence passed in a sort of robust rural isolation.

The old English gentleman—fond of fox-hunting and other field sports, and pursuing them as they were formerly pursued, in a manner equally conducive to his health and independence, and the well-being of his friends and dependents, was a national asset. Alas, the day has come when he is almost no longer known, and in a few years it seems likely that it will be recorded only as a matter of history that such men were once the pride of Old England.

The country gentlemen were the direct opposites of Horace Walpole and his school, once contemptuously dubbed ethereal essences of foolscap, and declared to be likely to hold their bergamoted cam-

brics to their noses should they be confronted with
the base crew, who, as the author of the famous
letters expressed it, " gallopped after a stink."

As a matter of fact, the old squires incarnated
healthy bucolic John Bullism, whilst the exquisites,
who drew inspiration from the school of Strawberry
Hill, were but cosmopolitan men of pleasure.

At the end of the eighteenth century and the
beginning of the nineteenth a veritable worship of
hunting prevailed amongst country gentlemen, many
of whom considered riding to hounds the most important thing in the world.

A certain sporting colonel chose Cambridge for his
son, because they made the best saddles and bridles
there.

Another fox-hunter entertained an adverse opinion
concerning University education owing to seeing
some young men in the hunting field rather shirking
their fences.

" Well, gentlemen," he shouted out, " all I have to
tell you is, that if you do not know a good deal more
about Latin and Greek than you do about fox-hunting,
your parents have sent you to college to confounded
little purpose ! "

Fox-hunting with many was a sort of religion.

The old Duke of Grafton, with a robust constitution and uninterrupted health, loved ease and sleep of
a winter's morning better than the music of the horns
and the hounds, yet he thought it necessary for a man
of his rank and fortune to be a sportsman and to keep
and follow a pack of foxhounds. He therefore ordered

his servants to call him at five o'clock in the morning on hunting days, and to pull him out of bed and dress him, though he should resist or be unwilling to awake. In this order his Grace was implicitly obeyed, though he defended himself from the assailants with blows and imprecations.

There even existed ardent supporters of the chase who knew nothing of hunting, and did not follow their own hounds.

About 1804 the Shropshire foxhounds were supported at the sole cost of Mr. Cresset Pelham, who never dreamt of such a thing as looking at them himself ! A bachelor, and possessing a fine fortune, he devoted the greater portion of it to this establishment. Mr. Pelham was a very eccentric character in many ways, having been most indifferent about his dress, whilst his household was conducted at a minimum of expense; nevertheless, he was by no means a miser, and was most generous to the poor. His benevolence in this direction sometimes assumed strange forms ; on one occasion he took off his shirt to cover a beggar woman.

When the Shropshire hounds were in Mr. Pelham's possession, the hunt servants rode in white, so that at any distance there was no difficulty in distinguishing them from the rest of the field.

Variations from the usual costume in the case of hunt servants was not uncommon in the past.

When Oldaker hunted the Old Berkeley, he and his men were dressed in yellow plush ; the members in scarlet with yellow collars. This dress had

originated with Oldaker on scientific principles.
He held, with a sure perception which after experience amply justified, that in any country, more
especially a woodland one, or where the coverts
were near one another, this difference of dress greatly
accelerated the work of the field : the hounds knew
the coat, and got much quicker to the men.

There were many characters to be found amongst
the sporting retainers of the squirearchy of the past.
Such a one was the keeper of Mr. Leveson-Gower at
Limpsfield, in Surrey, in 1830. This man, notwithstanding his calling, used to do all he could to preserve foxes.

One day towards the end of the season, however,
the hounds were unlucky in finding in some of the
gorse coverts on this estate, probably, as is often the
case, from their not being thoroughly drawn, and
some silly fellow, who knew nothing of Charles the
keeper's passionate love of fox-hunting, said in the
latter's hearing that the keeper must have destroyed
the foxes.

Charles said nothing, but went thoughtfully home.
He did not come near the hounds again that season,
but appeared at the commencement of the next,
when the hounds came to draw his master's covert
where the reflection upon him had been made.

On this occasion the hounds had found, and a
" Tally " was about to be given when, " Hold," said
everyone, " it's a hare ! "  " No," said an old farmer,
" it beant a hare ; younder be a fox's head."  " But
where's the tail ? " exclaimed a cockney, to the

amusement of the field. " It's a fox without a brush, gentlemen," shouted the keeper, " a fox without a brush, gentlemen ! Away after him ! He will beat some of you yet. You would not believe that I bred and preserved the foxes for you, and so I have taken care you shall know it this season, as I have docked all the young cubs, and you will now know " (with great emphasis) " *my foxes !* " And, sure enough, many breathless chases they afterwards had after brushless foxes, to the astonishment of strangers. One fox in particular they never could kill for some seasons.

Keepers of this type were rare, and not a few were ruthless as regards foxes. Many owners of large shooting strictly ordered their keepers to preserve foxes, and if it could be proved that they destroyed them they would be discharged. Keepers, then as now, knew well what such orders meant; they knew, too, that it could not be proved that they killed foxes. They had nothing to do but to dig a hole and bury them in the spot where they had caught them, and they stood a very remote chance of detection.

A large landed proprietor, who was very fond of shooting, once said to a friend who requested him not to destroy foxes : " When it is proved to me that a fox will not eat a pheasant, I will preserve them."

As a matter of fact foxes, where they can get other food, are not destructive to pheasants, except during the time the hens are sitting on their nests, and even then it may be obviated by a little trouble in feeding them.

# The Merry Past

There were many original characters amongst the sporting men of other days.

A certain huntsman was celebrated for his novel method of getting hounds out of covert when they were not disposed to obey the summons of the horn. His plan was to get hold of one of the hounds on the outside of the covert and to pull his ears so as to make him cry out, thereby inducing those which remained in covert to suppose that he was running a fox, when, by cheering and hallooing to the cry, he succeeded in getting them all away.

One of the best-known hunt servants of the past was Tom Snooks, who was whipper-in to many masters of hounds—Mr. Simmonds (when he had hounds in Berkshire), Lord Kintore, Lord Moreton, Lord Radnor, John Warde (when he hunted the New Forest), and afterwards to Mr. Villebois. Tom was a first-rate rider to hounds, having a quick eye and light hand, and could beat most men ; and may with truth be said to have lived all his life with hounds. He afforded considerable amusement to the field one day after the death of the deer, which he had jumped into the water to secure, and come out thoroughly drenched ; he asked some of the field how he was to get the water out of his boots. " Take them off, to be sure," said some. " Oh ! I know a trick worth two of that," said Tom : upon this he stood upon his head by the hedge side, and thus got rid of the water, much to the amusement of the spectators.

A similar anecdote used to be told of the celebrated

# *The Merry Past*

Matty Wilkinson, master of the Hurworth Hounds, who—

> Stretched supine upon the plain,
> With legs erected there has lain
> The water from his boots to drain.

Matthew Wilkinson had the reputation of supporting a pack of foxhounds upon smaller means than any other master in England. At one time the mastership of the Hurworth Hounds was shared between him and his brother, but after the latter's death Matty became sole master.

His love of hunting was a ruling passion, which relegated all else in life or even death to a subordinate place.

When Mr. Wilkinson's eldest brother was on his deathbed, he was asked by a friend for the fixtures of the forthcoming week. His reply was : "Why, Tommy is very ill, and if Tommy dees we can't hunt till Monday ; but, if Tommy don't dee, we shall hunt at —— on Friday." A brother sportsman died and left Matty five pounds to purchase a black coat to his memory. Matty purchased a red one, thinking thereby that he had shown still greater respect to his departed friend.

He himself died in 1837.

Another sportsman of considerable originality was a Mr. Stubbs, an intimate friend of Mr. Corbet, the well-known Warwickshire Master of Hounds, who was celebrated for his two packs—one of gentlemen and the other of ladies, the latter affording much the better sport of the two. Mr. Stubbs, who was a sporting squire, kept a small pack of fast beagles, and was not less fond of the sports of the field than his friend, who had two packs. It so happened that the jolly old gentleman had a fox brought to him on a Saturday, which he placed in a tub, promising himself great sport on the Monday following. Mr. and Mrs. Corbet were constant attendants at church, the latter being a very strict Protestant, and a lady of most regular and exemplary habits. Mr. Stubbs usually spent his Sabbath in a less edifying way, being only booked for an outside-place at the house of prayer. Full of his sporting anticipations for Monday, he could not refrain from taking a sly look at Reynard during the time of service: and he accordingly paid a visit to the tub, in order to see how the animal fared : there, to his great disappointment, he found that the fox was more cunning than those who had confined him, and that he had actually bolted. The old sportsman was furious at this ; but he swore that he would not be done. His horse was at hand, saddled and bridled, and the thought came into his head that he was still in time to have a bit of sport. He accordingly went to the kennel, let out his famous beagles, laid them on the scent, and ran through the churchyard. The scent was breast-high, and the clattering of his horse's hoofs, together with the cry of the pack, naturally alarmed and astonished both the clergyman and congregation. The former, indeed, was so astounded that when he was about to pronounce "The righteous man shall flourish like a green bay tree," he mistook and said a *green bay horse:* the "Amen" stuck in the clerk's mouth at an after-part of the service : whilst the sexton, unable to control himself, actually ran out after the pack. The church *belles* were all put in confusion, and Mr. Corbet was scarcely able to re-strain himself from following the pack and joining in the chase. Meanwhile old Stubbs, after a capital run of three-quarters of an hour, killed the fox.

According to Osbaldeston, who had as much ex-perience of hunting counties as any man has ever had, Lincolnshire was the best scenting county in England, and consequently the best hunting county of all. The better the scent, the better it becomes, because it enables hounds to be near their foxes : the nearer you are to your foxes, the more chance there is of their running straight : the nearer to a straight line a run approaches, the more it is of the best character of fox-hunting. In all these perfections the nature of the soil of Lincolnshire conduces, added to which, as Osbaldeston said, the rasping drains which were occa-sionally met with thinned a troublesome field, and made the county a fox-hunter's paradise.

Lincolnshire was the scene of Osbaldeston's début, and he ever spoke of it with enthusiasm.

Excellent sport was enjoyed in old days by small private packs, and about 1820 a pack of rabbit-hounds, kept by a gentleman in Dorsetshire, acquired a con-siderable reputation. This pack consisted of seven couple of the most diminutive of the blended blood of the beagle and the harrier, as prima facie exempli-fied in the round pending ear, generous dark spots, edged with a finish of tan colour, a feathered tail arched over the back when the animal was in motion, and above all, in such assumed consequence in the gait and carriage of the senior part of them, at least, as failed not to attract observation and interest. Their general size may be conjectured from a prevailing report as to the whole pack having often received a full meal from a common wash-hand basin once filled. One, however, as an inch or so taller than the rest, and which would have been drafted but for his inestimable qualities, was loaded with a shot collar of two or three ounces weight, to prevent his being too forward when in chase. This lilliputian pack killed upwards of four hundred couple of rabbits in one year. So great was its reputation that one hundred pounds was once offered for it, which was refused. The feats performed by these tiny chiders, for several successive seasons, drew forth resounding plaudits from sporting spectators, together with many a justly merited eulogium on their proprietor, by whose sole skill, judgment, and perseverance, they were brought to a state of unrivalled perfection.

Between 1770 and 1820 a complete revolution took place in everything connected with fox-hunting. The style of the hound, the horse, and the man who rode him, all underwent a change in the course of time, and fox-hunting, like everything else, altered its character. The speed of hunters greatly increased, for as hounds went faster in 1820 than in 1770, the horse had to go faster too.

# The Merry Past

This originated in a great measure from the change in the hours of hunting. A fox found, as was the custom in former days, as soon as it was light, and before he had digested his chicken, could not be supposed to run so fast as one whipped out of an acre of gorse at one o'clock in the afternoon, as was the more modern custom. Harriers now go the pace which foxhounds went in old times, and foxhounds that of greyhounds. The style of horse, the seat of his rider, and much else has been revolutionised, and fox-hunting, in some countries, is now little else than " racing after a fox."

The equipment of the sportsman has also completely changed. An old-fashioned squire used to say that a modern fox-hunter, stepping out of his carriage by a covert side, looked more as if he were going a-courting than fox-hunting. The old school disliked a luxurious equipment. Old Mr. Forrester, of Willy Hall, in Shropshire, who hunted that country many years, gave his coverts, when far advanced in life, to a pack of foxhounds set up in his neighbourhood by some farmers. Having ridden out one day to see them, he was asked how he liked them. " Very much, indeed," replied the veteran : " there was not one d—d fellow in a white-topped boot among the lot."

He was very contemptuous of "Mahoganites"— men who, he said, rode at a most infernal pace about the introduction of the second bottle of claret, with their knees under a semicircular mahogany table, comfortably placed before the fire.

# The Merry Past

Fox-hunters' dinners were then of a very solid though simple kind.

The following is the menu of a typical dinner which was given at Calverton in honour of a Nottinghamshire sportsman in the early part of the last century.

Course the first: a salmon and a quarter of lamb, flanked by every vegetable in season. Course the second: a goose, a ham, and a leash of chickens, flanked as above. Course the third: a couple of ducks with green peas, turkey poults, and three hunting puddings. The display of cheese was the finest of the season—Alfreton and York, Colwick and Stilton.

The only thing which seems to have interrupted the harmony of this evening for a second was the expression by two or three of the diners of a wish for claret, after the consumption of a couple of dozen of port. The chairman, having declared his intention of sticking to the truly British liquor then before him, said "he should not object to the introduction of claret late in the evening, but he had no idea of anything of the sort being usual in good society until each gentleman had completed his three bottles of port." This excited a little hubbub at the other end of the table where a gentleman rose, with more heat than the occasion demanded, and said "he did not know what the chairman meant by his insinuation about low company; that the gentlemen then assembled represented South Notts, and no man should cram 'Day and Martin' down their throats." This speech was received with loud cheers; and the president, perceiving his error, politely expressed his sorrow that an idea should have gone about that he there or elsewhere could possibly dream of anything like dictation, which he would show by immediately ordering a magnum of claret.

Many excellent songs were sung after this Gargantuan meal.

The general dress and equipment of a squire of the old-fashioned type was of an original description, more adapted for use than ornament.

His boots, which were only worn upon very special occasions, being reserved for full dress, generally served him for some twenty years ; when they were well greased with neat's-foot oil they would defy a week's rain, came up to the point of the knee-pan, and were well secured by a strap round the thigh, and the spurs just large enough in the necks for the rowels to turn.

Many of the old squires never rode their hacks to cover, their practice being to be at the rabbit-warren, or other place where the fox was expected to feed, by break of day, and to trail up to the cover, so that it was frequently necessary to be on horseback by four in the morning ; and, from the hounds being much slower than those of the present day, it was frequently starlight when they reached home.

Hunting in old days was not the expensive affair which it is at present. Of late it has in a great measure become the relaxation of the rich townsman, rather than the natural pastime of the squire of moderate means.

# The Merry Past

So recently as the beginning of the nineteenth century there were poor country squires who contrived to enjoy all the sporting delights of the country, and hunted their own hounds. Such a one was Captain Saich, whose picture was painted by Henry Alken. The Captain is represented on his old white-faced black horse, together with his three favourite hounds, Danger, Dauntless, and Darling.

Captain Saich was descended from an ancient Essex family who for many generations had been masters of hounds. He possessed little beyond his pay, but followed in the track of his ancestors, and for several years hunted part of Suffolk. He was fond of the sport; and it was gratifying to see him working through a strong covert cheering his hounds, his old horse walking round. The Captain might be termed slow, and so was his horse; but he was able to go straight through a long day in any country. The horse was supposed to be worn out before he came into Captain Saich's possession. At the Captain's death the animal was sold, and the last account known of him was as leader to the Coggeshall coach.

One of the last of the real old school of sportsmen was Squire St. John of Odiham, who to the very end of his life used to come out with the hounds of Mr. Pointz at Midgham in Berkshire. Squire Pointz himself always drove (he was near eighty) to covert in his chariot-and-six, attired in cocked-hat, bag-wig, and a green-and-gold suit. His huntsman, old Topper, was nearly as old as himself, and could ride but one horse, a hawk-nosed, dark chestnut. The whipper had but one nag too; the whole concern, old Squire and all, looked as if provender of all kinds was not over-plentiful. Anything so slow cannot be conceived. Old Squire St. John had been one who in his day could go; he was near seventy-five, and scorned the luxury of his brother squire, and stuck to the pig-skin to the last. As soon as the hounds found he used to trill out his best cheer, wave his hat, and shout as loud as he was able, " Ride, ride ! you devils, ride ! I'll jog home to dinner; damn your eyes, ride—thank God, I've had my day."

The political views of old squires such as these are best shown by the election address issued by one of the last of them. " Countrymen " (it should be added that a friend suggested gentlemen, but the candidate had retorted, " Damn gentlemen—they are not all gentlemen—say countrymen "), I'm for the King and Constitution; I'm for the Church, but not for tithes, unless they go to the landlords; if I get a seat, I'll keep it as long as I can, so I'm for long Parliaments. I'm for nobody but gentlemen learning to read, but let them work that there may be no poor-rates. I'll vote for corn at 100s. per quarter, and none of your mouldy foreign stuff; that every squire shall have as many horses and dogs as he likes without paying taxes; and that every poacher shall be hung or shot. God save the King ! "

The four golden rules which one of this class set up in his house and adhered to were : " Fear God ;

Honour the King; Love your neighbour; and preserve your foxes!"

In conversation they were, to use a mild expression, somewhat blunt, and did not scruple to call a spade a spade.

A certain squire who had just married, was, in due time, blessed with a fine thumping boy. The neighbours were all very kind in their enquiries after the infant and its mother, to which the usual answer of "As well as can be expected" was returned. This did not satisfy two old maiden ladies, who wished to know which the child resembled—papa or mamma? The squire politely informed them that, at that early age, it was impossible to determine the point. In a short time, however, they repeated the question, when he sent them word that, for their satisfaction, he had just been examining his child, and that "he was very like his father before, and very like his mother behind." This ended the correspondence.

Perhaps the worst fault of these men of another age was their heavy drinking, which sent not a few of them to a comparatively early grave, though many a one counteracted the evil effects of his Bacchanalian habits by an open-air life, and lived to a green old age.

The general sign of the influence of their deep potations upon these squires was their becoming very noisy, hallooing, and tally-ho-ing, and when in an advanced state of this kind it was most difficult to move them or get them to bed. One of them being once asked to withdraw from the table and join the ladies, where he would hear some excellent music, said : " Damn all music, except the music of a pack of foxhounds." This individual was like the man who was fond of his garden, and who, when asked by a lady to give her some choice flowers, replied, " Madam, I cultivate no flower but a cauliflower ! "

Fielding's Squire Western was, it is said, more or less a true portrait drawn from life at a time when this was no uncommon type. As the eighteenth century waned Squire Westerns grew rare.

Mr. William Leche of Carden, in Cheshire, who died in 1812, a country gentleman of original habits, was the squire who was called " the last of all the Westerns."

He led a somewhat eccentric life, according to modern ideas. Though a rich man, he did not keep a carriage of any sort till far advanced in years ; eventually, however, he was prevailed upon to do so in order to convey him home at night, he having met with several accidents from his nocturnal rides home. He called this carriage his drinking-cart.

The whole of Mr. Leche's life was centred in the enjoyment of field sports in the morning, and the society of his friends at night. He dined at three o'clock, if by himself, or if he had only a few of his intimate friends staying in his house.

Mr. Leche's usual practice was to breakfast at five in the winter ; he hunted up his fox's trail while the stars were in the sky, got over his day's sport, and was often at dinner by noon.

This practice he continued to follow even when

a later hour of dining had come into fashion. When
invited to dine out he would still have his own dinner
as usual previous to starting, in consequence of which
he used facetiously to say that there were two houses
at which he had often tried to arrive too late for
dinner, but never could succeed—these were Wynns-
tay and Emral.

Mr. Leche hunted his own hounds, but occasionally
the care of his pack devolved on his whipper-in Sam,
who was a wet soul, and often came home drunk.
The Squire, however, at length declared that he
would endure this no longer, so told Sam he must
quit his service, and that he should look out for a
new whipper-in. " Very well, sir," said Sam ; " and
if you was to look out for a new huntsman, it would
be quite as well for the hounds." This admirable
reply disarmed his master, and Sam continued in his
place.

Curiously enough, though Mr. Leche kept foxhounds, and hunted them himself for a long series
of years—possessing also abilities quite above the
common standard—he knew very little about fox-
hunting.

The harriers which he kept at one time were
hunted in a somewhat original fashion.

Contrary to the general custom, Mr. Leche and
his guests used to dine first and hunt afterwards.
This arrangement was thus effected: About three
miles from Carden was a pretty retired little villa
called Holywell, belonging to the Squire. It was
untenanted save by servants. Thither every hunting

day a pony, laden with meats, wines, and strong beer, was duly dispatched. About eleven, or half-past, the hounds usually turned out; sometimes a hare was put up, but most generally nothing was done till towards one, when, as was the saying, "Now, then, the Squire's making the right cast, we shall find directly"; and off the field would trot for Holywell. As the half-dozen men who on most occasions formed his field were all known to Mr. Leche, a general invitation to luncheon was uniformly the consequence; indeed, it was shrewdly suspected that a deep old file, who never missed a meet, from Chester, went there expressly with the view of feeding, as he was never seen after the banquet. The table groaned under a spread—all cold—fit for the Corporation of Bristol; meanwhile the horses were regularly stabled, and the hounds shut up by the veteran Joe, and a salvo of corks fired. The Squire was a lover of toasted cheese, and this dish always came bubbling in by way of dessert. The party then drew round the fire, "just to have something warm before starting, for luck." Tobacco was placed upon the table, and every man was furnished with a yard of clay.

Mr. Leche's company was sought after more than that of any other man in his neighbourhood; and so original was his wit, and so happily was it applied, that he was ever the very life and soul of every party he was in. Although naturally abstemious—so much so that when alone he drank but two glasses of wine after his dinner—yet in a party he never failed to sacrifice most freely to the god of wine, and his wit and good-humour seemed to increase with every glass he drank. The signal of enough—and he generally went the length of his tether—was an attempt to sing the first verse of a song, beginning with—

Women and wine the heart delight.

A witty man, Mr. Leche's sayings were often quoted about the countryside. One of his bottle-companions of the sacerdotal order asked him to go to church and hear him preach. He afterwards wished to know what he thought of his sermon. "Why," replied Mr. Leche, "I like you better in bottle than in wood."

This was another way of expressing the view which the old Scotchwoman took of her minister's oratorical powers. The unfortunate man having got wet to the skin on his way to the church, was about to receive the offer of some dry clothes from one of his congregation when an old lady interposed, saying, "Na, na, woman, ye need na fash yoursell; wait ye a wee till he gets into the pu-pit, he'll be dry enough there."

Mr. Leche was always ready for good-humoured chaff.

Walking round his paddocks one day he came across a poor young Irish haymaker, who was hanging about in a somewhat suspicious manner.

"Well, my lad," said the Squire, "where do you hail from?" "From County Mayo, your honour!" "And pray, what the devil brought you all the way into my premises ? " " Beg your honour's pardon, I was ounly looking for a bit of work to give me a morsel of bread, and a divil a friend in the world have I ! And sure I can handle a pitchfork or a spade pretty, your honour ! " " What ! such a hearty fellow as you get no work ! Then go and enlist— they want such lads as you." " Sure, and that I would, your honour, but I'll not be long enough for them." " Well, but you'll grow, you're young." " Grow, did you say ? Och ! by Jaisus, I don't know how I'm to grow, except it'll be thinner that I'll grow, walking about day and night, and a divil a copper to comfort me ! "

Possessed of a robust constitution, rising early in the morning, pursuing the sports of the field, and generally of temperate habits, Mr. Leche lived to the age of eighty-three ; and as a proof that the charms of conversation and the pleasures of a social glass lived as long as he did, it is only necessary to observe that the year before he died he sat down to dinner with a friend of his at Chester at one o'clock in the afternoon, and at two o'clock the next morning he got into his carriage to go home.

Another well-known Cheshire sporting character was Sir Harry Mainwaring, who, in spite of the fact that his sight was extremely feeble, was master of the Cheshire hounds during some part of the early portion of the nineteenth century. Sir Harry was a most enthusiastic fox-hunter.

Many stories used to be told of the queer results of this master's defective vision.

# The Merry Past

On one occasion, as they were running their fox across a gentleman's park, Sir Harry, who was the best-tempered man alive, was found in desperate dudgeon with his horse. A friend who was riding by his side enquired the reason of his wrath. "This unruly brute," said the baronet, "has been plunging with me every hundred yards since we entered the park . . . there again, confound the beast! you see he won't be quiet." "Lord bless you!" said the querist, "Sir Harry, that's not plunging; why, the horse is only leaping over the iron palings, that's all." "Oh, ho!" was the rejoinder, "there are invisible fences here, are there?"

On another occasion a party of hard-riding men had come from some other hunt to see the Cheshire, and, of course, to criticise. This put the master on his mettle, and he had been riding in the dark with his hounds all day, as though he valued his neck as little as a pipe-stopper. They had come to a check, and just at the moment when an indiscretion hazarded the fate of the day, and his own honour and glory, in went the rowels, and over a flight of rails flew the M.F.H. to the dismay of the field. "Mainwaring's run mad," shouted a brother sportsman. "What on earth ails him? See what's the matter with your master instantly," speaking to one of the whips. By an extraordinary effort the man contrived to come up with him, and breathlessly asked where he was going. "Going, you blockhead!" was the answer, "where should I be going? Don't you see the hounds before you?" "Oh, Lord, Sir Harry," cried the man of thong, "them's not our hounds, them's a flock of sheep."

A somewhat different type of squire succeeded the old Westerns of the eighteenth century. In the early years of the nineteenth there was many a plain English country gentleman who, possessing full ten thousand pounds a year, never left his seat, unless he was called to his county town, or went to visit his friends.

The longevity of many of the old school of sportsmen was amazing. A striking instance of this was Eleazar Ashton, who died in 1840 at the age of ninety-eight. In his latter years Ashton was well known to followers of the Hopwood Beagles, a little pack all of about the same height—15 inches—which up till 1838 had as huntsman another veteran, Jack Mathews, who himself pursued his calling till past seventy.

Eleazar Ashton attributed his health and long life entirely to his love of following hounds, which he did on foot. On the 12th of August, the opening day, he went as usual to keep his ninety-seventh birthday at Hopwood, walking three miles from his residence at Dilsworth and back, and on that occasion his voice and laugh were as strong and hearty as ever. In October he was out two or three times with the hounds when near his own house, but his powers were then fast failing. Up to this season he was always found at the place of meeting, his hands upon the hook of a long hazel stick, on which he rested his chin, with an admiring circle surrounding him, the majority of whom were not infrequently his own descendants. About four years before his death, when so standing, on the arrival of the gentlemen, and after the usual greetings, he addressed Mr. Hopwood : " Mester Hoppud," said he, " will you step this way, and I'll just show you a queer touch." The old man led the way to a house, and gave a shout ; out came a fine young woman (a great-granddaughter), with a child in her arms. " There now," said he with some pride, " you may go home and tell 'em you've hunted with five generations i' the same field." His interest in sport continued to his last day ; and on the very evening of his death a grandson, who had been out with the hounds in the morning, called to see him. The old man asked where the hounds had been, and what they had done ; and on being told that after a good run and killing their hare they had gone home at eleven o'clock, he expressed great surprise, and said quickly, " What could mak' 'em do so ? " In two hours after he was dead.

Eleazar used to declare that he had never missed a chance of following hounds since he had been a lad, whilst laying great stress upon the importance of putting on dry shoes and stockings on reaching home. He had been an early riser, and never a hard drinker, though, as he admitted, not averse to an occasional bout, though never to such an extent as to damage his health. He had a fresh complexion, and honest, open countenance, with a carriage upright to the last ; his appearance, indeed, was a faithful index of his health and character. He married his first wife the year George the Third ascended the throne, and lived like an ancient patriarch, dying full of years and—in his own humble way—of honour. He had eight children, forty-two grandchildren, one hundred and twelve great-grandchildren, and eleven great-great-grandchildren.

The passionate love of fox-hunting which distinguished so many humble village characters in old days was well exemplified in the case of old Daniel Cross, a well-known character in the neighbourhood of Thorndon and Ingrave, Essex, as an earth-stopper, thatcher, and mole-catcher. He died aged eighty-five, in 1827, surviving his wife (to whom he had been married sixty-three years) about a twelvemonth. His remains were followed to the grave by his relatives, consisting of children, grandchildren, and great-grandchildren. He had often latterly expressed an anxious wish to see one more fox killed before he died. Though he did not exactly attain his desire, the hounds crossed the field opposite his house a day or two previous to his death ; and on seeing the attention of his attendants drawn to the spot, and learning the cause, he insisted on being taken to the window, from which he was with difficulty removed back to his bed.

A remarkable instance of longevity was reported from Ireland in 1797, when there died at Irreagh, in the county of Kerry, Daniel Bull Macarthy, a gentleman who had reached the age of 112. He had been married to five wives, and married the fifth, who survived him, when he was eighty-four and she fourteen; by her he had twenty children, she bearing a child every year. Mr. Macarthy was very healthy; no cold affected him; and he could not bear the warmth of a shirt in the night time, but put it under his pillow for the last seventy years. In company he drank plentifully of rum and brandy, which he called "naked truth," and when, out of complaisance to other gentlemen, he took claret or port, he always drank an equal glass of rum or brandy to qualify those liquors; this he called a wedge. He used to walk eight or ten miles in a winter's morning, with greyhounds and finders, and seldom failed to bring home a brace of hares.

The class of whom Squire Western was the type, lingered in Ireland long after it had disappeared in this country.

As late as the beginning of Queen Victoria's reign there existed in Ireland men who, from the rising up of the sun until the going down of the same, thought of nothing beneath heaven save field sports and whisky! With frames naturally iron, and become as steel by the constant practice of every hardy, invigorating exercise, such men could perform almost inconceivable feats of physical endurance, and drink a stupendous quantity of liquor. Most daring horsemen, and imbued with the devil-may-care spirit characteristic of their race, they made it a point of honour to attempt the most impossible leaps when out with hounds.

In those days an Irish hunt was the noisiest, most rattling, merry, break-neck scene imaginable. The gentlemen sportsmen of the country were well mounted on horses of the highest courage. They, however, only formed a small portion of that field; the rest consisted of horse and foot, boy and man, regular and irregular sportsmen of all grades and appearances; some mounted on saddle-horses without saddles, and some on draught-horses with saddles; whilst boots, shoes, and hay-bands protected these Nimrods' sinewy legs according to the means of purchasing either. Then there was such emulation in the field either to gain the brush, or to brush before a rival hunter; such galloping and leaping, such shouting and authoritative commands from patrician to plebeian, or rather from squire to cotter and labourer, to " howld his tongue, and be d—d to him ! " It was really like a galloping masquerade, or a carnival on horseback.

The tremendous drinking-bouts in which many Irish sportsmen indulged not infrequently lasted right through the night.

" Good morrow to your honour, Captain ! " said a village character, smoking a dudeen at his door, to a certain young squire whom he perceived riding through the village towards his house at a very early hour in the morning. " It's yourself that's up brave an' early the day." " Morrow, kindly ! " was the reply; " it's early enough in troth, but it's home to bed I'm going, Barney. I've been dining with the officers in Newry over, and by the Piper of Blessinton, I'm after carrying away with me eight-and-twenty tumblers of punch, to say nothing about the port and sherry." " Ah ! well, any way," rejoined the smoker,

" you won't pass my door widout tasting a dhrop, just for look, Captain ? " " I'm obliged to ye all the same as if I drank," replied the punctilious squire ; " and I'd do that same with all my heart, Barney dear "—at the same time putting his mare into a walk—" only I'm in dread my mother would find the smell of spirits on me at breakfast ! "

" There is one thing I had clane forgot to till yez," said an old Irish squire to his son on his death-bed, after he had given him sundry good advices ; " and 'tis will it came into the hid av me, or I cudn't have died aisy. Mind whin yu are out dining, in the winter time ispicially, always to come clane an sober off after the tinth tum'ler of punch ; an' that's the way yule's nat be breaking yure nick by rason of tum'lin' in ditches like a dhrunken blackguard ; now mind that, jewel, an' my blissin' be wid yu ! "

A typical old Irish squire—it was said—the last of his kind—" a raal ould crack o' the whip," as he was familiarly termed by the peasantry of his immediate vicinity—was a certain veteran sportsman of seventy, who lived in Munster at the commencement of the nineteenth century.

This gentleman had received a rather rough education, but had in some degree been polished by a short residence abroad, had thence gone early into the army, where he had fought (according to the usage of the times), and killed not only his man, but nearly three at once, as he used to narrate with something of eccentric emphasis and whimsical melancholy. He had then run away with the girl of his choice from a fire-eating rival, and having married, retired to his family domain, where he hunted, shot, fished, farmed (after a fashion), drank, danced, and begat sons and daughters like a patriarch. A patriarch he was in practice, as, besides a large family by the wife of his bosom, those by his handmaids and others of his people would have disgraced no Israelite of ancient days. Many of these last served him as domestics and in other occupations, for he acted conscientiously, emulating those wonderful men of remotest antiquity, in particular taking good care up to the very last piously to obey the mandate to increase and multiply.

His appearance is described as having been peculiar in the extreme.

The Squire was a short, stout man, wearing a powdered wig with two tiers of coachman's curls appearing from below a hunting-cap, around which was tied a white handkerchief, with a large bow in front, to be in readiness to defend his neck in case of rain. To this wig was appended a natty pig-tail, which, from a habit he had of inclining his head a little on one side, always got between his coat collar and his neck, and stuck out under his left ear. The countenance was that of a hardy, hearty, hard-drinking country gentleman, the cheeks being streaked with red veins like a winter apple, but there was no appearance of a sot. His eye was small, volatile, keen, and expressive. He wore a long grey frock coat, evidently nailed together by the household snip, and a pair of leather breeches, which he boasted had never been cleaned since he first put them on.

# The Merry Past

His nether limbs were cased in a pair of black boots without tops, similar to a heavy dragoon's, though reaching only to the knee ; and these were garnished with a pair of solid silver spurs.

The "Ould Squire's" harriers—or "bagles," as he called them—were like the rest of his establishment (with the exception of a beautiful daughter), more useful than ornamental. They packed well together, and carried a good head ; but they were of all sorts and sizes. His dog language (for the huntsman was more properly whip) was of the most extraordinary kind. Whenever on a trail two or three staunch hounds denoted to the "Ould Crack" that they were near the quarry, he used to sing out, "Go to her, my babbies, 'the little red bitch'; now let every man rason (rosin) his bow." This he accompanied with suitable action : playing on his bridle with his fingers like a fiddler, and drawing his whip bow-fashion across his elbow, humming the while a stave of the "Kilruddery Hunt." The inimitable absurdity of his look and manner beggared all description. Nevertheless he rode well, his favourite mount being a mare which was a counterpart to himself—low, muscular, flinty, and flippant—with an eye indicating plenty of pluck, though she showed little of what is commonly termed blood.

The old Squire was a capital snipe shot, and his eccentricity failed him not there ; he shot in reflecting glasses, having had an eye turned in his head by a pike wound at the storming of Vinegar Hill. Whenever a fair shot rose, his " Be Dad, I'll have yu on a bit of toast," or, " Come here, my tight fillow, yu must sup with me to-night "—were almost certain death-warrants.

As he hunted and shot, so did he tell many a good anecdote, and his powers as a conversationalist were well known all over the countryside. One story of his, describing a treble duel in which he had taken part, was especially characteristic of his fire-eating youth.

As this sanguinary combat was an absolute fact, and highly illustrative of a certain phase of Irish life in the past, it may be of interest to give it in the Squire's own words.

" Feth (faith), sir, I was a jolly young cornet in his present Majestee's (George the Fourth, then Prince of Wales), God bless him, fincible cavalry, and quartered at Kilkenny. It happened, sir, that I had bin, and alone, at the thaatre, and returning to the barracks, I lucked (looked) in at the ' Hole in the Wall '— it was a tavern, sir, noted in those days for mutton kidneys and raspberry whisky-punch. I was taking my tumber (tumbler) when Lard ——, Colonel ——, and Captain ——, interred—all afficers in the Kilkenny militia. Feth, sir, I percaved they were flustered, and quarrels were plinty as swords thin. So I only bowed ; on which his Lardship asked me if I was too drunk to spake. I wished to take this in jist, but he repated it, and gitting angry I tould him, though he had the title of a Lard, he wanted the manners of a jintlemon. On this they all three threw their glasses (they had got a battle of claret) at me, and I rose and struck his Lardship with my sheathed sword, and desired the other two to concave themselves struck as well, and lift the room. The nixt morning we ware out, yu may be sartain, but I had the advantage, though they were three to one, being sober, which they were not. The first man who tuk his ground was the Colonel; he fell at the first fire, nivir stirred hand or feet. The Captain was the nixt. I hit him in the right hip, and lamed him for life. Though my blood was up, I could not help feeling a little sarious now, but what cud a man do, and his second handing him the third pistol without a word? His Lardship nivir tuk his ground, but coming up to me, said enough blood had been shed, and that he begged my pardon. I thought so to, but my blood was up, and I thought him a mane (mean) fillow at the time; but I have since percaved I was in the wrong. It was the fashion of those days, howivir, and no man knew whin it might be his own turn."

The Squire was something of a dandy in the evening, when he always appeared in silk stockings and dancing pumps. Notwithstanding his advanced age, he was a very tiger to dance, and would do so the whole night through, always taking special care to get hold of the prettiest girls in the room. He was such a wonderful gay hero for his time of life that he was a universal favourite.

A character always out with the Squire's hounds was Jack Mara, the groom and colt-breaker. The "Ould Squire" bred his own horses, and Jack was celebrated even among that desperate set of centaurs, the Irish horse-breakers. On one occasion the "bagles" found a fox, and ran into him on the banks of the Shannon, in an orchard which a gentleman had been newly making, around which a stiff stone wall, upwards of six feet high, had been erected. Over this wall, after a sharp run, Jack rode a young mare, got by Kildare; and though such hops were not miracles in Munster, it caused some talk among the sporting gentry, one of whom happened to meet Jack a few days after. " The top of the marning to yure Honour ! " " Well, Jack, how is all at home ? That was a raal skelp you had on Monday. Is it true that you rode the Kildare mare over Harry Cahill's garden wall ? " " Is it true ? " cried Jack. " Is there water in the Shannon ? and the divil a word of lie in that." " But tell me, Jack, now in arnest—was it as high as they spake about ? " " By Jazus," roared Jack, " an' is it yure honour's silf that's after áxing that ar of me ? Blud and nouns, wasn't it a wall for nailing paches (peaches) aginst?"

Another prominent figure in the field was the huntsman Tim, who at dinner always stood behind the " ould Crack's " chair. Tim had a grin like a satyr, and a fiery red nose which in a hot day it was absolutely painful to look at. He was attired in a long green coat with a hare on the buttons, red waistcoat, clean leathers, and shoes. This uncouth attendant was badly crippled, owing to severe falls. He made a shift to wait, however, which produced rather a disagreeable effect on strangers not used to him.

# The Merry Past

On hunting days Tim had always to be helped into the saddle; but when he once was there, and his "morning" (a stiff glass of whisky, which the Squire administered in person) tucked into him, he was "by the powers, a disperate fillow all out intirely."

He seemed, indeed, to have joined the field for no other purpose than spanking a one-eyed, cock-tailed "chisnut" mare—more like a deer than a horse—over every break-neck thing that could come in his way, to the interminable delight and appro-bation of the Ould Squire and his sons.

As a huntsman Tim had won the sincere regard of the Squire. He had broken almost every one of his bones in desperate falls, but was still the "bouldest" horseman in all Ireland.

## III

MANY English hunting expressions are of French
origin, and were used by the Normans, who
were ardently devoted to the chase. "Tally ho!" in
spite of its essentially British ring, is probably nothing
more than the old French cry, "*Dans le taillis en
haut*," "up in the brushwood," which rang o'er our
woodlands for many a long year after the battle of
Hastings had decided the fate of England.

The Conqueror himself was particularly fond of
hunting, and most of our English monarchs, including
the present King, have at one time or other turned
their attention to this sport.

William III was a keen follower of hounds, and is
said to have made it a point of honour never to be
outdone in any leap, however perilous. An adherent
of the Stuarts, Mr. Cherry by name, who was heart
and soul devoted to the exiled family, is said to have
taken advantage of this to form what was surely the
most pardonable plot ever devised against a king's life.
He made a practice of following the Royal hounds,
ever riding in the first flight, and took the most
desperate leaps, in the hope that the King might
break his neck in following him. One day, however,
he took a leap so imminently dangerous, that William,

when he came to the spot, shook his head, and drew back. It is further said that Mr. Cherry at length broke his own neck, and thereby relieved the King from being beguiled into danger.

George III was an ardent votary of the chase, and took great interest in the details of the hunts which he favoured by his presence.

On one occasion, when hunting near Basingstoke, he got into conversation with Mr. William Chute, of the Vine, who was member for the county, and well able to gratify the King's curiosity as to who was out with the hounds, besides knowing all about the places through which the hunt passed. When they came to a certain old manor-house which had some curious fragments of antiquity, the King exclaimed : " What is that, Mr. Chute ? What ! what ! what ! " Chute smiled and hesitated. The King repeated his question. " Why, please your Majesty," said Chute, who was bluntness itself, " that is a manor held of your Majesty by the tenure of finding your Majesty a concubine whenever you come this way ! " The King exclaimed : " What ! what ! what ! Mr. Chute ?— eh ? eh ? Mr. Chute !—I believe I shall stop my horse and take some refreshment there. But are there pretty girls there, Mr. Chute ?—are there pretty girls there ? " " Please, your Majesty," with sufficient familiarity, " shall I go and see ? " But a loud " Tally ho ! " sounded at that moment, and off they all went at a full burst. At the end of a famous run, which delighted the King, His Majesty again found himself by the side of Chute. " Ah ! ah ! Mr.

Chute," enquired the King, "where are we now?"
"Please your Majesty," Chute replied, in a droll
enough manner, "we are twenty miles from the
Master of the Concubines." The King burst out
into a loud laugh, and said : "Very well, Mr. Chute :
very well, indeed!"

George IV, when Prince of Wales, used to hunt a
good deal with the Cottesmore, at the time that
Sir Gilbert Heathcote was master of that pack.

Ranksboro' gorse was one of his favourite fixtures,
as it afforded a commanding view, and if they went
away he could keep them in sight for a great distance.
His Royal Highness, too, would sometimes go pretty
fairly ; he would fence boldly enough, but he was not
fond of galloping.

Sir Gilbert hunted what is now the Cottesmore
country for seven seasons, owing, it is said, to certain
family reasons which induced Lord Lonsdale to give
up his hounds during that period.

George IV, in spite of the severe criticisms which
were so often levelled at him, was no unkindly man.

When this Prince kept foxhounds at Critchel, in
Dorsetshire, he became much attached to Parson
Butler, the sporting vicar of Frampton, who was an
unconventional character of considerable originality
of dress and phrase. The parson in question soon
became a great favourite, and generally rode pretty
close to the Prince in the hunting field.

On one of these occasions, the Prince remarked to
him, that he rode a very bad horse. This the divine
took rather in dudgeon : even his John Bull stolidity

could hardly stomach such a remark, for he was by no means rich. "How comes it," again demanded the Prince, "that you, Doctor, who are so keen, and, let me add, so good a sportsman, ride so bad a horse ? " Thoroughly roused, the doctor bluntly replied : " For the same reason that your Highness rides so good a one." " How so ? " rejoined the Prince. " Because Providence has made you a Prince, and me a parson." "You have exactly defined it, Doctor," said His Highness, in high glee, " and we must see how it can be amended." The sequel was that one of the best horses in the royal stud was made over to the parson, to have and to hold for his own.

On another occasion—a certain Saturday night— when, after a long day and a late dinner, the bedroom candles were brought in, all, of course, waited until the Prince called for his—except the doctor, who, as soon as ever they appeared, grasped one, and was about to depart with clerical, but uncourtly, haste, had he not been deterred by one of the most ceremonious of the small household, who saw no joke in breaches of etiquette, but regarded them with utter horror. Just at this moment the Prince had, on the sudden, fallen into earnest conversation with some person of consequence, and the colloquy lasting some time, the doctor began to evince manifest and manifold signs of impatience—coughing, scraping his feet, and ever and anon casting unutterable looks towards the Prince. He stood thus for about half an hour, when all-powerful Nature broke out, and, shaking off the punctilious functionary above mentioned, who again endeavoured to restrain him, as a terrier would a rat, he seized his taper, and, striding up to the Prince, thus addressed him : " Please, your Highness, it may do very well for you to stand here all night talking, as you can lie as long as you please in the morning ; but I have many a long mile to ride to my parish, and there is no help for it : there's an old woman to be buried that ought to have been put in the ground last week, and she'll keep no longer, and there's a young couple to marry that I put off last week—by George, they'll keep no longer ; so your Royal Highness will excuse me, but you must not keep me any longer!" This was all in such " good keeping " that there was no standing it any longer—even the punctilious chamberlain was not proof against it ; and amid peals of laughter the triumphant doctor strode off to his roost.

Some of the old fox-hunting parsons held very peculiar views as to the performance of their duties. One of these, the Reverend Mr. Wright, who had a small living in the West of England, refused to read the Athanasian Creed, though repeatedly desired to do so by his parishioners. The parishioners complained to the bishop, who ordered it to be read. The somewhat curious Creed in question is appointed to be said or sung, and Mr. Wright accordingly, on the following Sunday, thus addressed his congregation : " Next follows Athanasius's Creed, either to be said or sung, and, with Heaven's leave, I'll sing it. Now, clerk, mind what you are about." After this they both struck up, and sang it with great glee to a fox-

hunting tune, which, having previously been practised, was well performed. The scandalised parishioners again met, and informed their diocesan of what
they called the indecorum ; but the bishop said their
pastor was right, for it was so ordered, in consequence
of which they declared that they would dispense with
the Creed in future.

Another sporting parson, the brother of an earl,
having had the misfortune to lose his pointer and his
Bible, caused a placard to be put up upon the church
door next day, in which the Bible was described as
being dog-eared, and the pointer lettered upon the
back.

Perhaps the best description of the qualities most
thoroughly appreciated in a popular parson of the
old school was that given by an old servant, who said
his master was " an excellent clergyman, and a truly
good man, for he always kept a capital tap of ale, and
was remarkable free with it."

Most of these reverend gentlemen were simple folk.
One of them, having been unwell for some time, con-
sulted his doctor, who told him that he must give up
eating bread as his digestion was weak. " Things are
come to a pretty pass," said he, when he got home, to
his wife. " Here have I been praying to God with an
audible voice, twice every day of my life, and ten
times on Sundays, to give me my ' daily bread,' and
when I go to my doctor, he exclaims, ' Don't touch
it, or it will poison you.' "

Queen Victoria in her younger years rode well, and
many other sovereigns have known how to bestride

their steeds in a capable manner. The French nation, it was said, always regretted that Louis XVIII could not be seen on horseback, calculating that he who has to manage the reins of government ought, at least, to know how to handle those of his horse—they remembered that Henri Quatre, the Roi Soleil, and Frederick the Great, not forgetting Alexander of old, were all first-rate riders. A king cannot show himself to his army and people without this, nor a queen either : the Empress Marie Louise rode the high-horse in great style, although Napoleon took her down upon one occasion when she was enceinte and forbidden to take this exercise.

Hunting with the old French kings was always the occasion for much spectacular display.

The equipage or hunting establishment and turn-out of Louis the Fifteenth was splendid, in carriages, horses, guards, and attendants. Many of the nobility had what they called a *voiture de chasse*, frequently drawn by three horses abreast, like some of our omnibuses. The idea was taken from the four-in-hand of the Romans, which were driven abreast instead of by leaders and wheel-horses. This lasted up to the time of Louis the Sixteenth, when considerable importance was still attached to the chase, where even ambassadors and courtiers paid their duty to the monarch, and where sometimes intrigue and politics were mixed up with the day's sport.

The more closely to unite devotees of the chase together, there was instituted on the Continent the Order of St. Hubert, the patron saint of hunters, which gave distinctive decoration to the knights of the Order. The Duc d'Aumont was, it is said, the last Grande Croix, or Grand Master of the Order, which is now fallen into decay.

In the eighteenth century a number of great ladies disdained the side-saddle when hunting, and were habited *à l'Anglaise* down to the waist.

This jacket was a riding habit, but having very large loose trousers for their lower garment, and sometimes all buttoned down the side.

In Italy, when the first British female was seen on the side-saddle, the passers-by exclaimed : "*Pater de Bacco! ecco una donna a Cavallo con una gamba*" : "By the power of Bacchus" (a substitute for an oath), "behold a lady on horseback with one leg!"

The costume of a gentleman hunting with Louis XV was of a most ornate description. A plain cocked hat, heavy boots, a blue coat of great dimensions with covered buttons, a scarlet waistcoat with broad gold lace, blue velvet inexpressibles, knee caps (*manchettes de bottes*) as white as snow, a *couteau de chasse* by his side richly mounted in silver, and with a crimson velvet scabbard. The saddle was of a sort known as "demi-pique," with a crimson saddle-cloth bordered with rich gold lace. The hair was dressed in large curls on the head and bagged in a rosette behind, which mode of hair-dressing survived till the reign of Louis XVI, though anyone wearing it as late as that date was derisively called a "Crapeau."

In England, also, there have in the past been magnificently turned-out hunts. When Lord Barrymore first started during his minority with his stag-hounds and sporting equipment it resembled the hunting establishment of Louis the Fourteenth at Fontainebleau, rather than the private hunt of a British subject ! Four Africans were in this spend-thrift's retinue, superbly mounted and dressed in scarlet and silver. They were skilled performers on the French horn, and occasionally, to quote a con-temporary writer, " in the woods and the vallies, gladdened Diana with Handel's harmony, and at once alarmed and pleased the browsing herds within the compass of their mellifluous sound."

The royal hunt as it existed under Louis XVI was a fine sight.

About a hundred and twenty horses would start for the rendezvous in relays of three, a groom form-ing the centre, with a led-horse on either side, the grooms in royal livery, dark blue, deep red, and silver, huge silver-laced cocked hats and demi-jack boots, heavy enough to frighten an English horse to look at. Then came the King in a carriage and eight, with his *gardes du corps.* In due course, he mounted his strong, bony, bay hunter, surrounded by nobles and courtiers dressed in the royal livery, and in similar manner with heavy boots and silver-laced hats. Many of them had the seams of their coats laced, and some had three stripes of alternate gold and silver lace, disposed in the same way as certain grooms had alternate red velvet and silver stripes. The King wore his own livery, was very fat, very easy-looking, and very healthy ; he sat back in his saddle, rode at almost full

speed, and seemed as if he thought that his horse had
no feeling. The whole appearance of the royal hunt,
amounting to nearly three hundred horse, had a very
curious quaint appearance; the noise, the bustle,
the pomp and parade, the clattering of heavy boots,
the flapping of the men's pigtails, together with an
air of importance and ceremony, produced an extraordinary effect. The hounds were English—very fine
dogs, and purchased at Tattersall's—they ran well,
but were not as well hunted; there was too much
bustle and exertion in the matter. The horses of the
King's establishment, as well as those of the nobility
who accompanied the royal train, were mostly
Norman, although a great many were English, and of
high price. The former were very stout and bony,
more calculated for a stiff country, or for the fatigue
of a long and arduous journey, than for fleetness,
fencing, or other active performances, in getting over
leaps and crossing a country. Bone was a great
recommendation in France in those days, and a cross
between the British and Norman breeds was much
sought for. The Duc de Lauzun, the Duc de Pienne,
and the Prince Charles de Ligne had some of the
finest English horses in the country, not forgetting
Philippe Egalité's stud.

At that time there were in France a number of
most magnificent *voitures de chasse*, hunting carriages,
very fancifully constructed, resembling our caravans,
and having sometimes a stag's head and fore-quarters
in front; over which a coachman, all gold or silver
lace, and his hair highly dressed, used to take his seat,

driving either four-in-hand, the horses all too far
from their work, the leaders with very long traces,
seldom tight (for these dressy coachmen did not know
how to keep the tits up to their traces), or with five
horses, the leaders having a postilion, with cocked hat
and jack-boots. The nobility mostly went to covert
in close carriages, the horses being led, like those of
the royal hunt, each led-horse being covered with a
rich cloth, corresponding with the livery of the owner,
and with the family arms, or cipher and coronet, at
each corner. That of the Comte d'Artois was dark
green with splendid gold lace ; the livery being that
colour and crimson, laced richly with gold. It had
a fine effect in the field, although an unsporting
appearance, being more military-looking than anything else. The Prince de Condé's trappings were
buff and crimson velvet, with silk embroidery of the
latter colour.

Marie Antoinette wore the uniform of the royal
hunt, with a quantity of gold lace, and as great a
profusion of fine white ostrich feathers in her riding-
hat. She generally arrived in a *voiture de chasse*,
drawn by eight fine English bay horses, driven by a
giant of a charioteer of most uncoachmanlike appearance—a desperate driver, but a bad whip. The
animals went at a furious rate, and Her Most Christian
Majesty had much the appearance of a sovereign of
ancient times making a triumphal entry into some
conquered state.

The Princess Elizabeth, sister to the King, who
afterwards fell a victim to revolutionary fury, was

dressed in a plain blue riding-habit, made in London, and an English riding-hat with black feathers ; she wore an open collar, like our young boys, and displayed a neck as white as the most polished ivory ; she rode *à l'Anglaise*, and was mounted on an English horse.

When the quarry had been taken and killed, the woodlands rang with loud fanfares, played upon French horns, whilst the Queen rose in her triumphal car and graciously bowed her recognition to the admiring noblesse.

The hunt being over, the royal party would adjourn to a *pavillon de chasse*, where refreshments were prepared and the Queen conversed with a few privileged persons.

Although Marie Antoinette had, when serious or displeased, a most disdainful haughty air, she very often unbent into the most playful familiarity. This betrayed her into what her enemies called levity or giddiness, but it was nothing but a natural vivacity, which Imperial pomp and etiquette kept down.

At a royal hunt the Duke of Dorset, then English Ambassador, was near Her Majesty, who, laying her hand upon his arm, said, in a playful tone : " How d'ye do ?  Go dem ! " which excited universal mirth.

On another occasion, having condescended to dance with a young Englishman of the name of Conway, and being a good deal heated and agitated by the exertion, she made him observe the palpitation of her heart, in an attitude which half seemed like an inclination to place his hand upon it.  The

act, however, was not done, nor did Conway attempt
to take advantage of this momentary, almost in-
voluntary, indiscretion. The King came up at this
juncture, when the lovely Queen naively said : " I
was just showing this young cavalier how violently
my heart beat." To which His Majesty sternly
replied : " *Et il y a bien-fait de prendre votre
parole.*"

Napoleon, though in his own way he enjoyed a
stag-hunt as much as any of the Bourbons, dispensed
with the retinue which accompanied the monarchs
of that line in the chase. The individuality of his
character showed itself here as in more serious matters,
and when he was in the mood for a stag-hunt not even
his most intimate friends knew of it till he was ready
to start. The grand forester of Fontainebleau and
his men were in consequence continually on the alert,
as they never knew when the Emperor might appear
or his orders arrive for this reason; even when His
Imperial Majesty was staying at Paris or St. Cloud
the circuit of the forest was made daily, and a report
as to the deer which were harboured within its limits
prepared.

At one time hunting was regularly carried on in
the Bois de Boulogne, near Paris, and the Comte
d'Artois once ran a stag right into the present Rue
Royale.

As late as 1814 there was hunting almost at the
walls of the city. Bagatelle was a favourite rendezvous, and here the Duc de Berri was wont to entertain
those ladies who were in at the death of the deer.

# The Merry Past

The Comte d'Artois, afterwards Charles the Tenth, from his eminence as a shot and his love for the sports of the trigger, to which he dedicated to the latest hour of his monarchy a great portion of his time, acquired the nickname of *Robin des Bois*.

Though after the Revolution there was considerable diminution in the splendour of the royal hunt, a day with Charles X, in 1828, would have seemed somewhat extraordinary to sportsmen of the present age. The King went to St. Germain in state. First came a strong advance body-guard, consisting of twenty or thirty lancers, riding at a hand gallop, clattering over the stones and making a most tremendous row; immediately after them followed a splendid coach, the whole body gilded, with the white fleur-de-lis and the arms of France upon the panels, with four footmen in state liveries stuck up behind. It was drawn by eight short-tailed, bay, English horses, six-in-hand, and a postilion on the leader, in a cocked hat, blue and silver-laced coat, and immense jack-boots, with a sort of thing like a trunk at the top of them in which a man might carry a day's provision. In the carriage were His Majesty and one or two others, and by the doors rode the equerries and all sorts of state officials. Then came another carriage-and-eight in the same style, only without anyone in it, and another strong body of heavy cavalry brought up the rear.

The cavalcade halted by some houses on the roadside, where the saddle horses were waiting, together with the hounds, the lieutenant and sub-lieutenant of the forest in uniform, *gardes*, rangers, both horse and foot, a large mob of people, and a party of *gendarmerie*.

The King now stepped out of his carriage and mounted his horse (a fine thoroughbred grey, with no end of trappings and nets to keep him warm) with all the activity of a man of twenty.

His dress was like that of an English country gentleman on a market-day—an old white hat, a cutty green coat, and pair of old drab breeches and an antiquated pair of top-boots.

The hounds, though the hunt servants swore the contrary, were mostly large English foxhounds, or at least had been so originally, some of them appearing to have a cross of the bull in them. There were plenty of attendants upon them, both mounted and foot, all dressed in the royal livery (dark blue and silver), some of them wearing badges.

There were also three or four huntsmen, all capital fellows in their way, with immense great saddles, great bits, and jack-boots.

When the hunt began the King set off galloping, the gendarmes scrambling after him as fast as they could, whilst keeping the rest of the field at a considerable distance. Everyone went tearing up one avenue and down another, and round a third, for a couple of hours, the stag every now and then popping across the road with the hounds in full cry, till at last he fairly left the forest. When at last run to bay and the King arrived on the spot, one of the *gardes* would hand the monarch a blunderbuss, with which he shot the stag dead, amid the playing of horns and bellowing of hounds.

This ended the day's sport, and the remains of the unfortunate stag were left to be mangled by the keepers. The coach-and-eight and all the guards were brought near the spot, the King dismounted, and, stepping into it, rattled off just in the same state he arrived.

After the Revolution of 1830 all the sporting appurtenances of Charles X were sold. The King in question had certainly been rather extravagant. Everything was by wholesale : two hundred shooting coats, two hundred pairs of gaiters, three hundred "Joe Mantons," six hundred powder flasks, and the rest in proportion. Perhaps there never was such a display of accoutrements, the property of one individual, before. They were all " George Robins'd," as the phrase originated by the celebrated auctioneer went, but the French carried their dislike for the man to his chattels, on a sort of love-me-love-my-dog principle, and things sold very cheap. The hounds went for a mere nothing. The largest purchases, it was said, were made on behalf of the King of Saxony.

In the days when there was such a close connection between France and the young American Republic, Lafayette sent to Washington a pack of French hounds of very great size, some of which were treated as household pets. An old hound, called Vulcan, in particular was allowed to take great liberties.

On one occasion, when a large party were sitting down to dinner at Mount Vernon, the lady of the mansion discovered that the ham—the pride of every Virginian housewife's table—was missing from its accustomed post of honour. Upon questioning Frank the butler, the latter portly personage observed that a ham, yes, a very fine ham, had been prepared, nay dished, agreeably to the madam's order ; but, lo and behold, who should come into the kitchen while the savoury ham was smoking in its dish, but old Vulcan the hound, who, without more ado, fastened his fangs into it ; and although they of the kitchen had stood bravely to such arms as they could get, and made a gallant fight, yet Vulcan had finally triumphed, and borne off the prize right under the keeper's nose. The lady by no means relished the loss of a dish which formed the pride of her table, and uttered some remarks by no means favourable to old Vulcan, or indeed to dogs in general ; Washington, however, having heard the story, communicated it to his guests, and with them laughed heartily at the exploit of the old hound.

During the hunting season, Mount Vernon contained many sporting guests, whose visits lasted for weeks, at which time they were entertained in the good old style of Virginia's ancient hospitality.

Washington used to hunt about three days a week when the weather would allow him to do so. On hunting mornings breakfast was served by candlelight, the General always breaking his fast with an Indian corn-cake and a bowl of milk ; and before cock-crow the whole cavalcade would often have left the house. Those who saw Washington on horseback declared that he was the most accomplished of cavaliers, in the true sense and perfection of the character : he rode, as he did everything, with ease, elegance, and power. The vicious propensities of horses were of no moment to this skilful and daring rider, who always said that he required but one good quality in a horse—" to go along," and ridiculed the idea of its being even possible that he should be unhorsed, provided the animal kept on his legs. The perfect and sinewy frame of Washington gave him such a surpassing grip with his knees that a horse might as soon disencumber itself of the saddle as of its rider.

He was always superbly mounted, and wore a very sporting costume of blue coat, scarlet waistcoat, buckskin breeches, top-boots, velvet cap, and carried a whip with long thong.

General Washington's usual mount was a horse called Blueskin, of a dark iron-grey colour, approaching to blue. This was a fine but fiery animal, and of great endurance in a long run. Will, the huntsman, better known in revolutionary lore as " Billy," rode a horse called Chinkling, a surprising jumper, and made very much like its rider—low, but sturdy, and of great bone and muscle. Will had but one order, which was, to keep with the hounds ; and mounted on Chinkling, a French horn at his back, throwing himself almost at length on the animal, with his spur in his flank, this fearless horseman would rush at full speed, through brake or tangled wood, in a style at which modern huntsmen would stand aghast. There were roads cut through the woods in various directions, by which aged and timid hunters and ladies could enjoy the exhilarating sport without risk of life or limb ; but Washington rode gaily up to his hounds, through all the difficulties and dangers of the grounds on which he hunted, nor spared his generous steed, as the distended nostrils of Blueskin often would show, always in at the death, and yielding to no man in the struggle for the honours of the brush.

The quarry was generally the grey fox, with one exception—this was a famous black fox, which, differing from his brethren of " orders grey," would flourish his brush, set his pursuers at defiance, and go from ten to twenty miles on end, distancing both dogs and men ; and, what was truly remarkable, would return to his place of starting the same night, so as always to be found there the ensuing morning. After seven or eight severe runs, " Billy " recommended that the black Reynard should be let alone, giving it as his opinion that he was very near akin to another sable character inhabiting a lower region, and as remarkable for his wiles. The advice was adopted from necessity ; and ever afterwards, in throwing off the hounds, care was taken to avoid the haunt of this unconquerable fox.

It may be added that the red fox is supposed to have been imported from England to the eastern shore of Maryland by a Mr. Smith, and to have emigrated across the ice to Virginia, in the hard winter of 1779–80, when the Chesapeake was frozen over.

Washington, after hunting (true to the rule of life which never permitted his pleasures to infringe upon the order and regularity of his habits), took a few glasses of Madeira, and retired to his supperless bed at nine o'clock. After 1787, having ceased to hunt, he gave away his pack.

One of the most intrepid sportswomen who ever followed hounds was the Marchioness of Salisbury, who was burnt to death in 1836 when eighty-six years of age.

Archery and coursing were also patronised by this sporting lady.

A feature of the coursing season at Hatfield was Bryant's day, as it was called, Mr. Bryant being then the landlord of the Salisbury Arms Inn at Hatfield, and having been complimented by the Marchioness with one separate and distinct day of coursing, in order to invite his friends to the sport, and afterwards to dine at his house.

Old Lady Salisbury was in early life prominent in the hunting field, and for many years presided over the destinies of the Hatfield hunt, which, in after years, developed into the Hertfordshire hounds.

Up to her seventieth year she was heard to say, if she could not hunt a pack of foxhounds, she was still able to follow the harriers. Her ladyship's ardour in the chase was excessive ; she was a constant attendant of the hunt for eighteen successive years, during which she was seldom absent a day from the covert side. She was an elegant and accomplished horsewoman, and rode with as much intrepidity as judgment : no day was too long for her, and she was ever anxious to give good sport to the field, which was

# The Merry Past

generally well attended. Her affability to all was proverbial, and during her reign Hatfield House was remarkable for its character of hospitality, maintained with the greatest splendour.

To the last Lady Salisbury scarcely ever omitted her daily ride into the park on horseback, except when the weather would not permit, and then she went to the King's riding-house at Pimlico for an hour; and so high did Lady Salisbury stand in the estimation of George IV, that he caused an opening to be made into the interior of the Green Park, exactly facing her garden gate, that she might have the exclusive privilege of enjoying her favourite exercise there undisturbed.

This sportswoman's death was extremely tragic. She had retired a short time before dinner to her dressing-room to write a note, and her attendant left her. The room by some means caught fire, and every exertion to save her was in vain. She perished in the fiery furnace, and the venerable lady found a tomb amid the mouldering ruins of the west wing of Hatfield, over which she had presided for more than half a century.

An old French sporting lady who was a great character attracted a good deal of attention during the English occupation of France, under the Duke of Wellington, when some officers were billeted at the Château of Zudguerke not far from Gravelines. This was owned by the Baroness de Draacke, a portly lady, of about fifty-five, of somewhat startling dress and appearance. She wore top-boots, black velvet breeches, a white waistcoat, with the uniform coat of "La Louveterie" (Wolf Hunt), of which she was the only female member. This coat was a green jacket with facing of white, gilt buttons, and gold lace; the skirts were tastefully turned up and fastened with two gilt hunting horns. Such was the invariable costume of the Baroness, whilst her hat was bound with gold lace, like that of a coachman. Under the *ancien régime*, "La Louveterie Club" had its ramifications through France. It was instituted for the extermination of wolves, and its members were of the high noblesse. There were many different grades and ranks, the funds were ample, and they possessed many packs of wolfhounds.

From an early age the Baroness, whose voice and manner were masculine, had been addicted to field sports, her education having suffered in consequence. She came of a noble family, and had a good fortune for a Frenchwoman of that day. She had been married to the Baron de Draacke, a famous wolf-hunter, who died before the Revolution, in the course of which the Baroness was imprisoned, deprived of the privileges attaching to her rank, and her estates confiscated. Of undaunted spirit, she petitioned the ephemeral Government of the day for the restoration of her liberty. She pleaded that she was a woman, that she never meddled with politics, and that she had performed important services to her country, as she had freed her own district from wolves. Strange to say, the Revolutionary Government allowed the force of her plea, and set her at liberty to enjoy one-half of her fortune : the remainder was otherwise disposed of. Out of gratitude to her hounds, to whom she owed her safety, she continued to keep them in honourable comfort at Zudguerke, though they never went out except for exercise. They consisted of about fifteen couple—large dogs, in colour black and white, a buckhound in the body, a foxhound in the head ; the ears somewhat large for the latter, but too small for the former. Their huntsman was a chubby-faced fellow, as much of a clodhopper as a Frenchman could be. Her plea of this pack having rid her neighbourhood of wolves was absolutely based upon fact, and on the doors of the kennel, stables, and great gate were nailed the emblems of the Baroness's daring achievements—in the form of several wolf heads, blanched and withered from their long exposure to the air.

She kept no good horses, but admired and understood the good points about one. She herself had always ridden astride, and according to an old picture looked when on horseback something like one of the " Blues."

The only sport she pursued in her latter days was cock-fighting, and there was a regular cock-pit in the courtyard, where mains were fought in the presence of several spectators, at which she always presided. In other respects her pursuits were those of a lady of the old school. For several hours every day she played at piquet with a female friend.

# The Merry Past

The Baroness had no musical talent herself, though there was an antiquated barrel-organ which played but one tune, " La Chasse Henri Quatre." The interior of the house bore every evidence of its owner's sporting tastes. Partridges and other stuffed birds exhibited in glass cases, bridles and saddles of every description, guns and pistols, powder-flasks and shot-belts in all varieties, but all out of date, and ante-diluvian, pervaded the house from dining-room to attic, as well as the stairs and landings, a strange medley of antiquated appurtenances of the chase.

Her living pets were a paralytic owl in a cage, and two little dogs somewhat of the King Charles breed ; these were a great delight to her, and she had taught them some tricks. " Fais dos-à-dos pour Le Roi " was the favourite ; but her pets were too fat and lazy almost to bark, being generally obliged to lean against the wall or the leg of a chair when they went through their exercises.

A bitter hater of Bonaparte, she would have seen him and all his dynasty hanged on the avenue trees; and she was the first to hoist the *drapeau blanc* on the steeple of Zudguerke when the Bourbons returned to France.

This brave old lady indeed was an ultra-loyalist, and overweeningly attached to the old Game Laws; the very thought of a poacher, it was declared, was enough to prevent her sleeping for a month.

Her only excursions abroad were to St. Omer in her carriage, as antediluvian as all the rest—a positive hen-roost.

87

# The Merry Past

Some years after the termination of the English occupation of this part of France several attempts were made to establish regular packs of hounds, the principal movers in the matter being English visitors to Boulogne, many of whom had come across the Channel for very pressing reasons.

Not a few English then appeared to think that everything was to be got for nothing in France, and generally returned home with the idea that they had been most shamefully cheated. Whole families came to Boulogne with little more than what would maintain them a few weeks, after which, of course, they got into debt, and went to the Maison d'Arret. The gaols both at Calais and Boulogne (with the exception of an occasional felon) contained nothing but our countrymen ; and so exclusively were these places considered the property of the English, that the French always called them the "*Hotels d'Angleterre.*"

Amongst the crowd of visitors there were several sportsmen, who determined to see if they could but manage to indulge in their favourite amusement of hunting.

After some scratch attempts at hunting, a number of hounds were converted into a subscription pack of twenty couple, twelve of which were foxhounds from the kennel of Mr. Oxenden, the East Sussex and Surrey, the rest harriers. The pack was managed and hunted by Colonel Charritte and Mr. R. S. Surtees. The hunting days averaged five days a fortnight, which were generally market-days, when the peasants were in the town.

# The Merry Past

Another attempt to establish a pack was made by Mr. Leigh Cross, but he met with a very hostile reception, and the authorities of that day actually issued an order forbidding the sportsmen to appear in scarlet.

The French at that time had a not unnatural antipathy to our national red, and at first the ears of the sportsmen were constantly saluted with " God dam!" accompanied by " *Monsieur Rouge*," or " *les soldats Anglais !* "

Owing to various reasons the experiment was abandoned. Five years later, however, in 1823, a regular pack of foxhounds was established at Boulogne by Mr. Cresswell, who, in addition to other sporting innovations, made a race-course, and built himself a sporting-box at Hardelot, seven or eight miles west of Boulogne.

At that time Anglomania raged throughout France. There was a certain count who lived near Arras, who was terribly affected by it. Everything he had was English, and everything he did was *à l'Anglais*. He had entered a horse for some plate or stake at the races at Hardelot, and it being made a favourite elated him not a little. "He is von dem fine horse," said he to an English friend, "von excellent vellow : I assure you he is a Roman." "Roman!" said the sportsman from across the Channel, looking at his head to see if he possessed the projecting forehead. "Yes, he is a rum vun," repeated he. And eventually it was discovered that he meant a rum 'un ; and moreover that he considered "rum 'uns" to be an especially good breed of horses.

At another time he flew into a tremendous rage with an English groom calling him a "dem hamburg." "No," said the fellow, "I'm English," indignant at the idea of being taken for a sausage eater.

Mr. Cresswell's field looked peculiar, for, with the exception of the gentlemen who hunted the hounds, there were never two coats alike. A glorious diversity prevailed in the way of collars, cuffs, and buttons, and, as the English papers observed, "the hunt was chiefly conspicuous for the scarlet jackets of the riders and the sorriness of the steeds"; and every man who could beg, borrow, or steal a horse for the day was sure to appear in a red coat, with, perhaps, his "lower extremities" cased in white ducks, or black dress kerseymeres and Wellington boots!

At the commencement of the season, when the hunting was chiefly confined to the warrens (a sort of sandy, bad-scenting, uncomfortable country), things went on pretty smoothly; but the drafting of the harriers, the assumption of the scarlet coat, and the breaking down a few fences, were the signals for the hostile powers to arise.

There were, nevertheless, several of the French aristocracy who were not only excellent sportsmen, but staunch supporters of the hunt. Among these may be mentioned one family in particular—that of the Baron Le Cordier (the Sous-préfet of the Arrondissement), and his brothers-in-law, the Messieurs de Trevis.

The pack eventually ceased to hunt, owing to an

unpleasant altercation with the owner of some land, its dissolution being hastened by a spirit of ill-will which existed among the English residents ; some of whom, either not being sportsmen, or else unable to join in the hunt, amused themselves by propagating malicious stories, tending to prejudice the mind of the public, and to arouse the peasantry. This was shown by the fact that shortly after the 15th of October, when the hounds went to hunt the country in the neighbourhood of Samer, some distance from Boulogne, where there were scarcely any English residents, not only were the sportsmen well received (the town on the evening of their arrival resembling an English borough during a contested election), but every Frenchman in the place who could muster a horse appeared in the field.

The country abounded in foxes, as almost every window in Samer testified—the sole article of commerce being gloves made of their skins ; and the sportsmen used to amuse themselves by buying brushes (for 5d. apiece) to send to Boulogne as trophies of sport.

The French at this place had some idea of hunting, and kept twelve or fourteen couple of old-fashioned, crooked-legged, long-eared English harriers. Whence they came it was not discovered, but such was found to be the case when the English fox-hunters took up their quarters at the " *Tête de Bœuf*," and a deputation of their leading sportsmen politely waited upon the English to welcome their arrival.

In the Boulogne pack were two dwarf foxhounds

—Marksman and Music—both infamously bad ; and these, it was thought, would make an excellent addition to the French one, and gain favour in the master's eyes, so, after a hunt dinner, to which the French deputation had been invited, as well as Monsièur Saurange (celebrated as being not only the most bibulous postmaster, but the most bibulous man in France), they were, after their great value and excellent qualities had been duly impressed upon the minds of the Frenchmen, marched off to their kennel.

A day of two after this the Boulogne hounds had an excellent run from a covert belonging to this jovial individual, who was the esquire of the place, three or four miles south of Samer, to a place called Dare, near the forest of Condet, at which several French were present ; and, being highly delighted, proposed a union of the two packs (having no regard to difference of speed) on the following day.

Accordingly in the morning there was a general muster in the " Place "; and, about an hour before the English thought of turning out, the French, in military order, had marched past on foot, all armed with guns, carbines, and other engines of destruction. Some of them played on immense French horns. This crowd was accompanied by the full pack of hounds, who joined in producing a most Babelish noise.

A large covert about five miles south-east of Samer was fixed upon as the place of rendezvous ; but, owing to some mistake, and the immense size of the wood, the French were not visible on the arrival of the Boulogne hounds ; and, after waiting some time, and hearing or seeing nothing of them, the covert was partially drawn, and they were about to return (most of the hounds having been out the day before, and having to go back to the home kennel that night), when the French horns were heard in the distance.

The wind being favourable, every now and then, between the blasts of the horns, the deep-toned baying of the hounds was heard ; but either being at a great distance, or the hounds excessively slow, it was full half an hour before they came in sight. At last the French were seen running and endeavouring to intercept the hare (for such proved to have been the object of pursuit), and shoot it—this being considered a tremendous piece of skill, and the *ne plus ultra* of a sportsman's ambition.

On this occasion, however, they were disappointed ; for puss coming down the hill, directly in front of the Boulogne hounds, which were standing in a green lane, headed back, and fell among her pursuers.

She was saved by an English gentleman, and handed over to the French on their coming up, who after the usual salutations, and having recovered their breaths, proceeded to eulogise the two hounds, which had been given them, adding, that they had changed their names out of compliment to the donors, and that they had christened one " Com here " (come here), and the other " G—d d—m."

After the close of the Napoleonic wars several

foreigners of distinction came to hunt in England, and took up their quarters at Brighton. The flower of the flock is said to have been the Saxon Baron Gablentz.

He was a light weight and generally kept in the front rank, not infrequently taking up a line for himself.

This Baron did not know what fear was, and did not care what sort of a horse he got on to, nor what sort of a place he rode him at: in consequence of which, and a naturally loose military seat, he seldom went out without saluting the earth a few times; one day, indeed, he had so many falls, that he himself said he could not count them.

It seemed, indeed, unfortunate that the Baron did not adopt the original plan for securing one's seat on a horse, which was invented by a Lord Tweeddale of the past—a nobleman who used to ride with plush breeches on a saddle made of the same material, the nap of this being turned the reverse way to the breeches, so that they worked in with one another.

The Baron's early hunting experiences on more than one occasion nearly culminated in a tragedy. He rode, for instance, at the Ouse about two miles above Lewes, observing, if his horse could not jump quite over, he would anyhow get part of the way, and might swim the rest. The result was that he got into the middle of it, where, as he said himself, his horse and he floundered about for a quarter of an hour, and only got out then with much difficulty. Of English gentlemen he had a very high opinion, and used to say, " By my word, an English gentleman is the first gentleman in the vorld." It was not, however, to everyone who claimed it that the Baron accorded this title, having as nice a discrimination in these matters as though he had lived in England all his life.

Though he could not speak a word of English on his arrival, he learned to express himself in a remarkably short time—his stories and descriptions were of a droll description.

Coming to covert one morning on a lame hack, someone said to him, " Why, Baron, your horse is lame." " No, my good friend, him not lame," he said, " but he beaucoup fatigue in one leg."

Another morning he appeared in a prodigiously smart red and gold waistcoat, fresh from Paris, in which he had been figuring at a ball the night before. A friend observed that it was too good to hunt in, to which the Baron replied : " So said my valet ven he dressed me ; but I told him, by my honour, there is nothing too good for foxing in." On the very same day, Captain Stanhope, the brother of Lady Southampton, was expected out ; but not making his appearance, someone asked the Baron, an intimate friend of the Captain's, where he was. " Oh, by my vord," said he, " poor Stanhope, I think he shall not come to-day. He got von criminal bootmaker, who make his boot so stout that he could no put his leg about ; and ven I call at Albion this morning I find him dancing about his chamber with one boot on, and demming Charles in the veritable nautical fashion, till at last he could not bear his foot any more, and got a razor and shaved it off."

The Baron passed the whole winter at Brighton, where he had a good establishment, which included a couple of valets, who, it was said, were kept, one to help the other to do nothing. He was a most agreeable and gentlemanlike young man, very popular, for he was always the life of any society in which he might happen to be.

# IV

A S the old fox-hunting squire typified a certain aspect of English life, the jolly tar, in the days of the Napoleonic wars, typified another.

Men-of-war's-men eagerly seized every chance of enjoyment during their sojourn on shore, and at fairs, race meetings, and the like were to be seen by hundreds in all their glory ; their sweethearts by their sides in their span new rigging, with streamers flying of every hue that fancy could devise, or beauty be decked in.

The eccentricities of tars ashore excited little astonishment, and unless their conduct was offensively outrageous, they were allowed to do pretty much as they liked.

In November, 1812, for instance, a decent-looking man, who wore the uniform of a warrant officer of a ship-of-war, and who had sacrificed too freely to Bacchus, was so completely overcome on reaching St. James's Church, Piccadilly, that he fell down and was unable to get up again. He seemed perfectly contented with his situation, and immediately composed himself to sleep, in such a manner, however, as completely to block up the footpath. He was accompanied by a large Newfoundland dog, who, the moment his master had lain down, took a position at his head, and on several attempts being made to remove the senseless body into a less inconvenient place, this faithful guardian rose with the utmost ferocity, and, with threatening growls, frightened away all who presumed to approach. In this situation the fallen hero remained for three hours, when, having slept off the fumes of his intoxicating libations, he awoke, and, on rising, was told of the care his dog had taken of him, upon which he exclaimed : " Oh, d—n his eyes ! This is not the first time he has *kept watch* with equal fidelity."

At that time drunkenness was not viewed with the same severity as it is to-day, when very rightly it has come to be regarded both as a social nuisance and a destructive malady. All classes were tainted with it, and a drunken sailor was considered no extraordinary sight. Many of these men, once they had landed from their ships, soon spent every penny they had in drink, which seemed to them the highest earthly pleasure attainable.

A poor drunken sailor being asked if he was sure of being gratified in three wishes, what they would be, replied : " My first wish would be *all* the brandy in the world." "Your next, Jack ?" " All the tobacco in the world." " Now for the third." " Why, d—n my eyes, *more* brandy."

Once his money was gone, Jack would set about to convert any earthly possessions he might have into the wherewithal to obtain a further supply of the fiery liquor, which from early years his environment had taught him to love. Even the most sacred things were put to this purpose, a practice which caused it to be facetiously observed when the Bible Society presented a large number of bibles to the sailors, that even if these bibles should not *convert* the sailors, the sailors would very probably *convert* the bibles—into *grog*.

Grog is not a very ancient drink, having been first introduced by Admiral Vernon in 1745, at which date he put an end to the use by the English navy of ale, and substituted for it rum diluted with water. The admiral was dubbed by the sailors "Old Grog," because of an old cloak of grogram which he always wore in foul weather, and hence it came naturally about that the new potation of the high seas acquired its present name.

Jack ashore was seldom unaccompanied by his lass, whom he often married before sailing away again. The responsibilities of matrimony did not oppress him, and he regarded the whole thing in a sort of casual good-humoured way, which sometimes went rather far.

The rough-and-ready marriages which these sailors contracted often turned out badly and led to trouble.

A young sailor, for instance, who was tried at the Clerkenwell Sessions for assaulting his wife, described his experiences of matrimony in a way which aroused some sympathy, for he certainly seemed to have cause to complain.

According to his statement he never could keep his wife in the same *berth* with himself, whilst often

catching her out at night, *cruising under false colours!*
Notwithstanding this provocation, he declared he had
still remained fond of his spouse; till finding her one
day in a house of bad fame, rage had conquered his
passion, with the result that he had beaten her with a
cat-o'-nine-tails. The jury, whose risible faculties
were provoked, acquitted him.

A sailor who was being married at St. Anne's, Soho,
when the clergyman came to that part of the ceremony which directs that the woman shall be supported in sickness and in health, said, in joke, to the
clergyman: "What shall I do with her, if she should
be lame or lazy?" Upon this the parson refused
to proceed with the ceremony, and the disappointed
couple were obliged to defer their nuptials to a more
convenient season.

Another sailor, at Liverpool, having just arrived in
the Jamaica fleet, applied to a clergyman for a licence,
it being his idea to be married the following morning.
Being asked the name of the lady, he declared he could
not tell, as he knew nothing more of her than that
she was called Molly, and lived at Edgehill.

On the other hand, the girls they espoused were
also somewhat casual. One of them, whose husband
had been three years at sea, having produced a son
and heir, was asked how, as her husband had been
away so long a time, such an event could possibly have
happened. "Why," she replied, "to be sure we
never met, but I had many comfortable letters from
him."

There was such an air of jollity about the old-fashioned tar when ashore that he was often made the medium of all sorts of jokes, to which his somewhat convivial habits were particularly suited.

A party of dandies in Leicestershire were once served a fine trick by a gentleman who, whilst at an inn, opened a door by mistake, and caught a glimpse of the convivial party wrapped in slumber. They had returned tired after a fox-chase, and in the place "of fighting the battle over again," in conversation, had quietly sunk into the arms of repose. The gentleman in question had observed a drunken sailor at the bar, who had come on the top of a coach, likewise fast asleep, covered with snuff and tobacco: with the help of his servant, he contrived to get the man into the room and place him amongst the sporting and snorting dandies, unperceived and unheard, and left him there. After sleeping some time very comfortably together, the sailor was awakened by the nasal music of one of the company, on which, stretching a dirty and fat paw over the soft countenance of a sleeping exquisite, he exclaimed: "What ho! brother messmate! What ho! if you do not stop the piping of your nose, we must tumble out of our hammocks, and go aloft." This sudden exclamation awakened the party, who, starting from their chairs, called out to know who had brought "this horrid monster amongst them." No one could tell, nor could the sailor give any account of the transaction. On being obliged to quit the room, he swore "they were the most uncivillist gentry he had ever slept with in his life."

Many of these men had very humorous turns of

speech. One of them, for instance, having killed a dog
with the sharp end of a marling-spike, was cited by
the owner of it before the magistrate, who asked him
how he could have taken the life of the canine assail-
ant. The sailor having answered that he had done
so in his own defence, the man of authority said:
" But you ought to have made use of the butt-end of
your weapon, and not the point." " Yes, I would
certainly have done so, plase your worship," replied
the accused, " if the dog had bitten me with his tail,
and not with his teeth."

Another, belonging to a man-of-war, having been
for his good behaviour promoted from a fore-mast
man to a boatswain, was ordered on shore by his
captain to receive his commission at the Admiralty
Office. Jack went accordingly, and afterwards thus
described his reception to his companions: " I bore
away large," said he, " for the Admiralty Office, and
on entering the harbour, I espied a dozen or two
quill-drivers. I hailed 'em; not a word said they.
' Hollo! ' again said I. Not a word said they. ' Shiver
my top-sails, but what can this mean ? ' said I. Then
I took a guinea from my pocket, and holding it up to
my peeper, ' Hollo!" again said I. ' Oh, hollo! '
returned they. ' So, so, my boys,' cried I, ' you are
like Balaam's ass, are you ? You could not speak
until you saw the angel ! ' "

A sailor who turned his sense of humour to a
prosperous purpose was Darby Alleyne, the Bristol
captain, who sailed for the West Indies at a time when
the Antilles were blockaded by the enemy. One

island being closely pressed, was actually in a state of starvation; and the Bristolian, who determined to get there if possible, after fighting in the most gallant manner, reached the port. The famished inhabitants enquired what his cargo was, and were answered, " Cheeses and grindstones." " Oh, d—n your grindstones ! " said they ; " our noses have been pretty well brought to that already—land your cheese, my boy, that is what we want." " I am sorry, gentlemen," said Darby; " you shall not have one without the other. But a cheese and a grindstone—a cheese and a grindstone—as long as you please ; you shall buy both or neither." What could they do ? There was only one shop to go to, and therefore, for the sake of the cheese, they put up with the grindstone.

When the brave Admiral Kempenfelt, unhappily lost in the " Royal George," was coming into port to have his ship paid off, a sailor eyed a gold-laced velvet waistcoat which his commodore wore with great earnestness, and, in his best sea fashion, begged to know who made it. The admiral, perceiving his drift, gave him the necessary information, and Jack went ashore. He forthwith applied to the admiral's tailor, who, knowing the humours of his customers, went with him to buy the materials, and at last asked him what he would have the back made of. " Made of ? " said Jack; " the same as the front, to be sure." The tailor remonstrated, but in vain ; so the waistcoat was made, and put on with an old greasy jacket over it. One day, in the High Street, the admiral met his man in his curious dress, which occasioned him to laugh heartily, and this merry fit was not a little increased when Jack, coming up to him, lifted up the hind part of his jacket, and showing his gold-laced back, exclaimed : "Damn me, old boy, no false colours ! Stem and stern alike, by G—d ! "

Some of the naval officers of Nelson's day were, on occasion, as unrestrained as the gallant sailors who fought under their orders. In October, 1805, a naval hero, the captain of a man-of-war, and the brother of a nobleman, was brought before the magistrate at Bow Street, from the boxes of Covent Garden Theatre, where he had been kicking up a row. He was charged with violently assaulting a youth of fourteen, the son of a respectable citizen in Coleman Street, who was also at the theatre, and now accompanied his son to the office. The noble commander had evidently been on a Bacchanalian cruise in the course of the evening, and had taken in a full cargo of the Tuscan juice, as his upper works were a good deal damaged. He was towed into the office between two of the Bow Street runners, with some difficulty, and immediately on arriving at that port endeavoured to assume the whole authority of the quarter-deck. The first salute to the bench was a whole broadside of damns and blasts, chiefly applied to the eyes and limbs of the officers. He vaunted his extraordinary pugilistic prowess; boasted an intimate acquaintance with the Game Chicken, Gulley, Belcher, and other celebrated bruisers of the day ; offered to box the magistrate or any man in the room, for a thousand ; swore great guns that if he had with him his first lieutenant and his boatswain, they three would clear the decks of every man there in two minutes, if the lubbers were twice as numerous as they were.

The magistrate, however, not being in a boxing humour, nor probably in training to meet such an antagonist in his own way, had other views as to the best way of settling the matter, and calmly began to examine the charge against the gallant commander. The captain, however, grew more and more furious, claiming as an officer and a gentleman the privilege of a private examination. In this, however, he was not indulged, and the Bow Street officer, who saw the assault, proceeded to give his testimony, as well as he could, under a tremendous discharge of oaths, intermixed with threats of gangways, round dozens, and double irons. The officer stated that the captain had been extremely riotous in the theatre, to the annoyance of the whole audience, and that he had violently abused a lady in one of the boxes, who from a very coarse illustration in the captain's own phrase, it seemed, was an old Cyprian acquaintance, and eager to lure him to a fresh engagement, which he declined. He was eventually forcibly taken from his moorings in the boxes, and in his way assaulted everyone he met, and amongst others the youth who now came forward.

The captain was still vociferous and unruly. Finding, however, that he could not bring his guns to an effectual bearing in this way, he put about on another tack, and proposed to settle the matter with the magistrate over a bottle of Madeira. The latter however, objected to be assisted in his decision by the influence of *grape* shot. Eventually, after much storming, the captain somewhat calmed down and said it was only a drunken frolic; he was released after making due amends for his escapade.

In 1809, Cheltenham was much disturbed at the doings of a certain Captain Brisac, a naval officer, who had formerly commanded the " Iris." Things at last reached a climax when the captain and his companions procured a set of workmen to erect four tall poles, with figures hung on them, in front of the villa of Lady Mary Lindsay Crawford, accompanied with a drum and fife playing, a gun firing, and the noise of a rattle. These figures were left standing several days, not only to the annoyance of her ladyship, but of all the company who frequented Mr. Thompson's public walks and rides, which adjoined the spot. Mr. Brisac and four others were indicted for this riotous proceeding, and after a long trial were all found guilty. The Chairman of the Quarter Sessions addressed the culprit on the impropriety of his conduct, but as he had made an apology for himself and the other defendants, the court only inflicted a fine of ten guineas.

Captain Montague, a brave but whimsical officer, incurred the displeasure of the demure magistrates of Philadelphia, by kissing his wife on her arrival, on a Sunday, and was obliged to pay a fine—the penalty of such a flagrant breach of decorum. To prove he had no malice in his heart, he invited all these stern models of virtue to dine on board his vessel the following Sunday, when these godly men indulged themselves, as godly men will sometimes do, in all the good things of this world, and drank to intoxication. He then told them he had submitted cheerfully to their customs when within their jurisdiction, and that they must now submit to his, one of which was to punish drunkenness. Accordingly the boatswain was ordered up, and he took leave of each of his guests with a round dozen.

A more decorous joker was Sir Roger Curtis, who having received orders, whilst in London, to take the command of a squadron, and hoist his flag on board the " Formidable," at Portsmouth, travelled for dispatch without servants, plainly dressed, in the mail-coach. As frequently happened in this sort of conveyance, the passengers were unknown to each other, and Sir Roger found himself in company with a young man who appeared, by his uniform, to be a mate belonging to one of the Indiamen lying at the Mother Bank. On the way, this young officer pulled out some bread and cheese from a bundle and invited his fellow-travellers to eat. During that repast he entertained them with sea-phrases, which induced the admiral jocosely to ask him many simple questions relating to nautical tactics. Among others, he demanded how sailors could see at night, and whether they were not compelled to tie the ship to a post or tree till morning. The mate was not backward in bestowing a few hearty curses upon the ignorance and lubberly lingo of the admiral, who laughed heartily at the joke. Not only did he bear the rough observations of the sailor with good humour, but also the contemptuous grins of his fellow-passengers.

On their arrival at Portsmouth, the admiral shook hands with the mate, and departed. Later in the day, Sir Roger came on shore in his broad gold-laced hat and uniform ; he was attended by all his bargemen, and while walking up Point Street he met his late fellow-passenger, the mate of the Indiaman. Before the latter could recover from his surprise, Sir Roger accosted him with "What cheer, messmate ? You see I am not the lubber you took me for ; but come, as I breakfasted out of your locker this morning, you shall splice the main-brace with me this evening, then you may square your yards and run before the wind to the Mother Bank." The mate, quite dumfoundered, apologised, as well as he was able, for the liberty he had taken with the admiral, who soon released him from his embarrassment, and advised him, after dinner, never to be decoyed by false colours, but to look sharply at the build and trim of every vessel he met before he suffered her to surprise him.

George III was very fond of a jolly sea captain, Captain Nagle (afterwards Sir Edmund Nagle), whose blunt wit made the good old King laugh. On a certain occasion this sailor was amusing the King with a story of a brother midshipman who had been a great enemy of his, but to whom he returned good for evil by jumping overboard one day and saving his life, he having fallen out of the rigging, after which they became fast friends. "That was noble of you," said the King. "I suppose after that he would have

done anything in his power for you?" "Yes," replied
the brave seaman, "that he would; he would have
gone to hell to serve me." "That's a great way to go,
Captain Nagle," observed the monarch, with a smile,
and, putting spurs to his horse, rode off, vastly enjoying the roughly told tale.

Naval officers, though ready enough for a joke,
were not men to be trifled with, as those who attempted anything of the sort soon discovered. A
sea captain, on his way home and travelling without
a servant, stopped to dine at an inn on the Chester
road, and ordered a pair of ducks, which he saw
ready at the kitchen fire, up to his table. The captain's desire had been just complied with, when some
country bucks came in, hungry as hawks, after a
morning's sport, and eagerly enquired what could be
had to eat. Like a true Boniface, the landlord
enumerated what he had not, in order to apologise
for what he had; among other things he mentioned
the ducks, which had been only a minute before served
up for the captain's dinner. "Sea captain, indeed!"
gibingly exclaimed one of the chagrined group.
"D—n me! I'll lay fifty to five the fellow does not
know a fox from a ferret. Here, waiter, take my
watch up to the son of a sea-cook, present my compliments to him, and request him to tell me what
o'clock it is." The captain heard the message, took
the watch, and, with great civility, returned his
respects, with an assurance that as soon as he had
dined he would endeavour to satisfy the enquiry.
The bucks, who were chuckling at the affront which

they imagind tehe sailor was going to support, sat down to regale themselves on whatever they could get; but their jollity was presently disturbed by the entrance of a stalwart figure, who advanced towards the table where they were all seated, and presented the watch. " Gentlemen," said he, " I wish to know its owner, as from a message sent me a little while ago I presume he is 'shortsighted,' and have brought him this pair of spectacles "—pointing to a case of large pistols he held under his arm—" to remedy his defect." This seemed a bad joke to the bucks. The captain deliberately put the watch into his fob, with a declaration that secured it to him for ever : " Gentlemen, I am sorry for intruding, as I find the owner is not among you ; whenever he claims it he shall have it, but never without a trial of my 'spectacles.' "

A gentleman from London had agreed with a landlord at Portsmouth for the use of three rooms,. for which he was to pay a guinea per day ; but immediately receiving a letter from home which demanded his instant attention in town, he wished to give up his lodgings, making some compensation to his host for the few hours he had occupied them ; but the landlord would not abate anything of the original agreement. A naval gentleman, who stood by, seeing the imposition about to be practised, offered to take the apartments on the original agreement, which tender was cheerfully acquiesced with. At night, he brought with him his boatswain and cabin boy, and gave them directions every three hours to *pipe all hands !* This order was punctually performed for three successive nights, to the annoyance of the landlord and his guests, who could not rest for the boatswain's pipe. The landlord remonstrated in vain ; the guests threatened to leave an inn so dreadfully haunted ; but the captain was inflexible, until mine host informed him, with many cringes and bows, that he was willing to forego any charge for the three nights' lodging if the captain would consent to sleep on board his ship, where he might *pipe all hands* as frequently as he pleased.

The sailors of the past, whilst generally bluff and good-natured, were capable of going to considerable lengths when provoked.

A naval captain being purveyor or commissary-general of the stores intended for the West India expedition, some delay in the necessary preparations occurred in his office. The admiral commanding the expedition called on him, and in harsh terms censured the neglect. The captain replied with warmth, on which the other collared him ; a scuffle ensued, in which the captain took the admiral in his arms, who bellowed lustily : " Don't strike me, you rascal, don't strike me." " No," was the reply, " but I'll be d—d if I don't have the satisfaction of roasting a rear-admiral," and so saying, he carried him towards the fire, on which he would have thrown him but for the interference of the clerks ; as it was, however, he was a good deal scorched.

Except when they had the good fortune to take part, or be concerned in, some rich capture, most of these officers were none too well dowered with the world's goods. Admiral Payne was first introduced to the Prince of Wales when a lieutenant; and on being asked by His Royal Highness if he had been *bred* to the sea, the gay son of Neptune replied that he had, but added, "the sea has not been *bread* to me."

A brace of lieutenants—one a naval, the other a military hero—rallying and firing their squibs and sallies of the brain at each other, the red-coated gentleman, taking out his pocket-book, said, "I will show you what you have not seen since the conclusion of the last war," and immediately produced a banknote of £20. "Very good," says the other: "but look, here is such a sight as you never saw in your life," taking a paper from his side-pocket; "here's a tailor's bill with a receipt to it!"

There were, of course, a few naval officers who had ample means, and these generally managed to get on to the same ships, their tastes and habits being naturally of a more luxurious kind than the usual run of officers, who only had just sufficient money to live.

When Sir Home Popham commanded the "Romney," in the Indian seas, one of his midshipmen wrote to him requesting his interest to get him appointed to a mate's berth in a country ship; on the receipt of which Sir Home sent for him, and asked him whether his request proceeded from a dislike to the service in general, or from his wish to serve under some other captain. The midshipman replied: "Neither, for he felt a sincere attachment to His Majesty's service; and had ever considered it as the highest gratification and pride of his life to sail under the command of Sir Home." "Well," said Sir Home, "I have a wish to serve you; but must insist on your explaining your reasons for this application." After some hesitation, he replied: "Sir, the gentlemen on your quarter-deck have all friends who can, and do, supply them with money; I have not; and my slender finances will not allow me to keep pace with their mess, nor can I bear the mortification of living by myself." "Well, well," said Sir Home, "if this is your only reason, I do not see why the service should lose a valuable officer for a little paltry cash; draw upon me for what you require for your mess and I will settle it. I know when you can you will pay me; till that time arrives, never consider yourself in my debt."

At welcome intervals most pleasant windfalls in the shape of good hauls of prize-money rejoiced the hearts of both officers and men; the distribution of this would appear at times not to have been entirely equitable as regards the latter, who did not always receive a fair share.

When the British, under Lord Nelson, were bearing down to attack the combined fleet off Trafalgar, the first lieutenant of the " Revenge," on going round to see that all hands were at their quarters, observed one of the men devoutly kneeling at the side of his gun. So very unusual an attitude in an English sailor exciting his surprise and curiosity, he went and asked the man if he was afraid. " Afraid ! " answered the honest tar, with a countenance expressive of the utmost disdain. " No ! I was only praying that the enemy's shot may be distributed in the same proportion as the prize-money—the greatest part among the officers."

Whilst the great admirals and captains received a full measure of praise, many humble heroes who displayed almost superhuman courage have now passed out of recollection. Such a one was David Bartleman, master of the brig "Alexander and Margaret," of North Shields, who on the 31st day of January, 1781, on the Norfolk coast, with only three 3-pounders and ten men and boys, nobly defended himself against a cutter carrying eighteen 4-pounders and upwards of one hundred men, commanded by the notorious English pirate, "Fall," and fairly beat him off. Two hours afterwards the enemy came down upon him again, when totally disabled. His mate, Daniel M'Auley, expiring with the loss of blood, and himself dangerously wounded, he was obliged to strike and ransom. He brought his shattered vessel into Yarmouth with more than the honours of a conqueror, and died there in consequence of his wounds on the 14th day of February following, in the twenty-fifth year of his age.

Crowds flocked to see the "Alexander and Margaret" in the harbour, where she lay riddled with shot, a mere wreck, whilst the house in which the gallant Bartleman expired was for some time a local centre of interest.

This hero was terribly wounded; his death proceeded from a shot which struck part of his large shoe-buckle into his foot, which gangrened and produced lock-jaw. Bartleman sleeps in Yarmouth churchyard.

At Yarmouth is the monument raised by the men of Norfolk to the memory of their immortal Nelson, at the foot of which for years, in a little oaken cabin, lived one of the tars of the " Victory," who had seen his admiral die. This man eked out a livelihood by keeping the steps clean, and doing little services for visitors.

The whole conditions of life at sea in old days produced a class of officers and men who were so constantly inured to danger and adventure of every kind that nothing moved them. When Lord Howe, who was very remarkable for his presence of mind, was captain of the " Magnanime," during a cruise on the coast of France, a heavy gale obliged him to anchor, and depend solely on his ground-tackle. It was on a lee shore, and the night was extremely dark and tempestuous. Captain Howe, at this time laid up with gout, was reading in his cabin, when, on a sudden, the lieutenant of the watch came in, with a countenance fraught with alarm, and said he was sorry to inform him that the anchors came home. " They are much in the right of it," coolly replied the captain. " I don't know who could stay out such a night as this."

The Honourable George Dundas, of Upleatham, in Yorkshire, once commanded a ninety-gun ship, when she took fire and blew up. He remained on board the last man, when, finding the fire so hot that he could stand it no longer, he took his knife out of his pocket, cut off his trousers, and pulling off his coat committed himself to the waves, whence he was picked up, unhurt, by his men.

The spirit of the old English seaman was unquenchable, as many records testify.

A brave, but economical, sailor, during a naval engagement on board the " Royal Charlotte," had his leg separated from his thigh by a cannon-ball, just at the knee ; some of his shipmates had taken up Jack's leg, and were going to throw it overboard, when he called out : " D—n my eyes, you may do what you please with the leg, but give me the silver buckle out of the shoe."

During a naval engagement the captain of a man-of-war asked one of his lieutenants for a quid of tobacco. It was in the very heat of the contest, and a cannon-ball carried off the lieutenant in the act of presenting it. "I must apply to you, now," said the captain, coolly, turning to another officer; "for, you see, our friend is gone away with his tobacco box."

A young midshipman, not more than thirteen or fourteen years of age, was employed during the engagement at Navarino in the charge of the ammunition of his deck. A cannon-ball passed so close as to knock him down, while it shattered the skull of a sailor doing duty beside him. The "young gentleman," on recovering his senses and his feet, observing that his trousers were bespattered with the blood and brains of the unfortunate tar, coolly exclaimed, "Poor fellow! 'tis a pity, a great pity, for—he has entirely spoiled my lily-white ducks!"

# The Merry Past

The lot of a sailor wounded in battle was terrible, for the rough-and-ready methods of surgeons on board men-of-war sometimes degenerated into sheer brutality. One of these men, after a severe action, gave directions to throw the dead overboard ; besides the dead, however, there were some wounded men whom it was supposed the surgeon wished to get rid of, who were also ordered to be thrown overboard. Some of the unfortunate men remonstrated against this cruel order, but the surgeon replied : " Come, throw away, if you attend to these fellows, they will all swear they are alive."

The medical treatment of illness on board ship was also crude in the extreme. Cases were known in which sea-water was employed as a specific for almost every ailment. A doctor who was a great believer in its efficacy, being on his way up a rope ladder to rejoin his ship, the rope broke, and he was precipitated into the water ; on which, bawling out lustily, one of the sailors enquired, " What's the matter ? " " Why," answered a messmate, " the doctor has only tumbled into his own medicine chest."

Many curious customs existed in the British navy in old days ; it was, for instance, considered contrary to naval etiquette for frigates to interfere in combats between ships of the line. There were several frigates present at the terrible action between the " Mars " and " La Hercule," in 1796, but they did not take part in the fight, which was of the most desperate nature.

The " Hercule " had four ports blown into one by

the " Mars' " guns, and after the action exhibited a cavernous gulf through which, as a country-bred sailor said, you might have shoved a haystack.

The " Mars " lost her captain, and many were killed and wounded, whilst the Frenchmen suffered very severely.

Much of the routine work on the old men-of-war was frequently done by a subordinate, who had a knowledge of figures. The captain's clerk, for instance, not unusually rendered himself indispensable. Many of those men could write fairly and glibly, were clever at an official letter, or a return ; and as writing was learning in those days, their betters winked at their imperfections for the sake of their capabilities. To read a book or to be seen with one upon deck or the booms at that period was a sin or crime seldom unpunished with mast-heading, or a severe reprimand from the first lieutenant ; and happy was the youngster who could stow himself away in the lee-chains of a sunny day, to beguile a few hours in the perusal of " Robinson Crusoe," or " Tom Jones."

Though the majority of seamen were rough, uncultured men, there were a few who, notwithstanding very unfavourable conditions, were possessed of artistic aptitude.

There was on board the " Undaunted," when commanded by Captain Usher, a seaman who had a remarkable taste for carving, and whose ingenuity had been conspicuously exerted in ornamenting the cabins and stern of that frigate. Another naval officer, the head of whose figure-head had been recently shot away, went on board the "Undaunted" in hopes of getting a new head supplied by this ingenious sailor. The captain in question was reputed to be somewhat harsh—even tyrannical amongst the men of the Fleet; and on account of having inflicted sixteen dozen lashes upon a sailor for drunkenness, he was commonly called by the foremast-men, "Sixteen-dozen-Jack." When he got on board, he asked Captain Usher to let his carver supply a head to his figure. The carver was called, and Captain Usher communicated to him the wishes of his fellow-officer. The blunt tar replied by a significant shrug of the shoulders. The officer was very urgent, and told him he should not care what he gave him, if he would replace the head. "Can't do it, sir—can't do it—it is no use to try at it—I am sure I can't do it." "I will give you anything you desire," said the captain, "if you will oblige me." "It's of no use, sir; for I couldn't do it if your honour would give me sixteen dozen."

Besides the real Jack Tar, there was a sham one who assumed nautical dress and bearing for purposes of gain.

The popularity which the British sailor enjoyed was the cause of disreputable landsmen resorting to various nefarious practices. After our great naval victories a swindle known as the shawl rig was much in favour with such gentry.

A fellow dressed like a seaman and having a flashy shawl wrapped round his arm, in a careless way, would roll into a shop in fine style and ask for a pennyworth of tobacco. He would soon be followed by a queer-looking fellow with a bag, having the appearance of a dealer in old clothes. Stepping up to the sailor, the latter would accost him with : " Well, shall I have it, or not ? " " No," would be the reply, with a shake of the head. " Well, I'll give you half a crown more." " No, I tell you, it won't do." " I'll give you five shillings more, I'll make it up to two pounds five shillings, and if that won't do, I wish you a better customer." The sailor being to all appearance determined not to part with his shawl, the old-clo'man would then disappear.

The shopkeeper, as likely as not, would be fully awake to all that had passed, and whilst the customer was rolling his quid, would enquire of him whether it was the shawl bound upon his arm for which he and the Jew had been bargaining. The sailor, shaking his head, with a sigh, would then answer : " Yes, I bought it for Sue, but she is false-hearted and shan't have it ; howsomdever, I won't sell it neither." " Then," in nine cases out of ten, would rejoin the shopkeeper, " you had better give it to your mother or sister, if you have one, for you will dirty and soil it by carrying it about in this way." " No, I have neither a mother nor sister, and Sue has played me false, and I can't help it." At this period of the farce the clo'man would return and say, " Well, to be sure, it is not worth more than I offered, but I must say the article is uncommon good, and I'll stand another half-crown, and that is my last word ; you had better let me have it." " No, I tell you, I

won't sell it," after which the man would make a
final exit.

The sham mariner now observing the gudgeon
nibbling at the bait, with eyes fixed upon the shawl,
would draw it from his arm, and display it upon the
counter in all its splendour of gaudy colours. " It
cost me five guineas in India, and there an't a better
piece of goods under the vault of heaven. Well—I
did not mean to part with it, but Sue is false : if
you choose to have the shawl at two guineas, which
cost me five in India, you shall, and split me if ever
I sell it for less. At that time I thought nothing of
the money, as it was for Sue. I did not intend to sell
it, but now I don't know what to do with it, and,
ma'am "—if the shopkeeper was a lady, would say
the importer of Indian shawls, looking sweetly in the
woman's face—" you so much resemble my poor
mother, God rest her soul, I would wish you to have
it beyond anybody." By this or some similar trick
the gudgeon was generally hooked : two pounds two
was paid, and the splendid Indian shawl delivered, to
be safely deposited in the bettermost drawer, among
the Sunday and holiday attire. The shawl, of course,
was worth only a few shillings.

Another trick was the lace rig. A man in seaman's
garb, purporting to have just come out of a French
prison, would exhibit some lace, which he declares
to have been secreted by sewing it into the lining of
his jacket, which has made it look yellow, though not,
on that account, a farthing the worse—real French
lace, and not to be got anywhere in England for

money. In due course, the fortunate, or unfortunate, buyer would find that he had purchased a piece of real " Buckinghamshire," at about double the price such goods would have cost him at any shop. The colour was easily produced by dipping the lace in coffee-grounds and raw starch.

England can scarcely be said to have been generous to her tars. During the war with France, poor crippled sailormen were frequently to be met on the public roads, trying to eke out a modest livelihood by selling little trifles.

Jack's store usually consisted of coarse hardware, some ink, garters, brimstone, broadsheets, and the like. The literary department was enriched with the "History of Jack the Giantkiller," "Tom Thumb," "An Account of the last illness of Mr. Pitt," and the dying speeches of some of the most celebrated heroes of the Old Bailey. He had also a collection of love songs for the amusement of the village girls, and to complete his stock, usually laid in a few dozens of prayers for pious customers.

Hobbling away upon a wooden leg and a crutch, many a gallant old sea-dog would tell how he had been fighting for his King and country ten years, and had crippled and destroyed as many " French dogs " as he could, and had he not in turn been crippled himself, would still have been fighting away as usual.

"I have fought devilish hard," said one of these men, " but the lubbers have crippled me now, so that I can fight no more, and I am trying to get an honest penny by selling a few articles of hardware, and a few godly books. If your honour will shorten sail and lay me alongside, you shall overhaul my stores." Thus did many a maimed hero eke out a living, though not a few sailors who had been lucky in coming in for a good share of prize-money, might, had they been prudent, have made ample provision for their old age. A provident sailor was, however, unheard of, and when flush of money men-of-war's-men were wont to indulge in wild extravagance. One Jack Tar, desirous of getting up to London from Deptford, thought it only seemly for a sailor who had just been paid off, and had plenty of money, to have a whole coach to himself ; of course, he took all the places, seating himself at the same time upon the top. The coach was about to set off when a gentleman appeared, who was holding an altercation with the coachman, on the absurdity of his insisting that the seats were all taken, and not a person in the coach. Jack, over-hearing high words, thought, as he had paid full freight, he had a right to interfere, and enquired what was the matter. On being told that the gentleman was much disappointed at not getting a seat, he re-plied : " You lubber, stow him away in the hold ; but I'll be d—d if he shall come upon deck ! "

It was, indeed, no uncommon sight to see a coach full of sailors and their girls driving about the streets singing : " There's a sweet little cherub that sits up aloft," which the rubicund old driver on the box, as a rule, seemed to construe as a compliment to himself.

Sailors, indeed, were very fond of the pleasures of the road. A party of tars just paid off from their ship after a lengthy cruise would often fill up a whole coach, and as many as sixteen jolly sailors—four inside and twelve out—were not infrequently stowed away; any discomfort being alleviated by a plentiful stock of liquor. A crowd of seafaring passengers such as this, however, was liable to lead to accidents, for the men were so accustomed to being swung about at sea that when the coach swayed over a rough part of the road or going down hill they would sway with it, and by their weight occasionally cause it to overturn.

## V

AN altogether different patron of the road from the jolly tar was the amateur whip, who often handled the ribbons with all the skill of a professional coachman.

In 1809 the mania for driving which seized the world of fashion was a never-ending subject of jokes. A dashing young Etonian, for instance, raised a great laugh against a detachment of the "Barouche Club" whips, by parading round Grosvenor and Berkeley Squares, in the rear of three of those fashionable vehicles, in a low phæton, drawn by a four-in-hand of well-bitten jackasses.

The procession of the Four-horse Club to Cavendish Square excited a good deal of hostile comment as being ostentatious; nevertheless, the drivers were good coachmen. Luncheon for thirty was always set out at the "Pack-horse," at Turnham Green, with cider cup, and the same at the "Magpies," on Hounslow Heath, eight miles further down the road. Here also the horses were watered. The animals in question went to Salt Hill and back the next day without being taken out of their harness. The number of teams generally amounted to about a dozen—each dragsman having an honorary member by his side.

# The Merry Past

The Four-in-Hand Club came to an end owing to the great expense which the members incurred. One of these being asked why it was broken up—very dryly answered, " It's not broken up, it's broken down; we hadn't enough 'in hand' to go on with it."

When coaching was the rage amongst fashionable bucks, the turn-outs of the latter were often mistaken for regular stage coaches.

A farmer living not far from the London road near Stamford, directed one of his labourers to take a basket, which contained a present for a friend in London, to the road, and deliver it to a particular coach which would be the first that passed upward. In two or three minutes, trumpeting along came what appeared to be the coach for which the man waited, and he delivered his parcel and paid for the carriage, as desired. The wag of a buck who drove the coach and his friends, exulting in their success, drove to the Fountain Inn, Huntingdon, where they dined well off a fine green goose and early peas (the contents of the basket), and afterwards packed up the bones and the pea-shells, and forwarded the present by a *real coach*, agreeably to the direction.

Whilst a gentleman of the Four-in-Hand Club was driving his coach (which had all the appearance of a stage-coach) from Richmond to town, with a few servants on the roof, a nimble tar, seeing the seats behind empty, immediately mounted and placed himself on the dickey, when the gentleman, on perceiving his breezy passenger, began to pull up : but

Jack, supposing himself on a stage-coach, hallooed :
" Go on, Coachee, go on, and I'll pay my fare when
we arrive in Piccadilly."

The fashion of gentlemen driving coaches for
pleasure greatly improved the conditions of travelling
just before the introduction of railways. The stage-
coach drivers came into close contact with a more
civilised type of humanity, and were seized with a
wholesome spirit of emulation, a creditable style of
dress and address, and an honest pride in the condition, neatness, order, and cleanly comfort of their
cattle.

Coach travelling changed (from what it used to be
in the olden time, a disgusting and tedious labour),
first into comparative comfort, and at last to something
very like luxury. A modern stage-coach was an
ornamental and beautiful object on the road. The
old coach was an unwieldy machine, loaded (or
rather overloaded) with luggage and wayworn
passengers groaning in concert with the surcharged
and crazy vehicle that lumbered heavily along.

The old Four-in-Hand Club, notwithstanding its
brief existence, and in spite of all the satire and ridicule
which was unmercifully bestowed upon it when it was
first started, did infinite good. Harness, if ill-con-
structed, is at once unsafe to travellers, and more
tormentingly punishing to horses than all the whips
and all the spurs which ever were sold. The Four-in-
Hand Club improved it in a thousand particulars,
of which the ordinary coachmen, without practical
experiment, could never have been judges ; and of

which coachmasters and their servants were too careless or too ill-informed to be aware.

Most of the amateur coachmen were good whips,
for which reason the regular stage-coachmen were
generally quite agreeable to yielding up the reins to
them for any particular stage or stages when they
might have a fancy to drive.

In consequence of this queer mistakes were often
made by passengers who were unaware that the reins
had been assumed by some sprig of nobility.

A certain nobleman, very fond of the road, had
been on a visit to the Marquis of Bath, and was taking
a lark one night on one of the Bath coaches. When
they arrived at Marlborough his lordship thought he
could not do less than perform the honours of the
supper-table, and a lady being of the party he was
particularly civil in paying her compliments. " Will
you allow me to send you some beef ? " said our
noble friend. *No answer !* " Permit me, madam, to
help you to some beef," repeated his lordship. *No
answer !* Once more, and a little louder, " Shall I
send you any beef ? " " *I never speak to outside
passengers !* " said the lady, with a contemptuous
toss of her head. Upon this the rebuffed carver rang
the bell, and told the waiter to send the landlord into
the room, when the following conversation took
place, to the great dismay of the fastidious lady :

" Landlord," said the peer, " order me a little supper
at another table, as I find I am unworthy of a seat at
this ! "

" God bless me, my lord ! fancy your lordship

being here and I not knowing it! Here, waiter! I hope your lordship left all the family well at Long-leat."

In solemn silence the patrician driver ate his supper comfortably, and after taking his " allowance " resumed the box, and drove as far as his coachman went. To keep up the joke, he opened the coach door as was usual for coachmen to do in order to obtain their tips, when the old lady, as if wishing to atone for her folly, put five shillings into his hand !

Though gentlemen often drove coaches for pleasure without attracting unfavourable comment, driving for remuneration was looked upon in a very different light. The difference between an amateur and an operative coachman was well exemplified in the case of poor Harry Stevenson, at one time proprietor and driver of the Age on the Brighton road. Not only was he a gentleman by birth and education, but his appearance and manner bespoke him one : and yet, though he was intimate with several of the first noblemen and gentlemen in England of that day, the colonel of a crack Hussar regiment read a lecture to the officers for having invited " a coachman " to dine at the mess.

Certain drivers were celebrated for their originality. Such a one was Wise of the Southampton Union, a coachman renowned for his quaintness of speech. His conversation with a young clergyman, the son of one of his respected clients, was typical.

The youthful deacon, who, in the language of that day, had just been " japanned," that is to say ordained, finding himself by old Wise on the coachbox, was interrogated as follows :

" Well, Mr. John, so you be got into orders."

" Why, yes, I am."

" All right : I am glad to hear it, for they tells me that's not quite so easy a job as it used to be. Now I've known your father many years, and have drove you many a mile, and I want to ask you a bit of a favour : Will you be so good as to explain to me a little bit about that there Trinity ? "

" Why, that is not exactly a subject for a coachbox, Wise : and perhaps I might not make you comprehend it clearly without entering more fully into it."

" Why, to tell you the truth, sir, I have thought a good deal myself about that there Trinity, and never could understand it : but I don't know how it is—I never meets three in a gig that I don't think of it ! "

The language of stage-coachmen was not unnaturally singularly bluff and direct; they had indeed a peculiar method of expressing themselves which was essentially British in style.

The following is a description of a wedding banquet given to a favourite stage-coachman by a sporting baronet, very fond of the road. On this occasion a brother whip, who had been invited to the festivities, spoke as follows :

" I walks in as free as air. Hangs up my hat upon a peg behind the door. Sits myself down by the side of a young woman they calls a lady's maid, and gets as well acquainted with her in five minutes as if I had known her for seven year. When we goes to dinner we has a little soup to start with, and a dish of fish they calls trout, spotted for all the world like any coach dog. A loin of veal, as white as Halley-blaster, the kidney fat as big as the crown of my hat, I ain't lying, so help me G—d! A couple of ducks, stuffed with sage and innions, fit for any lord: and a pudding you might have drove a coach around. Sherry white, and red port, more than did us good, and at last we goes to tea. I turns my head short around, and sees Bill—making rather too free. Stop, say I, Bill—that won't do. Nothing won't do here but what's quite genteel."

Stage-coachmen, of course, were, as a rule, somewhat illiterate, but strange exceptions were to be found, like the driver who, off his box, made a hobby of botany, about which he knew a good deal.

Another cultivated driver was Stockdale, of the Tonbridge road—a good whip, who was also a literary character, and beguiled the road with cockney slang and quotations from Pope! He drove to London and back six days a week—the Sunday, he said, he spent at home studying the Greek Testament. His translation of οὐαὶ ὑμῖν, ὁδηγοὶ τυφλοί was, "Wo, wo, ye blind leaders!"

Stage-coachmen were not particularly well paid, the most skilled not receiving more than eighteen shillings to a pound a week, whilst the ordinary rate of pay was from twelve to fourteen, from which in some yards eighteenpence was deducted for petty expenses. Drivers of coaches not running from London usually got sixteen shillings.

Though these wages may appear to have been very modest, some coachmen on first-class coaches made a very comfortable livelihood—say, from two to four hundred pounds a year. Those who drove into, and out of, London were allowed the privilege of not entering on the way-bill the passengers they might take up on the first stage off the stones. These they call their "short shillings."

A regular phraseology of coaching was used by those connected with the road. An empty coach was called the mad woman; asking the passengers for money, kicking them; a passenger not on the bill, a shoulder-stick, a bit of fish, or a short one; a passenger who paid shabbily, a scaly one; not paying at all, tipping the double; a glass of neat spirits, a flash of lightning, a drop of short, or "don't stop to mix it"; greatcoats, benjamins, or upper benjamins; putting on greatcoats and shawls, dressing; a white hat, a lilly shallow; good clothes, a good bit of broadcloth, or neatish toggery; a kicker, a miller; galloping horses, springing them; driving near to anything, feather-edging it.

"Shouldering," as it was called, was merely a mild form of robbery, and consisted in not including a passenger on the bill, by which omission the money paid by him went into the driver's pocket.

There were other terms for this: "You have no luggage, I believe, sir?" said coachee to a passenger, after having brought him about fifty miles. "I have none," said he. "Then if you please you shall get down at the turnpike, as I mean to swallow you."

This, however, was not altogether without an excuse, as it happened on a company's coach, where coachmen were not allowed to " kick," and there was no other way of getting an odd shilling on a cold night.

A little shouldering was generally winked at by proprietors of coaches, especially of those which ran at night.

The life of a stage-coachman was, of necessity, a hard one, whilst the lot of the men who drove at night was often anything but enviable, exposed as they frequently were to the worst vicissitudes of weather, almost in solitude, with perhaps a solitary passenger besides the guard, their team of a description unfit to show by day—with rotten reins and worn-out harness that not a few proprietors persisted in keeping for work in the dark.

Nevertheless, when guard and coachman pulled well together, there was sometimes a good deal of fun between supper and breakfast.

Jack Myers, who drove the Glasgow Mail, was especially noted for the fun which he managed to extract from night work ; he was a jolly coachman, who it was said went to a premature grave in the very prime of manhood, killed by want of rest, a pretty wife, and strong tea.

The guards of coaches had not particularly agreeable or lucrative posts ; some of them were so hard-worked that they were half the time asleep.

Those who went a moderate distance, sixty to eighty miles out, were relieved by others, and had a comparatively easy time of it, but others on coaches which went long journeys, such as London to Exeter, with only a short time allowed for stopping, led a very hard life, especially in bad weather. One hundred and sixty miles on a frosty night was terrible work for the poor men, who, not unnaturally, drank heavily, generally at other people's expense.

Many passengers complained of having to tip the guard, saying that they had already paid enough in their fares.

"Why should I remember you?" said one of these individuals; "the proprietors of this coach are answerable for my luggage, and I do not see what use you have been to me on the journey." "I took care of you, sir," was the reply. "What with?" "My horn." Nevertheless, guards generally got their tips.

About 1827 guards had ceased to carry firearms, which was much resented by passengers, who considered that their safety was not assured.

The Hereford Champion coach was attacked by a highwayman in the winter of 1826, and much irritation was manifested against the proprietor for not having provided the guard with a blunderbuss.

Many guards of light coaches, as well as of mails, were men of great integrity, who were constantly entrusted with bankers' parcels and other valuables to a large amount, and who well understood the duties of their calling.

During the hard winter of 1814, a guard distinguished himself much on the Holyhead road. There were fourteen mails due in Dublin, and the merchants and others were much distressed about their acceptances. The road was open as far as Corwen, in Merionethshire, but the passes through the Carnarvonshire mountains were blocked up. By extraordinary exertions, undertaken chiefly at his own suggestion, this man got the coach, filled with bags, to Holyhead, for which he received the thanks of the Post Office, accompanied by a reward. Several other guards more than once ran great risk of their lives in getting through flooded roads ; brave men in two instances sacrificed their lives to their duty.

Guards on mails, being servants of the Crown, did carry firearms, the idea being to protect the letter bags.

Female guards were not altogether unknown.

In 1815 a newly started stage-coach from Sunderland to Shields attracted crowds of people at both towns, in consequence of the unusual appearance of a corpulent, masculine-looking woman, apparently about sixty years of age, who officiated as guard. Her alertness in looking out for passengers, and the agility with which she ascended and descended from the top of the vehicle, were wonderful. Besides all this, the lady professed to be an expert pugilist.

Much connected with the coaching of other days is now enshrined in a kind of romantic mist, and the traditional stage-coachman is always supposed to have been a pattern of bluff geniality, whose most serious failing was a love of good cheer; as a matter of fact too many of these men were anything but estimable characters. No class of person was so little scrutinised on his initiation into office as the driver of a stage-coach, who, unlike the man on the box of a hackney cab, was not registered or licensed; in consequence of this many were men of indifferent reputation, whilst a few were in league with the dregs of society and, in their hours of relaxation, the associates of poachers and thieves.

Practically anyone was allowed to drive a stage-coach, and so frequent were the changes and resources of the fraternity, that in the event of serious misconduct, calling for punishment, the offender was generally able to put himself out of reach, and substitute someone else to take his seat on the box.

" Ah, Timothy ! " said a gentleman, to one who had been in his service ; " what, you on the box ? I thought you had the care of the plough, instead of the coach. What is become of old Tom ? " " Why, Tom, your Honour, hath lifted his whip hand so often to his head, that 'tis almost over with him." " And Frank ? " " Oh, Frank! Didn't your Honour hear of it ? Why Frank drove for speed against another coach for a crown's worth of punch ; both were upset ; Frank had his collar-bone and an arm broken— but that is a trifle, compared with what befell some of the passengers." " Indeed ! And Jack, what is become of Jack ? " " Jack is in limbo about that 'ere parcel as dropped out of our coach." " And Dick ? " " I saw Dick a few days since. Why, some pheasants were found yesterday in Dick's care ; the Squire made a terrible pother about it, and I'll be hang'd if Dick an't this very morning gone to 'list for a soldier. Before he set off, though, he went to master and tould him he knew as I could drive, and so I be come to take hee's place, but we have a 'rum 'un' coming in a day or two, one who is up to most things, and will have his way."

Drinking and bad company were the principal causes of ruin to many a stage-coachman; some were corrupted by rascals who travelled merely for predatory reasons, and in return for " lifts " gave the drivers surreptitious presents of game and pilfered articles as a means of ensuring their silence.

Other stage-coachmen were irascible, and given to bursts of unbridled temper. On one occasion the driver of the Bath coach, who had been indulging in an altercation with some men on the road, alighted from his box, and after pouring forth a volley of invective indiscriminately, interlarded with horrid oaths and execrations, offered to fight any passenger, to use his own words, " inside or outside, gentle or simple, for a one-pound note."

A celebrated coachman, notorious for his hot temper, having four " rum 'uns " to deal with, and unable to make them work to please him, threw the reins on the footboard and exclaimed : " Now, d—n your eyes, divide it among you, for I will be troubled with you no longer."

The lowest class of drivers were exceedingly apt to become intoxicated, when their insolence to passengers was often very offensive. A man of this sort was once well served out one Derby day by a dashing young officer, who having sent on his hack to Epsom had taken advantage of one of those " occasion coaches," as they were called, which started on race days horsed, as a rule, by a sorry team.

The officer had the box-seat on the coach, which conveyed a number of Frenchmen desirous of seeing the great race. The driver was an " occasion whip," with a dirty, villainous countenance, whose handling of the ribbons left much to be desired. It was a pelting wet day, and when they had reached Ewell the man handed over the reins to the officer, saying he was going to stop for a bit.

The latter, who had a good idea of what would happen, told the coachman that if he was going to get drunk he had better say so, and the whole party would get down and take shelter.

" Oh, no, young master," was the reply, " I be's only a going in whiles the horses gets their heads loosed, and wets their mouths a bit." The coach drew up, the horses underwent the usual process, and in due time the officer desired the ostler to call the coachman. That worthy soon returned with a broad grin on his curious frontispiece, and, cocking his eye : " Why, Lord," said he, " young man, that 'ere coachman says as how he don't care not a damn for yow or none on 'em, and yow may wait his pleasure." This would have led to an altercation, a scuffle, and probably a scene with most people ; the officer, however, was equal to the situation. " I tell you what, my friends," said he to the passengers, " I can drive you on to Epsom fully as safe as that dirty disciple of the goose ; and it is ridiculous to suppose we are to sit here, be drenched through, lose our money, and be too late for the race. If those people in the basket are not afraid, I will drive on." The Frenchmen, on the situation being explained to them, were unanimous in their approval, saying : " *Oui ! oui ! tous les Anglais connaissent bien les chevaux ; il n'y a pas de danger ; allez, monsieur, brave jeune homme, jusqu'a le champs de course.*" Throwing a shilling to the ostler, the officer bade him rein up the leaders, and, putting the whip suddenly into the rum 'uns, they darted off into the thick of the crowd of carriages and britschkas, gigs, and the like, and away they went spinning round the sharp turn at Ewell. Meanwhile the foreigners looking back began to shout, "*Regardez notre conducteur, qui vient au grand galop*" ; and sure enough, with a heavy box-coat on, greasy top-boots, and greasier in-expressibles, with his " shocking bad hat " raised in one hand, and a bird's-eye blue waving in the other, throwing up the mud abundantly, and shouting with all the power of his lungs, the angry tones of the irate coachman rose fiercely above the din of the crowd. " Stop that 'ere coach; I'll pay you off, you young devil ! " together with many other oaths, execrations, and entreaties, rent the air. The man's remonstrances, however, were all in vain, and served but to excite the mirth of the amateur whip and his companions, as he neatly cut round the corner, and lashed away best pace for the Downs. There he gave over the coach and rum 'uns to the booth stable-folk, took off his hat to the foreigners, who highly lauded his prowess, mounted his hack, and galloped off to the Warren.

Bad coachmen were well known along the road, and subjected to much chaff. An indifferent driver having brought his coach to the door of an inn, not in the most coachmanlike manner, a knowing boy in the street addressed him thus : " I say, Coachee, who feeds the pigs when you be from home ? "

The " White Hart," in Fetter Lane, was a great resort of the best stage-coachmen, who used to indulge in anecdote and song. A great favourite here was Tom Simcock, driver and part proprietor of the Lewes coach, who was well known for his singing of :

> Fortune's wheel goes round, round, round,
> And round goes Fortune's wheel.

Simcock's principal peculiarity was his dislike for everything French, so much so that he was never known to eat a French roll, and as for French beans, he would not allow them a spot in his garden. The military also were not favourites with him. On one occasion on a journey from Lewes, Tom picked up some redcoats, and on his arrival at the " Elephant and Castle," being on the look-out after the luggage of an inside passenger, the soldiers took advantage of the bustle and confusion attendant on the arrival and departure of the numerous vehicles of every description from the " second Babel," to take French leave, and by bolting did him out of their fares. A brother whip, known as " Tidy and Tight," an old pal of Tommy's, whose domicile was not a hundred miles from the British Museum, happened to pass at the time, and noticed the move, but was unconscious of any fraud having been practised on his friend. Ever after, however, when they came in contact, the un-varied salutation was : " Well, how get on the scarlet runners, eh, Tommy ? "

A great frequenter of the " White Hart " was Dick Vaughan, the driver of the Cambridge Telegraph, who had an odd mixture of roughness and dry humour, which made him a universal favourite.

Dick was very outspoken. Arriving one day at the " Sun " yard with his coach, a great dissenting brewer and banker, who supplied the " Sun " with beer, happened to be there. One of Dick's passengers, a lady, chanced to be very refractory about paying for some luggage. " D—n my eyes, ma'am," says Dick, not in the best temper ; " I can't stand here all night a-higgling." Upon which up marches the rich dissenter to remonstrate. " Pray, Mr. Vaughan, don't be too hard with the lady, now pray don't—pray, how did you find the roads to-day, Mr. Vaughan ? " " Roads ! " answered Dick, turning round to him in a voice of thunder ; " why, like your beer, d—d bad. Now, ma'am, I'll thank you for that three shillings."

In its day, the old Telegraph was the crack coach out of Cambridge, and most of its drivers were char-acters. Such was, besides Dick Vaughan, Will Elliot, Civil Will, who was also known as Quaker Will, on account of his great contrast with Dick, which could not pass unnoticed. Elliot was naturally mild and taciturn ; attentive and polite, if occasion called for it ; but if otherwise, so unobtrusive that he could scarce bring himself to " kick " (that is to say, stand waiting for a tip at the coach door) at the " White Horse," but would rather place himself in their way, to which his bulk and the premises remarkably conspired. Added to this, his round, dark, and complacent countenance—the very sombre cast of his toggery—the peculiarity of his castor, the serious, thoughtful, and deliberate way in which he collected his ribbons, his dignified ascent to the " bench " (all in accordance with the arms and motto on the panels of his drag), led to the supposition amongst his passengers that he was a Quaker.

The Telegraph, with Elliot over one half of the ground and Walton over the other, was the fastest coach of its day, and many a luckless Johnian " lost a week " in the books of the two amiable deans of his college by missing Hall, owing to taking up a position opposite to the " Sun," for the sake of seeing the latter workman tie up his nags preparatory to pointing his turn into the yard—a feat always executed at the rate of twelve miles an hour.

Another celebrated Cambridge coachman was Jack Remington, who had a very happy method of expressing himself. A Reverend divine, a great friend of Remington's, and a staunch supporter of the road, had to throw off for his first sermon at St. Mary's. Jack accordingly, as one good turn deserves another, booked a place to hear him. On being asked, after all was over, how his friend had got through, he answered : " Why, sir, he was a little groggy at starting, but by and by he took the bar, and went off like a good one," adding, " that he only pulled up to hay and water once," alluding to the use he made of his pocket-handkerchief.

Bob Poynter was another Cambridge coachman, said to be the best who ever drove, but he was intemperate, and had only a short career.

The coach of coaches that ever worked the Cambridge road was the Times, the motto of which, "Tempus Fugit" painted on it, was a most fitting one. When the Times was started, it was opposed by the Regulator, under Alexander, who also ran a coach to Brighton. No expense was spared on either side to do the thing in the best style. "Why do they call the opposition the Regulator ? " asked a passenger, of Joe Walton one day. " Why," replied Joe, dropping his hand and letting them out, " because we go by it," and passed his antagonist.

After the opposition had ceased, their coach continued to be worked in exactly the same tip-top form. Bob Poynter, son of old Poynter, of Sussex notoriety, and Joe Walton, were installed drivers of this famous coach, which left the " Eagle " yard as St. Mary's struck six, and, including a stoppage of twenty minutes for breakfast at Hockerill, made Shoreditch Church at a quarter before twelve—fifty-six miles. This was not done merely for a short time, but went on steadily for years without a minute's variation in time. Poynter was succeeded by Bennet, known as the "Astronomer." Joe Walton then worked the Times up and down (one hundred and sixteen miles) every day, barring Sundays, without assistance.

Joe was of spare make, nearly six feet high, and

did not turn twelve stone in the scale. Tough as wire, long-armed, and as firm on his box as a rock, he seemed to bring four horses across a road with as much ease as an ordinary man could twist a buggy, and in case of " cord-physic " being required, he was very punishing. On a wet or wintry day, he was an excellent specimen, although always workmanlike in dress, of the " damn-all-dandies " school. The rather low crown, and rather broad-leafed hat—the close-made " ben," a protection, not an encumbrance, the ridge-and-furrow breeches, the grey stocking drawn high over the knee, and the long black boot ; not forgetting the natural requisites for a workmanlike appearance—a good brown muzzle, quick eye, and short black hair—stamped him a dragsman all over.

" Joe," once said a passenger, " how many miles do you think you travel in a twelvemonth ? " " Why, sir," was his answer, " last year I did accidentally keep an account, and it was thirty-three thousand six hundred and seventy-six ! "

The University itself produced some capital whips, though perhaps the best amateur who handled the ribbons was an Oxford man, Sir St. Vincent Cotton, who worked the Times the whole way from Cambridge to London. Sir Vincent was an unlucky man, being the victim of a series of accidents. One of his horses put a foot in his mouth and demolished a considerable portion of his dining-room furniture, having been taken into the house for a freak; he was next floored from Mr. Wombwell's drag, and very much hurt by falling upon some iron spikes, whilst in after years he was seriously wounded in some street row in Lisbon, where his regiment (the 10th Hussars) was quartered.

A great Oxford amateur of stage-coaches was "Student" Atterbury, a lineal descendant of the celebrated bishop of that name. Possessing great talents, and not badly connected, he remained a student to the last, refusing all college livings. His great hobby was seeing the various coaches through Oxford arrive and start. From early in the morning till nearly midnight he was to be seen at the " Star," " Mitre," or "Angel " inns, on the look-out for the coaches. He lost his life on his way to London (as Graham once said he would) by the upsetting of his favourite opposition coach.

In all probability the best workman who ever sat behind four horses was John Richardson—" Sailor Jack "—a coachman well known to every northern disciple of the road on account of his extraordinary skill in managing any kind of team.

Like so many others, his fame was but the herald of his fall, and indirectly, owing to his peculiar talents as a driver, Sailor Jack eventually met with an accident which deprived the Northern Road of its most accomplished workman. Was there a kicker, jibber, bolter, or runaway within the precincts of any stage on which he worked, the understood order was, " Turn him over to Jack." " I used to have nice games with them, sir," he told an enquirer : " sometimes all down, one half under the coach, and the other on top of her. Coaching was not then what it is now : if I had two in a team that would go, it was as much, or rather more than I expected. 'Hit them as will work,' used to be the proprietor's maxim, 'there's no use in hitting them as won't.'" With such tools provided for his labour, there is little wonder that casualties became so common that they were as second nature to him, and an occasional runaway, in fact, a rather agreeable episode. Of the latter, poor fellow, he had one too many, and most extraordinary was the catastrophe in its relation to himself. When on the Edinborough Mail, a team was given to him that more than once was ominous of some catastrophe before its career was run. At length it came—the horses broke away with him in the neighbourhood of Grantham, beat him at every point, leaving him no move but the hazardous expedient of running them off the road, and bringing up his coach in the ditch. As she went over, he heard, as he described it, a crash as if his head had been riven to atoms. A mere momentary shock it seemed, and to all appearance completely recovered he was enabled to meet and remedy all the consequences of the accident. Soon, however, it became manifest that some mysterious injury had been sustained, for whenever Richardson mounted the box, at the end of a score of miles his sight would gradually fail him, till at last he would grow quite blind, a melancholy state in which the poor man continued. Sailor Jack was a splendidly made man, who bore about him all the signs of robust health and aptness for exertion of any kind, and even after his accident in ordinary life his sight betrayed no symptom of weakness, whilst he looked as little a subject for nervous affection as Hercules in his prime. Nevertheless, his nervous system was utterly overthrown, and his reputation as a driver became a thing of the past.

Whilst there were a number of first-class coaches, a great many were indifferently horsed and badly driven.

The Shrewsbury Wonder, the Dorchester Magnet, the Nimrod, Telegraph, and Independent Southamptons, the Norwich coaches and many others too numerous to mention, together with all the mails out of London, were exceptions : but alas ! when the magic circle was passed these were but Magnets without attractions, Flys that only crawled, most dangerous Safetys, and Regulators pre-eminently uncertain. Such coaches were generally driven by the worst specimens of coachmen of the old school, men weighing the weight of two outside passengers, and occupying the space, too : or shadows, nerveless and powerless from habitual dram-drinking, and who thought bad language, worse slang, hard drinking, and cruelty to their unfortunate cattle the essential requisites to establish the character of a stage-coachman.

The worst kind of coach was infamously turned out, whilst the wretched condition of the horses was sometimes such as to attract the attention of passengers and arouse a protest.

" By Jasus ! " said one of these, an Irishman, pointing to a particularly decrepit wheeler; " if you want to send him on his thravels, it's into the coach you should put him, and not into the harnish."

# The Merry Past

Certain coaches could boast of a considerable antiquity.

The York Highflyer, for instance, which was running in 1812, was the identical vehicle which had been pictured by Hogarth. It had, of course, undergone much renovation, and resembled the family relic which the Irishman kept in memory of his grandmother—" a knife which had had two new handles and three new blades."

On the other hand, the efficient manner in which some of the great roads were worked was remarkable.

One of the fast coaches which ran between Liverpool and Manchester in 1828, for instance, was celebrated for the speed with which the horses were changed, it being declared that this operation could be effected in thirty-four seconds. Seven men, it seems, were in attendance. Both wheelers and leaders were brought out coupled, with the reins through all the terrets ; but the novelty of the plan consisted in the management of the wheel traces. The chains at the ends of them were opened sufficiently to fit the roller-bolts on the splinter-bar, and kept open by means of straw stuffed in a link of each—which straw, of course, gave way as soon as the horses touched their collars, and then the traces fitted tight.

Another famous coach was the Shrewsbury Wonder. It was established in February, 1825, and was the first that ever attempted to perform so long a journey as one hundred and fifty-four miles in a day ; in fact, it was the wonder of the day, and thus the coach took its name. It started at a quarter before five, and arrived in London at a quarter before ten, stopping twice on the road for refreshment. Some years afterwards, in order to give those who preferred an extra hour for "sleep and a downy bed" that indulgence, their time for starting was postponed to a quarter before six, and their speed increased, so that the journey was terminated at the same hour. In 1834 an opposition was started, with the imposing cognomen of the Nimrod. On this occasion the Wonder party, with much sagacity, put on another coach called the Stag, to accompany the Nimrod, not allowing the Wonder to race or perform any of the dangerous exploits usually exhibited by oppositions. Thus the road was for about a year and a half supplied with three coaches, when the Nimrod party found theirs was a losing concern, and made overtures to consolidate it with the Stag, the latter having all along had the best of the chase. It is scarcely necessary to observe that the Stag did not long continue its course after the competition had ceased. The Shrewsbury Wonder itself ceased running in 1839, killed by the competition of the London and Birmingham Railway.

Many and loud were the curses which about this time were levelled at the "new-fangled steam-kettles" by the old coachmen and other lovers of the road, who could not bring themselves to believe that the railways had come to stay.

Until the appearance upon the Windsor road of the Taglioni coach, the most elegant public carriage that ever took the road in England, the strange fact seemed utterly unnoticed that the coach communication between the metropolis and the royal borough was conducted upon a worse principle than on any line from the Land's End to John-o'-Groat's. The old lumbering " blues " in pace and cut belonged to the eighteenth century, and were in sober fact a mockery of travelling in comparison with the style adopted by every other purveyor of locomotive conveniences. At last, upon the principle that " it never rains but it pours," the affair was taken in hand by those who could do it better than any others. It was decided that something " slap " was to be put upon the Windsor line, which resolution was come to somewhere about the time of Hampton races, and in a fortnight after date the Taglioni was started. At the end of a month this coach was doubled, starting from London and Windsor at twelve each day, Sunday excepted, and returning at four, the distance, twenty-six miles, done in two hours, " everything inclusive." What was probably the very perfection of a coach owed its existence to the taste and spirit of a triumvirate, the teams belonging to the Earl of Chesterfield, Count Batthyany, and Mr. Harvey Aston. The London end was driven by Mr. Richard Brackenbury, whose brother was so well known on the Age, Brighton; and the Windsor, by Mr. Charles Jones, also a star of the Brighton hemisphere. The Taglioni did not start from any yard in town, but, issuing from the sporting precincts of Chesterfield House, called at the principal West End booking places, and as the minute hand at the Gloucester Coffee House pointed towards noon set out on its gay career.

Mr. Warde of Squerries initiated the first coach-box placed upon springs. He prevailed upon the proprietors of the Manchester Telegraph to adopt the use of them, and thence they were called Telegraph springs.

The opposition between the Telegraph and Defiance was carried on with more spirit than any other upon record. Both coaches were worked in a very superior style. Two very swell coachmen drove them out of London about 1811, and may be said to have set the example of neatness in dress, and respectability of appearance and demeanour, which was so characteristic of the more modern coachman. These were, John Marchant on the Telegraph, and Bob Snow on the Defiance—the latter for some years past a proprietor of, as well as at work upon, a Brighton coach.

Whilst in the last days of coaching in England very great improvements were effected, the French adhered to the methods of their ancestors in the matter of travelling, right up to the time when railways became a general mode of conveyance.

The *malle* or French mail coach, drawn by five heavily-shod horses, was a very ingeniously contrived conveyance. It carried four besides the courier (a person of much higher rank than our guards) ; three in the body, similar to a chariot ; the other in a calash in front, where the letters were deposited in a bag attached to the apron, from which they could be easily distributed.

These *malles* went about nine miles an hour, and the changes were constant, which was uncomfortable at night, as people were awakened every hour, in addition to the tilting and swinging of the vehicle. A quaint figure was the *maître de poste*, in his nightcap, slippers, and shorts, often raw-boned, from a diet of *soup maigre*, or lanky with fasting, but not with praying. Nevertheless, he was always a courtier, whether hungry or not ; as were the two *hommes à cheval*, who lugged at the heads of five creatures, high-backed, low-necked, and stiff-legged, which were, when thus used, also stiff-tempered. These horses, though certainly not crammed like turkeys, but rather more like rats half starved, had light and airy hearts ; with but a good word, " *mon petit garçon*," or " *ma belle fille*," back would go their ears, and a smile and a kick would at once indicate that they were ready to go.

The postilion was equipped in striped linen trousers —in jack-cases or jack-boots for the legs, wanting only a jump to get into. The jacket was lancer-like—blue body, red facings, and a multitude of *fleur-de-lis* buttons in bright brass—a glazed hat over a white nightcap, just touching the head of a *bien poudré*—tail of hair. In his mouth was a short pipe, and a devilish long whip was ever present in his hand. The three stallions before him, all in a row, were generally under excellent control.

The decadence of English coaching was but the fulfilment of that law of Nature which ordains that once perfection has been accomplished decay should begin.

At the time of the introduction of the railway

system, the coaches and the roads on which they ran had never been better.

The roads, indeed, had reached what was practically perfection, their condition being a great contrast to that which had prevailed at the beginning of the eighteenth century, when they had been in a terrible state. In 1703 when Prince George of Denmark went from Windsor to Petworth to meet Charles the Third of Spain, that journey, a distance of about forty miles, occupied a space of fourteen hours, although those who travelled it did not get out of their carriages, save when they were overturned or stuck fast in the mire, until they reached their destination. At times the coach had literally to be carried over impassable stretches of road on the shoulders of sturdy natives. The last nine miles of the way took six hours to negotiate. When communication by roads was in such a condition as this, it is clear that even in the equipages of the nobility, the only description of horse that could have been used was such as we now find occupied in the severest labours of farm husbandry. In the middle of the eighteenth century, travelling by public carriages was in a deplorable condition, the best scarcely accomplishing four miles an hour, and many of them not reaching that rate of pace.

Even in 1811 it was no very unusual thing for a gentleman to find himself obliged to return to his coachmaker an open carriage, in consequence of its fore-wheels not being high enough to keep the bed off the crown of the road.

# The Merry Past

As late as 1814, when Jack Richardson first went on the Glasgow Mail, the depth of the ruts and wheel-tracks was such as to defy any team to lift their coach out without assistance, when once it was fairly let in. The plan then adopted when two carriages met in the same track was for a joint effort to be made to fill up the rut in front of one of them with large stones, by which an inclined plane was constructed to lift it from out the slough. And yet they kept time in those days !

All this had been changed by 1838, when the main coach roads rivalled the smoothness of a billiard table.

The change produced by the introduction of railways was bitterly lamented by old-fashioned people, who complained that the coach offices were deserted, whilst an omnibus to the railway station alone supplied the place of the gallant teams of high-bred horses which formerly were seen issuing forth at all hours of the day and night, with well-appointed coaches to all parts of the Kingdom.

The days of travelling for pleasure appeared to be about to disappear for ever—the glories of the road to vanish in a puff of smoke.

For some years before railways had seriously begun to supersede coaches, " posting " had dwindled to the shadow of what it once was. As late as 1839, it is true, family men still travelled with post-horses to their own carriages ; and now and then one encountered a solitary individual in a britschka, rolling along with a cigar in his cheek for company's sake : but such sights became rare; and as for post-chaises, they were scarcely used, save in towns, and here but seldom. In the country, when one of these " yellow ochres " was seen, its inmate was more often than not an accoucheur, or a churchwarden, with a job in hand that the parish paid for. The great travelling public had by this time taken freely to making use of the public coaches.

As railroads began to increase, nearly all the old coaching and posting inns lost their business. The advent of steam, indeed, caused a good deal of ruin to numbers of people who had drawn their main sources of livelihood from the road.

Small towns and villages, hitherto kept alive by the necessary accompaniments to stage-coach travelling, began to assume a deserted look, and the inhabitants, downcast and dejected, gloomily viewed the few remaining coaches merely as belated relics which recalled to their memory " the brave doings of bygone days."

Fittingly enough, in 1838, just as the coaches were disappearing before the triumphant forces of steam, died that Prince of Jehus, old Sir John Lade, at the age of eighty. Fifty-nine years before, when this sporting Baronet had come into his inheritance, Doctor Johnson had written the famous lines :

> Long expected one-and-twenty,
> Ling'ring year at length is flown;
> Pride and pleasure, pomp and plenty,
> Great (Sir John) are now your own.

# The Merry Past

Call the Betseys, Kates and Jennies
All the names that banish care,
Lavish of your grandsire's guineas,
Show the spirit of an heir.

Sir John Lade in the course of years became totally
ruined, and would not improbably have ended his life
in the most abject poverty had it not been for
George IV, who granted him a pension when the
gentleman jockey, the pearl of coachmen and the
companion of the Prince's festive hours, was driven
to ground. This pension Queen Victoria, to her
eternal honour, insisted on continuing, and poor old
Sir Jockey John, owing to her bounty, ended his
days in peace.

George IV was at one time in the habit of constantly passing part of the evening with Sir John, on
whom he bestowed many a kindness, as the following
will show. Finding the sporting Baronet one night
unusually low-spirited, he kindly enquired the cause,
which, after some reluctance and hesitation, was
explained, and which was on account of Lady Lade's
nephew (a great favourite of her husband and self)
being embarked and about to sail immediately for
India, in which service His Majesty had procured him
a cadetship. The ship was already at Gravesend, and
there were many probabilities of its being then in the
Downs. George IV nevertheless said, "Johnny,
there is still a chance left; send down immediately,
and if he is not beyond our reach, I will provide for
him otherwise." A friend of Sir John's undertook
the task: one of his fleetest horses was saddled, and

after the first stage he rode post, and actually brought back young Daly, having fractured his collar-bone on the way to seek him. George IV kept his word, and gave the young man a commission in his own regiment, the 10th, where he served with credit to himself, but unfortunately fell a victim to the fatal retreat from Corunna.

In the distant days of the eighteenth century, poor old Sir John, then "as wild as the wind," had been the finest whip of his time, and was celebrated for the manner in which he would drive the off wheels of his phaeton over a sixpence.

The following very appropriate lines were written at the time of his death:

> The father of Jehus, Sir John Lade, is gone!
> As a Whip in his day, he was beaten by none.
> Though with tits, four-in-hand, he so long shew'd his
>    graces,
> He has bolted at last, and kicked over the traces.
>
> His coach was a fast one in life's early stage,
> Yet its run had been long—the best part of an age;
> But its speed has decreas'd, the machine got more weighty,
> Though it never broke down till its years number'd eighty!
>
> Thy leaders and wheelers no longer could save,
> Whatever their speed, thy frail form from the grave;
> Death has taken the ribbons, that coachman of gloom,
> And has taken thy drag, four-in-hand, to the tomb!

# VI

WITH the advent of railways disappeared the Corinthian or buck, whose day and night sprees have been celebrated in many a volume—the most famous, of course, being Pierce Egan's "Tom and Jerry."

The exploits of the not particularly estimable type in question would appear to have vastly interested a past generation, who regarded the smashing of lamps, wrenching off of knockers, and the like with comparatively good-humoured toleration.

As a rule the buck was essentially a townsman, though hot-headed young squires were generally quite ready to emulate his ways. These latter, however, were for the most part men of a better and more sterling type than the ordinary London buck, who in many instances was nothing but a spoilt child of fortune, with a limited intelligence which had never been developed.

Whilst possessing all the faults and vices of the squire, the buck too frequently lacked his merits; at the same time it must in justice be said that many a box-lobby lounger became a first-class officer when at the wars. The natural companion of the eighteenth-century buck, of course, was the dashing Cyprian who was such a familiar figure in the pleasure resorts of that day.

# The Merry Past

She exercised her dangerous blandishments from Piccadilly to Temple Bar, whilst in the streets about the Haymarket and Covent Garden her resorts were almost publicly recognised.

The over-righteous, it is true, held up their hands in horror as her gay curricles wept by, but the reign of the hypocrite had not yet dawned, and whilst youth and beauty lasted, the Betseys, Kates, and Jennies lived pretty well unmolested, and were not, as to-day, hounded from pillar to post by zealous reformers on the mendacious plea that they were but carrying out the dictates of Christianity.

The London buck when travelling about the country was very apt to give himself insupportable airs, which rendered such wild spirits not over-popular with innkeepers and others whom they were apt to browbeat.

Not a few of the latter, however, were well able to hold their own. A dashing blade once strode into a well-known inn in the city of York, and ringing the bell with violence ordered a chaise to the door instantly. The waiter naturally asked, " For what stage ? " " What's that to you ? " replied the dandy ; " be off, and do as I tell you." The waiter immediately went to his master, and said there was a queer customer in the coffee-room, who wanted horses, but wouldn't say where to. " Aye," said the innkeeper, who was particularly mild in demeanour, and a man who held the doctrine that more flies were caught with honey than vinegar, " I'll go to 'un ; he don't know we must make out a ticket for the horses ":

and proceeded to his guest to make the necessary enquiries. " I be tould, sir, ye do want a chaise : where to, pray, may I be so bould to axe ? " " To hell ! " responded the exquisite. " Oh, then I can accommodate thee directly," replied mine host : and walking quietly to the window threw up the sash, and called out, " Ostler John, here be a gentleman in a desperate hurry to go home—harness Thunder and Lightning, put them into the Brimstone chaise, and tell Hell-fire Dick to drive like the Devil. And now, young gentleman," turning to the astonished dandy, " I'll go and make out the ticket, and ye'd better come down with the ' blunt ' before ye starts, lest I should never see your face again ! "

The old posting inns were queer places, and most of them had some character well known for his originality and quaintness of phrase.

The disconcerting reply which one of these—a waiter—made to a somewhat pompous pillar of the law excited considerable amusement amongst those who heard of it.

The learned and saintly judge in question having retired into one corner of the public day-room to indite an epistle, and seeing the waiter bustling about, called him in his usual grave and mysterious manner. " Waiter," said he, in an undertone, " pray is there a ' w ' in Harrogate ? " " I don't know, my lord," said William, with a shake of his head, and putting on one of his slyest looks ; " master is very particular, but I dare say I can manage it for you ! "

A notorious buck of his day was Lord Lyttleton,

a nobleman celebrated for his high spirit and strong attachment to the pleasures of life. He was once much piqued by the remarks of a certain antiquated lady, well known for her strong predilection for beauty and athletic form in her footmen, and in consequence fixed upon the following comical mode of revenge. A friend of his had an Irish servant, of remarkably fine presence, with a great fund of native humour. This man my lord borrowed, and instructed to play the old lady off, who, the parties previously knew, had advertised for a footman. It must be observed, her ladyship either was, or affected to be, of the most delicate and irritable system of nerves, which could not endure the slightest disturbance or noise. The new servant, handsomely dressed and *bien poudré*, presented himself at the lady's door, and his errand being announced, he was soon ushered into her salon. My lady was alone, and after asking the young man a variety of questions, the ready answers to which seemed to be highly satisfactory, her ladyship told him she liked his appearance much as he stood, but she wished to see him walk, to know whether he did that gracefully, a main point with her : on this he walked up and down the room, the old woman's eyes seeming to devour every part of him. The man, it should be understood, was full six feet, and very lusty. He was now ordered to turn on this side, now on that, then to make his bow, then to carry a fan and book ; last of all, to walk the length of the room again. Here he was prepared to finish the joke. Having walked the last time, he made a profound bow, and said, "Your ladyship has examined some, but not all of my motions, which are all equally excellent. You have seen me walk, now you shall see me trot." With that, he trotted up and down the room with his utmost force, until the glasses, china, chairs, and everything else danced as if bewitched, and the lady was seized with such a fright as took from her all power of utterance. Then stopping a moment, the hopeful blade repeated, "Now, my lady, you have seen me trot, I'll next show you how I can gallop." This he also performed with his utmost energy; and running downstairs, bolted fairly out at the hall door.

The old lady was found by her servants in hysterics, partly from affright, and partly from rage and disappointment. Two physicians were called in, and she did not get about for several days; but the first day she could possibly get out, she spent in driving all over town, to inform her acquaintance with what brutality and insolence she had been treated.

An advertisement appeared in several public papers, with a reward of fifty pounds for the discovery of the offender.

In the meantime Lord Lyttleton was convulsed with joy at his success, for which he rewarded the humorous Irishman with a twenty-pound note; and to clinch the joke, offered the fellow twenty more if he would himself appear to the advertisement, and claim the reward, to which his master, who valued him, would not consent.

Wild freaks of the most reckless and extravagant

description were not uncommon amongst the bucks of that day, who did not always confine their eccentricities to the metropolis, their own country houses sometimes being the scene of mad outbursts.

In 1780 a considerable sensation was created in the neighbourhood of Axminster by an act of vandalism performed by a young Baronet who owned a fine old mansion in the vicinity.

Together with a band of wild companions, Sir John, who was annoyed at being prevented from hunting by the weather, set to work to destroy the pictures of his ancestors with a hunting whip, in which work of destruction he was ably seconded by his friends, with the result that every sheet of canvas hung in strips and tatters, and the once magnificent hall presented a scene of purposeless destruction.

Masterpieces of Rubens and Vandyke were here treated with as little respect as any daubing upon the door of a pothouse.

Just as this famous exploit had ended, in came George Ralph, the painter, who, with a sorrowful countenance, like a sad herald from the vanquished, obtained permission to dispose of the dead. When the conquerors had left the field, this saddened artist and the lady of the mansion, greatly to the credit of her gentle heart, put together the venerable ancestors, but for whom the degenerate young Baronet would never have been in existence.

The young buck of that day was, as a rule, riotous, loose, and wild, making little secret of his love of dissipation and pleasure. The following lines,

# The Merry Past

written in the eighteenth century, convey an admirable idea of his chief characteristics:

A man of *ton*—eh, dam'me! who's afraid?
In public places, fit to shine and sport,
With beauty's charms to flirt and pay my court;
Through the box-lobby, mellow, blythe and reeling,
I'll show my wit and sentimental feeling;
Out-roar the play'rs in dialogue and singing,
And hear my voice through all the boxes ringing.
An't this delightful, frolicksome and smart,
Enough to conquer any woman's heart?
With cash and spirit for the world's career,
I'll have my name in all the clubs appear;
At whist, and faro, I'll my shiners stake,
And seven's the main shall through the dice-box shake.
Then how I'll sport my curricle and ponies,
Drive out *ma chère amie*, or friendly cronies;
I'll shake my noddle, and I'll crack my lash,
Gee-ho my nags, through thick and thin to dash.
In coat with seven-fold cape, and coachman's art,
'Gainst ev'ry driver in the town I'll start,
Whirl'd here and there, nor posts nor people heeding,
For that's your sort—and shows your sense and breeding.

As a rule he commenced the arduous labours of the day at about ten in the morning, when he rose, and having taken a slight breakfast, put on his riding-coat and repaired to his stables. Having inspected his horses, asked a thousand questions of his coachman and grooms, and given as many orders, he either rode on horseback or in his curricle, attended by two grooms, dashing through all the fashionable streets into Hyde Park. If, however, the weather was unfavourable, he would take his chariot and visit the shops of the most noted coachmakers and saddlers, who never failed to receive him with profound respect. After bespeaking something or other, he would then repair to Tattersall's, where he would spend his time with his friends seriously studying the pedigree or merits of horses, or in discussing the invaluable properties of a pointer, setter, greyhound, or other sporting dog.

Afterwards driving from one exhibition to another, he would stop at the caricature shops, and about three drive to a fashionable hotel, take his lunch there, read the papers, and arrange his parties for the evening, till he strolled home at five to his toilet, which he found prepared by his valet. At seven he was dressed, and either went with a party to dinner, or returned to the hotel where he had previously arranged with some friends the order of the day. At nine he went to the play—not to see it, which would have been a shocking infringement of the laws of fashionable decorum, but to flit from box to box, to ogle ladies whom he knew, and to show himself to others whom he did not know; to lounge about the lobbies, take a review of the frail, fair ones in the coffee-room, and saunter back to his carriage. He then drove to a rout, a ball, or the faro-bank of some lady of distinction, who was wont to conceal her own poverty by displaying the full purses of others. About four in the morning, exhausted with fatigue, the buck would return home, to recommence the next morning the follies of the day which had passed.

# The Merry Past

The man of fashion at the West End of the town was aped by many a young cit from the purlieus of the Royal Exchange (whose father had amassed a competence by the rigid observance of the laws of economy, and who transmitted his property, though not his prudence, to his son); such a man deemed it necessary, as a stylish lad of spirit, to buy a bit of blood, keep his gig, his girl, and his lodgings on the skirts of Epping Forest; and, as his keeping his gig and his girl afforded him but a restricted pleasure, unless all the world saw them, he made it a uniform practice to take Bet, as he familiarly called her, to all fairs, reviews, camps, Epping hunt, and the races at Epsom, Ascot Heath, Egham, and the like.

A lower type of pleasure-seeker was the greengrocer from St. Giles's, who, deriving his important being from the auspicious efforts of a link-boy and a barrow-woman, could not think of descending to the grave without being stylish and participating in the fashionable amusements of the age. This gentleman thought it supreme felicity to procure a light cart, drawn by a raw-boned blind pony, or a donkey; into this vehicle he conveyed three chairs, some geneva, hung beef, tobacco, pipes, and a tinder-box, and then mounting with his favourite doxy and sandman Joe, drove rapidly to a boxing-match, an ass-race, or a bull-bait, at Ball's Pond, Tothill Fields, or Bow Common.

The buck of the beginning of the nineteenth century was altogether different from his predecessor of a quarter of a century earlier, who was of a more vicious type.

# The Merry Past

The Corinthian, as a rule, could drive a coach full of ladies as well as the most experienced coachman; did not often overturn the carriage, and very seldom rode down old people or children; could trace the pedigree of a racehorse through one hundred descents, and enumerate all the dams, grand-dams, and great-grand-dams, with the most fluent accuracy; could tell the good and bad qualities of a horse at first sight; and in the refined employments of the stable could vie with the most expert groom or stable-boy.

He was an adept at swearing. As to the fair sex, the elegant society of the stable was preferable in his estimation to that of the drawing-room, and the lounge among brother fine fellows in the coffee-house, or the tavern, superior to the company of the ladies, in whose conversation his accomplishments did not enable him to bear a part. He paid his debts of honour much in the same manner as the fine fellow of 1783; and, like him, could drink three bottles of wine, kick the waiter, and knock down watchmen with much the same good grace.

His dress, however, was not so picturesque.

The beginning of the decadence of the picturesque eighteenth-century costume dates from about 1787, when round hats began to come into general use, and men's clothes to lose those decorative features which have since been completely eliminated.

At first evening coats still retained some traces of ancient splendour, but it was not long before all costly fabrics were discarded in favour of a costume which gradually evolved into the present funereal evening dress.

After the French Revolution the dress of the upper classes in England totally changed. Those who regarded the new ideas with favour affected a studied negligence in their personal appearance, and there was an assimilation between the dress of high and low in sympathy with the prevalent doctrines of equality. Knee-breeches and the small sword were then, as to-day, seen only at Court, wigs had disappeared, and powder, which had taken their place, was fast following. We read in 1795 of the Duke of Bedford and his household at Woburn, including the stranger within his gates, undergoing a general shearing, as a protest against Pitt's tax on hairpowder. The cocked hat had gone, and the present tall hat had come in; muslin cravats, waistcoats, and pantaloons were beginning to be worn. Masculine dress indeed, after 1794, consisted, as now, of coat, tall hat, waistcoat, and trousers.

Up to the latter part of the eighteenth century dress and equipage were considerable badges of distinction; but as this waned the rich citizens, incited by a laudable ambition, soon broke through their old restraints of economy and deference, and as Mrs. "Flounder" transferred her residence from Cornhill to Cavendish Square, it was no longer possible to discover her origin, either from her jewels or her liveries. The barrier being thus broken down, an immense gap was left in the fences of the fashionable world, through which multitudes from Change

Alley and Pudding Lane flocked into the West
End.

Rich dresses now began to be given up; and a
rapid succession of whimsical fashions, often something new for every day, became the distinguishing
badge of fashionable ladies. The industrious direct-
resses of the *Magasins des Modes*, however, rendered
all these measures abortive; for the nobodies were
never above a day behind in their imitations, and
the very waiting-maids were apt to be mistaken for
their mistresses. The ladies of the first fashion,
indeed, at one time made a bold effort, in which
they thought none of the middle class could have
the assurance to follow them; and, in order to set
all competition at defiance, actually appeared in
public somewhat more than half naked. The enterprise, however, was not attended with that success
which its boldness merited; for instantly the whole
necks, arms, shoulders, and bosoms in the kingdom
were thrown open to the eye of the gazer.

Fashionable men adopted a more vigorous mode of
revenge for the encroachments made upon their
dignity in the way of dress. They began by direct
acts of retaliation; and as their valets and grooms
had most impudently aspired to their dress and
manners, they, in their turn, usurped the garb and
habits of the individuals in question.

As the nineteenth century ripened all memory of
the gorgeous costumes which the aristocracy once wore
became dimmed, and men at the West End gradually
gave up wearing even the blue coats and brass buttons

which struck such a pleasant note of colour in the streets.

Though his costume was more subdued, the nineteenth-century buck could be as insolent as his predecessor of a quarter of a century before.

" I believe," said one of these gentlemen, entering a room full of his friends, " that I was drunk enough last night to ask some of you fellows to dine."

" Possibly," said a quiet man in the corner ; " but, if you are referring to me, I may tell you that I never could have been drunk enough to accept."

" Damme, sir," said a young buck to a country gentleman in a coffee-house, " you look like a groom." " I am one," was the reply, " and ready to rub an ass down."

Another sporting dandy found that his carriage could not be driven up to the house, in consequence of a heap of stones lying in the way. Irritated at the circumstance, he leaned out of the window, and, with a volley of oaths, asked an Irish labourer who stood near why those stones were not removed. " Where can I move 'em to ? " " Move them anywhere—move them to hell ! " " I think," rejoined Paddy, " they'd be more out of your honour's way if I moved 'em to heaven."

Even more crushing was the repartee of the bargee, who in a slanging match was begged to remember that he was talking to a gentleman.

" Gentleman, indeed," said he ; " you a gentleman ! Then, damme, if I beant a lord."

# The Merry Past

With the fair sex the buck was enterprising in the extreme, but sometimes he met his match.

A couple of dashing bucks having made violent love to some girls who were inappreciative of their attentions, the latter determined to rid themselves of their importunities by a stratagem of a novel kind.

They invited the young men to supper, and then having procured and killed a tom-cat, the cook flayed and washed it, dexterously cut it up, and with proper seasoning put it into a pie. The beaux were invited to supper, and had each partaken very heartily of the pie, when the girl who did the honours of the table, poked from the bottom of it the nether extremity of poor Tom, curled up like a spitch-cocked eel, and begged the two swains to pick a joint or two of tail to finish with! The latter beat a precipitate retreat, and the story getting about, they were in consequence so laughed and mewed at, that soon both of them, to avoid the scoffings of the multitude, were induced to quit the neighbourhood!

A more refined snub was that administered to the youthful Marquis of Bath, who, when quite a stripling, had behaved rather rudely to one of the chambermaids. The girl complained to his mother, who, being extremely angry, the Marquis exclaimed, " Upon my soul, mother, she had so neat an ankle, and so pretty a foot, flesh and blood could not resist the temptation." His mother, looking at him, said, " That may be true—but skin and bones can have no such excuse." Lord Bath was remarkably thin.

According to a modern estimate a number of the

# The Merry Past

Corinthians were not particularly well off, many, indeed, were chronically hard up. Such a man was the Irish baronet, a buck with more tenants than acres, and more bogs than both, who had rattled through life on that great principle of economy which once induced a veteran dandy, in talking of some person whom he disliked, to say, " A low fellow that—damme, sir, I owe more than ever he was worth."

The baronet in question, who, as he used to boast, certainly had not the soul of an accountant, for his affairs were always in the greatest disorder, at last determined to put things right by a good marriage, and being agreeable enough, did actually succeed in paying successful court to a lady of considerable fortune. Settlements, however, were required, and though the baronet agreed to settle his very unsettled Irish property upon his fair intended, some extra provision of ready cash was insisted upon by her relatives.

At his wits' end to raise the money, the buck applied to a friend to furnish him with an introduction to a well-known banker, who might possibly accommodate him.

Going into the City, he stepped into the office with a free, jaunty, dashing air, and asked for one of the partners.

It happened to be Rogers the banker poet's day for business, and the baronet was ushered into that curious character's sanctum.

His easy demeanour and general appearance of a

man of fashion pleased Rogers, who with his most winning smile enquired what his visitor's needs might be.

"I want about two or three thousand pounds. Can your house accommodate me?"

"Without doubt, sir. We shall have great pleasure in doing so. May I ask on what security?"

"Oh, personal security, personal security," replied Sir Frederick, adjusting his cravat.

Mr. Rogers smiled. "Will you walk this way, sir?" He then opened a small door and led the way through various apartments and passages, until they arrived at a small room fitted up with fireproof deed cases and other places of safety. Here he took a small gold Bramah key from his waistcoat pocket, and opening a large iron safe or closet, courteously waved his hand. With a small sly look of the eye, Mr. Rogers turned to Sir Frederick and said:

"I must trouble you to walk in here, Sir Frederick."

"Walk in there? walk in there! What for, sir? what for, sir?"

"Oh, my dear sir, we always keep our securities in that closet."

The poor dandy was completely nonplussed by this novel method of showing a client what value was attached to personal security.

Another well-known frequenter of the West End, a dashing colonel, who had run through a decent fortune, became so encumbered with debts that he had to resort to the most elaborate expedients to escape the bailiffs who were employed to arrest him. By constant practice he became an adept at this somewhat unpleasant sport, the most ingenious bailiffs being baffled in their efforts to entrap him. One day, however, these men, who had come to regard the capture of the Colonel as a veritable trial of skill, obtained information that a son of the Colonel was expected home from the East Indies, and they determined to utilise this circumstance and capture their quarry by stratagem.

In accordance with a preconcerted plan four of the catchpoles, whose faces were not much known, disguised themselves in the dress of sailors, and taking a couple of trunks to the Colonel's house, requested admission. An old corporal, who mounted guard regularly in the area, demanded their business ; they answered, that "Captain ——, who had just arrived from the East Indies, had sent them forward with his trunks, and a letter, which they were to deliver into no other hands but his father's." This deception succeeded to the utmost of their expectations, for abating for a moment some of his usual caution, the Colonel ordered them to be admitted.

No sooner, however, did he perceive that the direction on the letter was in a strange handwriting, than the trick stared him in the face, and he resolved, if possible, to turn the tables once more in his favour. Bursting therefore into a fit of laughter, he said :

"Well, gentlemen, at length the chance is yours. There is an end of your trouble and my anxiety. But as I am going to a place whence I may not very soon return, you will drink a glass of wine with me, whilst my servant brings up a couple of dozen bottles to take away with us."

Then turning to his servant, he said significantly : " Go, call a coach immediately, and bring me up a dozen of wine of the *blue* seal, and a dozen of the *red*." The old corporal took the hint, and repairing to two press-gangs in the neighbourhood, one of which was distinguished by *blue ribbons*, and the other by *red*, he brought two strong parties, which finding four stout fellows in sailors' dresses, immediately impressed and took them on board a tender.

A more peaceful character was the Bond Street buck, who being, as he thought, at the point of death, thought it right to settle his worldly affairs. Accordingly he sent for a neighbouring solicitor to make his will. The solicitor, who was a wit as well as a lawyer, having been informed by the sick beau of all his circumstances, said he had a precedent for his will in that of the famous Rabelais, which he should adopt, and which was in these words : " I owe much ; I have nothing ; and I give the rest to the poor ! "

In spite of penniless bucks and long outstanding accounts, West End tradesmen did very well, far better, probably, than to-day.

In the early days of the nineteenth century Pall Mall and St. James's Street were crowded with the shops of tailors and of bootmakers, instead of the magnificent palaces which now occupy their site, and the man who lived in the West End led a very different life from that now in vogue. The buck

or " swell " spent much of his time in one of the few
fashionable clubs, membership of which was an indispensable adjunct of his life. When he lounged down
Bond Street or walked in the Park, he bore himself as
a dandy of the first water, and the anxiety he evinced
as to his dress, and the assumption of a certain swagger,
plainly proved that his promenade was an event in his
own opinion, at least, of some importance.

As late as 1806 men about town still frequented
coffee-houses, which were crowded in the evening.
The resorts in question, whilst greatly promoting
sociability, could not in any way compare in comfort
with the clubs—coffee-houses were stuffy, ill-ventilated
places.

At that time there were in London many small
clubs which held their meetings at a late hour of the
night in cosy taverns, where the rooms were carpeted
with sawdust, and the tables were of the darkest
mahogany, stained by the marks of pewter-pots and
the blemishes caused by heated tumblers. Prints
of famous racehorses, of ex-champions of the ring, of
jockeys, statesmen, and sportsmen hung on the walls.
The food served was simple, being limited to kidneys,
chops, and steaks, together with the whitest and
most floury of potatoes. Wine was at a discount,
but the beer and the spirits were of unimpeachable
quality.

Such clubs as these were enlivened by much wit-
ticism and song, whilst many a good story, generally
unfitted for sensitive ears, was retailed by members
afflicted with much dryness of throat. Membership

was composed of actors scarcely a remove from supers ; journalists who were really little better than penny-a-liners ; artists sketching for magazines, or painting for the dealers at famine prices ; stage-managers of unknown theatres ; authors who slaved for the publishers as hacks ; and barristers who had never held a brief. In addition to these the company as a rule included one or two men whom drink had " broke," and who were picking up a livelihood as best they could ; and a sprinkling of " swells from the West End."

The multiplication of clubs has caused a veritable revolution in the life of the bachelor living in the West End, the old tavern dinner being a thing of the past. In a club, after paying his entrance fee, a member finds himself part owner of a most splendid town house, where the tax-collector never intrudes, where repairs and dilapidations never concern him, where attentive servants wait upon his every order, where everything provided is of the very best (when it suits the committee to give satisfaction), where retirement can be obtained without the depressing sense of solitude, and where companionship can be enjoyed without the dangers of intrusion.

A fashionable hotel in the days of the Regency was Stevens', in Bond Street, the head-quarters of many a man about town. A number of saddle-horses, tilburies, and other smart turn-outs, were generally outside its doors, belonging to well-known habitués of the house, where a prodigious amount of wine was consumed. Stevens' was one of Byron's haunts.

Close by, in Cork Street, was the " Blue Posts," a favourite dining-place for bachelors in old days, Certain hostelries, instead of the customary signboard. adopted different coloured posts as distinguishing signs of the good cheer to be found within, and this originated the name of the place.

Hatchett's, much frequented by country gentlemen, was a bustling, crowded, noisy hotel. Visitors were furnished with the accommodation which their funds and social position seemed to warrant. A bachelor, for instance, without a servant, who arrived at the "White Horse Cellars" on the outside of a coach, would be shown up into a miserable little dirty attic, the best rooms being reserved for the county squires, who arrived in a post-chaise, or in their own carriage.

Blake's Hotel, afterwards the " Brunswick," in Jermyn Street, was a favourite bachelor resort.

Louis Napoleon took up his residence here under the name of the Comte d'Arenenberg, after his escape from the fortress of Ham in 1846. The " Brunswick " continued to be frequented by the sporting world up to its demolition a short time ago.

Other popular hotels in the early years of the nineteenth century were Limmers', Long's, Fladong's, Stephens', Grillon's, and Mivart's, which afterwards became Claridge's.

Limmers', though much frequented by rich sporting squires, was generally said to be the dirtiest hotel in London. It was famous for its gin punch and old port. Long's was another sporting hostelry which a certain group used almost as a club. Stephens' (in Bond Street) was a fashionable hotel much frequented by men about town. Fladong's was a favourite resort of naval officers.

The " Clarendon " (which ceased to exist in 1870), between Old Bond Street and Albemarle Street, was once the only public hotel where a well-cooked French dinner could be obtained. Its reputation as a resort of epicures was made by a cook, Jacquiers by name, who had amassed a considerable sum in the service of Louis XVIII, a royal gourmet, who was a worthy gastronomic successor to Louis XV. It was his custom, for instance, to have his chops and cutlets broiled not only on the grill, but between two other cutlets, in order to preserve their juices. His ortolans and small birds were also cooked inside of partridges stuffed with truffles, so that he often hesitated in choosing between the delicate bird and the fragrant esculent. The ortolan was termed by him *la bouchée du gourmet*, as it was never to be eaten in two mouthfuls. He had even established a testing-jury for the fruit that was served at the royal table, M. Petit-Radel, Librarian of the Institute, being the tester of peaches and nectarines.

The King in question, rather prematurely, perhaps, deplored the decadence of cooking generally.

" Gastronomy is passing," were his words to Dr. Corvisart, " and with it the last remains of the old civilisation. It belongs to organised bodies, such as physicians, to direct all their energies towards preventing the disruption of society. Formerly France was filled with gastronomers because it numbered so many corporations, the members of which have been annihilated or dispersed. There are now no more farmer-generals, no more abbés, no more monks."

Louis XVIII could not foresee the coming of that Napoleon of hotels, " M. Ritz," who, in addition to the very finest cooking, introduced an altogether higher standard at the various hostelries of which he became the guiding spirit. To him and his lieutenants is due the enormous improvement which has taken place in the way of hotel accommodation in London and Paris. The increase of comfortable flats has also done much to enhance the amenities of town life.

The inefficient attendance, the dirt, neglect, and wholesale .fleecing to which an unwary bachelor used to be exposed, can hardly be realised in these days of first-class hotels and luxurious flats.

As late as the middle of the nineteenth century bachelors' lodgings in the West End were of a kind which to-day would scarcely be tolerated by anyone. The paramount objection, as a rule, was the dirty, dowdy maid-of-all-work, who often ruled the bachelors who had rooms in her mistress's house with a rod of iron.

Most of these maids were superlatively bad servants, and anything but remarkable for cleanliness. " Lawk, sir," said one of these mop-squeezers to a lodger who had made some remonstrance, " do you call these hands dirty ? You should see my feet ! " Others were frankly insolent, like the one who said, " Please, sir, your tailor called this morning and left his compliments, and says you'll oblige him by paying his bill, and if not, sir, he says he'll oblige you."

Those were the days before bachelors prided themselves on the artistic decoration of their rooms, and it was certainly fortunate that the mania for collecting had not yet begun to rage, for most of these maids were wholesale slaughterers of crockery ; they seemed, indeed, to have sworn a war of extermination against china.

## VII

THE London of the past was full of fine old mansions, the abode of the great noblemen who lived there in a certain state. Formerly the custom of hanging out hatchments, which is now so rarely seen, was general. Probably the best description of the significance of these picturesque survivals of a stately age was that once given by an Irishman who, being accosted by a comrade with, " Arrah, Pat, look up ; what is that sign ? " replied, " Oh, botheration, 'tis no sign at all, at all, 'tis only a sign that somebody's dead that lives there."

A number of the aristocracy lived in Lincoln's Inn Fields, which was planned and laid out in the time of Charles the First, one or two of the houses being designed by Inigo Jones, though the greater number were completed at different times afterwards. This square is remarkable from the circumstance that its area is said to be of exactly the same dimensions as the base of the great pyramid of Egypt ; and was laid out of that size after Graves returned from Egypt, and made those dimensions known. The whole of this square, and everything that surrounds it, were built upon St. Clement's Fields.

Within our own times many of the great town

houses of the nobility have been demolished. Northumberland House, Harcourt House, and many others are cases in point. Numbers of others were removed years ago, amongst them Salisbury House, which was taken down in the eighteenth century, when Salisbury Street, built by Pain, the architect, covered its site. Cecil Street was built upon the Salisbury property at about the same time as Beaufort Buildings ; part of Cecil Street was built upon the site of Salisbury Exchange, which was a collection of shops or standings, similar to Exeter 'Change, which has now long been taken down. Salisbury Exchange was the scene of a remarkable affair during the protectorate of Oliver Cromwell. The Exchange was then a lounging-place for idlers, and some foreigners were parading it, and acting in a manner that was offensive to the English gentlemen who were present. Swords were invariably worn by gentlemen at that time ; in the scuffle the disputants drew, and one of the foreigners killed an Englishman. The culprit was seized, and committed for trial at the Old Bailey. It was clearly proved that the prisoner did kill the deceased under such circumstances that the jury found him guilty of murder, and sentence of death was passed upon him.

It then transpired that the offender was brother to the Portuguese ambassador, who, of course, made great exertions to save his relation from a disgraceful end. He influenced the ambassadors of other courts to join in procuring his pardon, and threats were made, the object of which was to prove that the execution of the criminal would be an infringement of the privileges of ambassadors. In spite of everything, however, Cromwell ordered the man to be hanged, without any deviation from the customary method of executing a common criminal for the same offence. The Protector was determined to show that, whatever he might choose to do himself, neither the ambassadors nor their brothers should murder English subjects with impunity.

At one time the most easterly point in which any of the nobility lived was Devonshire House, in Bishopsgate Street. When Lord Burlington was asked why he built his house, on the site of what is still Burlington House in Piccadilly, so far in the country, he said he was determined that no one should live beyond him.

Lord Burlington was a nobleman of great public spirit and fine taste. He it was who repaired St. Paul's Church, Covent Garden, and published the designs of Palladio with the idea of stimulating the taste for classical architecture in England.

When the citizens determined to build a palace for their chief magistrate, the peer in question, the great amateur and Maecenas of the arts of that time, offered to supply them, without expense to themselves, with an excellent design, which he proposed to extract from the works of Palladio. Instead, however, of receiving this offer as it should have been received when the matter was debated in the Common Council, a wiseacre rose in his place and asked if Mr. Palladio was, or was not, free of the City. When he was told who and what " Mr. Palladio " was, he moved that the offer should be rejected, because, as a citizen of London, he thought it was their duty to give every profitable order to a member of their own corporation, in preference to a foreigner of whom they knew nothing. The argument was thought unanswerable, and the job was given to Dance, the City Surveyor, who built the still existing Mansion House.

In spite of Lord Burlington's boast, the Duke of Devonshire built further on still, and Devonshire House was erected about 1737 by Kent, at a cost of something over £20,000. The entrance was originally up a double flight of stone steps, forming an external staircase to the central window on the ground floor. This arrangement was, however, altered during the last century, when the present insignificant entry was contrived. The general appearance of Devonshire House would be vastly improved were the original staircase to be replaced and the central portion of the dreary expanse of courtyard converted into a grass plot. The latter portion of this scheme, it is understood, may possibly be carried out, and should this be so, the alteration will, without doubt, greatly add to the amenities of Piccadilly.

Some twenty-three years after the Duke had beaten Lord Burlington, a private gentleman beat him, and in 1760 a good house was erected in Piccadilly, beyond Devonshire House. This gentleman proceeded with his design till he got it roofed in, and then discovered that it would require the expenditure of more money than he was willing to lay out, and he got rid of it by selling it, in its unfinished state, to the Earl of Coventry. The agreement was that he should produce the bills of what he had paid for the work, so far as it had gone. This the Earl repaid him, and then finished it himself, and called it Coventry House. The price that Lord Coventry paid for it, in its unfinished state, was ten thousand pounds—a fact which shows the moderate expense of building in those days. It may be added that this house is now the St. James's Club.

Apsley House was erected from the same idea as the other mansions which have been mentioned.

Lord Apsley, afterwards Earl Bathurst, when he was Chancellor, procured a gift from his royal master of a piece of ground within Hyde Park, being determined that his residence should be the last mansion of the town on that side.

It should be mentioned that till 1825 there was a toll-gate at Hyde Park Corner, and near here once was the inn known as " Hercules' Pillars," where Squire Western is described as having alighted on his visits to London. The tavern in question stood near the site of Apsley House, and in its day marked the extreme West End of London. The exact situation of this inn was probably between the present Apsley House and Hamilton Place.

After Apsley House was finished, it is said that King George the Third called upon his Chancellor and desired to see the new building. After he had gone over it, His Majesty turned to the Chancellor and wished him joy of his promotion. The noble lord, not having had notice of anything of that sort,

humbly but gratefully thanked His Majesty, and begged
to be informed what that promotion was. The King,
with equal gravity, replied : " My lord, you have
made yourself master-general of the dust, and I wish
you may live long to enjoy it." The observation,
if it was made, contained much truth, as the art of
laying the dust in that neighbourhood was not at
that time well understood.

When Lord Apsley began to build this house, he
employed people whose carelessness put him into a
situation that compelled him to pay a large sum of
money. The road, and the wall at the side of the
road, were kept in very bad order, and encumbered
with rubbish of various kinds, among which an old
woman put up a stall or stand to sell fruit. She
did this so long without being noticed by any but
her customers that, by degrees, she collected a quantity
of such materials as enabled her to make a kind of
hovel, in which she slept and lived, and having been
unmolested for so long a time she regarded the place
as her own. When the workmen prepared to build
the Chancellor's house, they cleared away this hovel
with the other rubbish in order to lay the foundations.
The old woman, much upset, would have protested
had not a relation, who was clerk to an attorney,
advised her to keep quiet till an auspicious moment
should occur. Following this advice, she bided her
time until the house was raised above the first storey,
and proceeding rapidly towards the roof, when she
went and enquired, in a formal manner, what had
become of her home. Those in charge of the works

treated her with ridicule and neglect; but she seriously asserted her claim, and referred to the men at the turnpike gate, who vouched for the fact that within their own knowledge she had lived unmolested in that place for several years. The young lawyer then drew his pen, and threatened the Chancellor that if he did not make satisfactory reparation, he would take such steps, in his own court, as would stop the building till the complainant was satisfied. His lordship saw clearly how the matter really lay, but finding he was legally caught, thought it would be better to give the old lady a sum of money than suffer the inconvenience of having the progress of his building interrupted, for which reason he paid a certain amount on the spot in full satisfaction for the loss of her dwelling.

The changes of fashion as regards locality in London are very curious.

When King George the Second kept his court at St. James's, his son Frederick, Prince of Wales, kept his court, in opposition, at Leicester House, then standing in Leicester Square, and the neighbourhood was crowded with persons of considerable rank and importance, whilst the taverns and houses of entertainment were popular. Among them was then (at the west end of Cecil's Court, in St. Martin's Lane), a house known by the name of Pons' Coffee House. In its most flourishing days it was frequented by the best class of foreigners, principally French, who were then in London. For their accommodation Monsieur Pons established the first table d'hôte *à la mode de Paris.* It was frequented by the superior classes of foreigners in London, who were desirous of living there in the same manner as they were accustomed to live in Paris, and as nearly as might be upon the same terms as they did in the capital of France. It was likewise frequented by English gentlemen, who, as men about town, were fond of a tavern life, and officers in the army and navy, willing to enjoy good company upon moderate terms.

The whole length of the house, on the ground floor, was laid out as a coffee-room in the usual way, and opening into Castle Street, behind the house, was a more select coffee-room, for parties who wished to dine in privacy; over that, on the first floor, was a large room fitted up for the table d'hôte, or ordinary as the "John Bulls" called it. For the convenience of the company dining a large table filled much of the room, surrounded by chairs numbered and fixed in regular order, and upon the wall were rows of pegs, fixed and numbered to correspond with the seats. A suitable seat was placed at the head of the table for the president, and another at the bottom for his deputy.

It was the rule of the house that the first gentleman who entered the room when the time for dinner was near should take the president's chair, and be president for that day; the next became vice-president for the day, in the same manner; the other company as they arrived seated themselves regularly in the vacancy nearest to the president. Each gentleman hung his hat and sword (all gentlemen wore swords whenever they were absent from home in those days) upon the hook numbered the same as his seat, and he was thus at his ease when the dinner commenced ; those who came in late took their seats below those who were already seated.

The harmony of this place was, after some time, interrupted by the foreigners, who being constantly there, contrived to get one of their own number into the chair, as perpetual president, and the rest on each side of him in succession, according to their notions of their relative importance.

Leicester Fields, now Leicester Square, passed through many vicissitudes before they became the decorous site of palatial music-halls and fine buildings such as it now is. It was Baron Grant who converted the square, formerly disfigured by a tumbledown statue and a singularly ill-kept spot, into the public gardens which exist to-day. Londoners of the past were not very enthusiastic about statuary.

When the statue of the Duke of Bedford in Russell Square was first exposed to public view in August, 1809, it attracted a good deal of attention and controversy, besides incidentally causing a fierce combat between two Irish art connoisseurs in a humble walk of life.

An exceedingly rough crowd having assembled near the statue, it was not very long before differences of opinion began to make themselves felt.

Mr. O'Flannagan, who was a composer of mortar, insisted it was made of cast stone, and represented the Duke of Bedford ; and Mr. O'Shaughnessy, who was a rough lapidary, vulgarly called a pavior, contended it was made of cast iron, and intended to " raprisint Charley Whox." The dispute ran high, and, as it advanced, became mixed with party and provincial feelings.

With such provocations of mutual irritation, the two Hibernians quickly appealed to the law of arms ; and after putting the eyes of each other into half-mourning, they agreed to adjourn the battle till the next Sunday morning, and to decide it like " jontle-men " by the cudgel. The meeting took place at Chalk Farm, and each was attended to the field by a numerous train of partisans, male and female, from the warlike purlieus of Dyott Street and Saffron Hill. They were armed with blackthorn cudgels of no ordinary dimensions, and having set-to, without ceremony or parade, each belaboured his antagonist for above an hour in a style that would have struck terror into the stoutest of the Burkes and Belchers, and enamelled each other from head to foot with lasting testimonies of vigour and dexterity. The air was rent by the triumphant shouts of their respective partisans, as either alternately bit the ground. At length Mr. O'Shaughnessy yielded the victory, and Mr. O'Flanna-gan was borne off the field with his brows enwreathed by the Sunday shawl of a milk-woman, his sweet-heart, who witnessed the combat, and crowned the conqueror with her own fair hands.

Another statue, erected on the site of Carlton House in 1837, attracted much unfavourable comment. This was the Duke of York's column, the designs and proportions of which were ironically said to be those dictated by the Committee of Taste—not of taste itself.

It had been debated by this committee whether the statue on the top (which is of red granite, and represents the Duke in the costume of the Knights of the Garter) should face the Park or the metropolis. The former was eventually decided, because, it was wickedly said, the overwhelming majority of His Royal Highness's creditors being resident in the metropolis, no one could expect that he should face them.

The whole thing was denounced as a job in which contempt had been shown for the public at large.

Nevertheless, the statue in question is not at all unsuited to the neighbourhood of Pall Mall.

The street in question was never used for the game from which it derives its name. This was played in the Mall, which is now the Processional Road, which originally sloped downwards towards the centre a foot or two deeper than either of its sides. Here, in its whole length, was laid a stone gutter, hollowed into a form approaching to a semicircle, and made perfectly even, being united smoothly with the gravel walk on each of its sides. Through this gutter, in its whole length, and at equal distances, were made holes, in such a manner that in hot weather they allowed the water to pass from the surface into the drain below, which carried it into the canal. These holes, likewise, held the hoops that were set up in them when the game was played. The reasons for the decay of the game of Pall Mall have never been made very clear ; its rules, according to tradition, were as follows : In the

holes, which have been mentioned, were temporarily
fixed hoops similar to those which are used at croquet.
The players stood at one end of the walk, with "malls"
—implements nearly resembling, if not identical with
croquet mallets. The contest was, who should drive
the ball (like the croquet-ball) through the greatest
number of the hoops. This must have required both
strength and dexterity, for if the ball touched either
side of any of the obstacles, it would be stopped.
Charles II is said to have been such an adept in
the art, that he could drive his ball right through the
whole length of the walk. When the game was
ended, the hoops were removed till next wanted.
The game of "pall mall" in course of time fell into
gradual disuse and was eventually forgotten; the walk,
however, where it had been played remained in the
state that has been described till, in making the improvements in 1770, its concave form was changed to
convex, by raising it about four feet in the centre.

Another favourite pastime of Charles II was playing
tennis at the court which, till 1863, existed on the
south side of James's Street, Haymarket. When
the building was finally destroyed, the pavement of
the court in question, it is said, was removed to
another tennis court, where it still serves its original
purpose.

In the Merry Monarch's day St. James's Park presented a very different appearance from what we now
see. Great alterations were made in 1770, before which
date the ornamental water was a long canal. As Le
Nôtre left it, it extended from the parade, where it

formed a straight line from the road that passed from
Carlton Gate to opposite Princes Court. The distance
of that line from Suffolk House did not exceed thirty
feet, and the distance of the other end of the canal,
by being curved to allow persons to walk round it,
did not exceed forty or fifty feet. These ends of
the canal were within the same wooden rails which
surrounded the whole of the lawn; and the rails in
question were supported by uprights at moderate
distances, which allowed anyone who chose to stoop
under them to get either to the grass or to the water.
The consequence of this arrangement was that the
end of the canal nearest the parade frequently became a scene for executing rough-and-ready justice
upon pickpockets. When any of them were detected
in their evil deeds, either in the Park or streets near
it, the crowd, instead of sending them for trial, to
the watch-house, or the Old Bailey, took the execution
of justice into their own hands, dragged them down
to the parade, and plunged them into the canal;
and when they attempted to get out, the children of
justice repeated the plunge, till they thought they
had given them enough. The only chance the
poor wretches had to elude this correction was to
wade up the north side of the lawn till their tormentors ceased to follow them, and then, getting
upon dry ground, run away as well as they could.
If they succeeded in this, they had to cross the Park
to that gate which allowed the best chance to escape
further torment; but their dripping clothes and
heads showed where they had been, and unless they

were so lucky as to get into the street, where there
were no mischievous persons who would raise the hue
and cry, "A pickpocket!" they had the additional
exertion of being the subject of a chase, till they
either ran themselves dry, or escaped by some lucky
turning which enabled them to baffle their pursuers.
Many of these unfortunate wretches, when approaching the fatal canal, would humbly petition not to be
thrown in, ejaculating, "Pray, gentlemen, don't
throw me in. Indeed, if you will give me leave, I
will jump in myself, and duck myself as often as you
please. Indeed, indeed, gentlemen, I will, but pray,
pray don't throw me in." If leave was granted, the
poor wretch would jump from the kerb into the
water, wade into such a depth as he was ordered to
remain at, face his tormentors, and crouch till his
head was under water, rise again, and repeat the
plunge as often as the order was given. If he was
dilatory, stones were thrown at him to enforce
obedience. He then ducked willingly to avoid the
blows, and this discipline was repeated till the tormentors were satisfied that he had had enough.

The canal was done away with during the early
part of the nineteenth century, and during the time
the alterations were being made the King used sometimes to superintend them. Amongst the workmen
there was a man who, being esteemed a kind of wit
among his brethren, longed for an opportunity to
speak to the King. His Majesty coming near the
spot one day where this man was at work, he seized
the opportunity, and, looking directly in his face,

" hoped His Majesty would give them something to drink." Displeased at this intrusion, but unwilling to appear to resent it, the King felt in his pockets for some coin, but finding none, he at length replied, " I have got no money in my pockets." " Nor I either, by G—," said the workman ; " and as you have none, I wonder where the devil it all goes to."

South of the Le Nôtre's canal there was originally a moat, thirty or forty feet wide, and more than that distance from the rail of the lawn. Its water came out of the canal, and ran parallel with it, preserving its regular distance till it approached the Bird Cage Walk ; it then turned and went parallel to that, till opposite to the gate from Queen Square. It then made another return, and ran straight towards the north, about half the distance between the rail on the outer side of the lawn and the edge of the canal. Again it turned to the west and ran parallel to the Bird Cage Walk, about half the distance from Queen Square to the end of the walk ; it then turned once more to the north, and ran direct into the canal.

Within this moat, and in its whole circumference, the ground, close to the water's edge, was thickly planted with willows and other trees. Within the western end and wide part of this enclosure the ground was laid out in three channels, running into one in a clever way : one received the water from that end of the canal nearest the parade, within the hedge that surrounded the ground, within the moat ; a footpath passed round the whole enclosure, which consisted of water, intersected by other footpaths.

Within the angle formed by the return of the moat, opposite the gate of Queen Square, and within the hedge, stood the Fishing House, a large building, which had been charming, but for years before its removal had fallen into decay. In its general appearance it resembled the orangery in Kensington Gardens. But although it was a very large building it was very much smaller than that greenhouse. A moderate-sized dwelling-house adjoined the great room, and had been in all probability the residence of Governor St. Evremond when he commanded the island, as well as devoted to any other purposes which might have commended themselves to Charles and his merry companions.

Before the alterations of 1770 this spot had become very desolate, everything having a forlorn and untended look.

The water was crowded with reeds and rushes, but still contained fish and some ducks. The small walks which surrounded the water, and had been gravelled, were overgrown with high grass and weeds. In what had been their borders were some degenerate flowers mixed with the weeds, with some bushes and willow or other trees, some of which had grown to a great height, giving the place an appearance of being deserted. The island, once the scene of so much unrestrained gaiety, was situated on the neglected side of the Park, and as admission to it could not be obtained but by application, which few were willing to make, it had acquired from the public the name of the Wilderness. What had been St. Evremond's House was inhabited by an old man and woman, whose business was to take care of it, as well as the grounds, and what live stock still existed.

In the bend of the moat nearest the house a punt was stationed, and on the opposite shore was a post to which a bell-wire was fixed. Anyone who wished to see the place rang the bell, when the old man would appear and punt the visitors over into the Wilderness, through which they rambled at pleasure till they were tired, and then they were punted back again to refresh themselves where they could, because no refreshments were to be had in the Wilderness. Those, however, who knew the secrets of the place took tea, and everything that was necessary for the tea-table, but china and hot water ; these were supplied by the Charon and Hecate of the place, who were not allowed to sell any refreshment. The old couple, however, always provided sufficient hot water, as well as a very decent tea-service and all the attention that was necessary. In return for this, it was the custom for visitors to present them with some adequate present at the moment of departure, and one way and another the old couple did a comfortable trade.

Such were the last scenes that took place at the spot where the merry Charles and his companions passed so much of their time.

At the south-west end of the canal was, once, to be found Rosamond's Pond, remarkable, for many

reasons, from the time it was made by Le Nôtre, till
it was finally destroyed by the improvements of 1770.

The lawn north of the canal was left as a pasture
for the cows that supplied the nursery-maids and
their charges with milk, at the east end of the park.
It will be remembered that when the Processional
Road was formed a few years ago the proposal to
entirely banish the milk stall from the Park raised
much indignant protest, with the result that the
descendants of those to whom the privilege was
originally granted were permitted to establish a new
stall to be held for their " lifetime only " on another
spot. The cows (latterly one only was kept) had
been a feature of this park since the sportive days of
Charles II. He it was who originally granted the
right of purveying milk here to an ancestor or ances-
tress of those still holding the existing stall. When
permission was accorded for this to be set up it was
stipulated that the cow should be banished, and so
about the last survival of the semi-rural ways of old
London disappeared.

## VIII

IN the London of other days a distinct line of
cleavage existed between the West End and the
City, where numbers of rich merchants had their
permanent abode; some of these latter indeed lived in
their counting-houses all their lives, and seldom left
the business premises in which they had been born.
Men of rank and fashion, though then as now by no
means unwilling to take unto themselves brides with
rich dowries derived from trade, seem rather to have
prided themselves upon having nothing in common
with the merchants and great traders of the City of
London, who in their own way were equally independent. Nevertheless there would appear to have
been little antagonism between the two classes. The
fashionable world regarded the City as a place which
somehow or other produced the wealth necessary for
the amenities of its existence, whilst those who
worked and made money there were quite reconciled
to the existence of a caste practically living apart and
indulging in all the joys of leisured ease—not a few
of which nevertheless scandalised the more sober of
the "Cits." Most of the merchants, however, were
very conservative at heart, though for all that they
were in reality in a state of perpetual change. The

older men of every generation firmly believed themselves to be perfect in every respect, and determined that all things should remain as they were. The junior members of the rising generation, on the other hand, were as firmly convinced that their improvements upon the methods of their parents were greatly superior, and determined they should be adopted in practice when the seniors were removed to a better world.

The modes of government, the principles, and the habits of the citizens generally, were, in certain respects, strictly patriarchal. The Lord Mayor was, in their opinion, the greatest man in all the world ; and though his office lasted but one year, it was the great ambition of most young men one day to fill it, and the retrospect made those who had served it happy for the rest of their life, by reflecting on the great honours they had received, and the great actions they had committed during the twelve months that their commands were as absolute within their own precincts as those of the Pope or the Grand Signor within their respective dominions. The aldermen were patriarchs, each in his own ward, as absolute as the Lord Mayor was over the whole city, and exacted equal respect in their own limited jurisdiction. The Common Council were the respectful advisers of the alderman in his own wardmote, and, when all were assembled in the Witenagemote at Guildhall, they constituted the parliament of the Lord Mayor.

Whilst the Lord Mayor of London was as a rule

an educated man, as things went in his day, the provincial mayors were sometimes almost illiterate.

The following was a letter sent about 1796 by a newly chosen provincial mayor to a correspondent in town :

" Dear Sur,—On Monday next I am to bee made a mare, hand should obliged to you if so be as you will send me down by the coach some provisions fetting the occashon, as I am to ax my brother the old mare, and the rest of the bentch.

" I am, Sur, etc.,

" ____."

This letter having fallen into the hands of a wag, the latter penned the following reply :

" Sir,—In obedience to your order, have sent you, per coach, two bushels of the best oats, and, as you are to treat the ' old mare,' have added some bran to make a mash.

" Yours, etc.,

" ____."

The merchants were the first class of unofficial citizens ; they were the peers of the City, and so great was their importance that the lesser orders of citizens could scarcely venture to look up to them. The next order was the wholesale traders, who did not venture to export on their own account. The retail shopkeepers followed next in order, and the manufacturing or working tradesmen were the last.

# The Merry Past

The brokers were considered the servants of the merchants, and all beneath them were thought scarcely deserving any name, though, to distinguish them from those still meaner beings who were not permitted to exist within its sacred walls, they were dignified with the title of Freeman of the City.

The City was divided into mercantile residences, private residences, warehouses, and shops, and such was their uniformity that the description of one quarter and the manners and practices of its inhabitants will give a correct idea of the whole. To begin with the lowest: the shopkeepers saw their shops opened and put in order, cleaned themselves for the day, breakfasted, and took their stations behind their counters for that day, and, when that was ended, closed again at night. Their women formed neighbourly parties at home; the men met in the back parlours of a public-house, to spend the evenings, as they called it, or in a neighbourly club; the wholesale men, who held themselves above that, congregated with the upper class of merchants' clerks in some coffee-house; all their different sets were sure to be at their parish church regularly on Sunday mornings clothed in their best; thence they formed neighbourly parties to walk in Moorfields, which had the imposing name of the City Mall; then returned home to dinner; again to church in the afternoon, and then, if they were quite at ease, a pleasant walk in the country, to Mile End, Hackney, Islington, White Conduit House, or Bagnigge Wells, whence, having had their fill of tea or coffee, as the night came on they returned home to sleep off the fatigue of the day. They went to business the next morning, and continued the same kind of life every day but Sunday throughout the year.

The middle class of citizens thought a good deal of themselves, and merchants and bankers carried their superiority with the very highest hand. They had country residences for their summer abodes, but in the winter they lived in the City; they associated, however, with their own class only, for they had not then found their way to the West End.

The magnates of the City had little idea of art, which was more understood and appreciated by the aristocracy, not a few of whom had travelled abroad.

When the hero of the Nile and of Trafalgar was the universal idol of the country, many public bodies resolved to decorate their halls with his life-size and full-length portrait, and as there was not at that time much employment for artists, orders for those portraits became serious objects for competition. A certain Worshipful City Company determined to purchase a portrait of Nelson, and on the suggestion of one of its members, the Court of Assistants gave a select dinner, to which an artist, with whom they were advised to treat for the picture, was invited, in order that he might state his price, and describe the proposed painting. The dinner was excellent, though there were certainly some very odd fish among the guests. After the feast was ended, and a good quantity of wine consumed, the business of the evening commenced; one member proposed one artist, another another. None of the proposers in all probability knew anything about the particular artist he mentioned, except his name. At last a member of the court, who had drunk enough wine to render him a bold speaker, rose and gave full vent to his oratory, which he concluded by saying that they might vote for whom they pleased, but for his part he was determined to vote for the artist they had asked to dine that night, because he knew that he had a large family, and was a very poor man!

The most striking characteristic of the citizens of London in the middle of the eighteenth century was pride; sometimes it was the pride of ignorance, sometimes the pride of wealth; and sometimes, as it related to the affairs of the City, it was the pride of rank. But though there were various kinds, pride was the universal basis upon which everything was founded. To be a citizen of London was, in the opinion of many a man, to be a member of the most important class of subjects in the British Empire; whilst to be the first magistrate was, in their opinion, to be the greatest man in all the British dominions, save and except the King alone.

"Once a lord always a lord" was their favourite maxim, and the lord of a single year, after he had passed out of his office, continued to be, in his own idea, as well as that of his family, only second to the ruling lord, the Lord Mayor; and as he, also in his turn, had to descend from his lordly rank at the end of the year, there was always a host of retired lords who claimed, each for himself in his private circle, the same attentions as he had exacted from the world at large when he had been the real great Lord Mayor.

In private life the middle classes never aspired to rank or to associate with the aristocracy, except when they were asked, for some political purpose, to a grand banquet at the London Tavern, or some place of the same description. On these occasions they were permitted to pay for their own dinner, and drink the toasts that were proposed by the chair, or the chip of aristocracy that sat in it, with three, or three times three, according as the circumstances of the case required.

At that time wealth and social position did not necessarily go hand-in-hand as now. Those were the days when, whilst birth had its sphere and bullion its own circle, commerce drew its votaries from its own set, leaving the higher things in life to those recognised as betters. An unbridged gulf stood between the moneyed plebeian and the aristocrat, who by a sort of prescriptive right danced at Almack's, played his rubber at White's, commanded his troop in the Life Guards, and was returned for a close borough, afterwards not infrequently receiving some fat sinecure. The limits of a City man's ambition were clearly defined; he might become a director of the East India Company or the Bank of England, a member of the Court of Aldermen, Lord Mayor, the warden of a company, or something similar, but his vulgar figure was not allowed to obtrude itself into society, or his plebeian hands to shuffle the cards in an exclusive club. His sons could not be attached to embassies or obtain commissions in crack regiments, nor oust the landed gentry from the soil, which many claimed to have held from the Conqueror's day.

Whilst the general spirit of the eighteenth century was essentially bluff and light-hearted, there was a certain ferocity about life which made people think little of much which would seem dreadful to-day.

This is perhaps best expressed by the following extract from an eighteenth-century book of travels, where the author, relating the particulars of his being cast away, thus concludes :

" After having walked eleven hours without tracing the print of a human foot, to my great comfort and delight I saw a man hanging upon a gibbet ; my pleasure at this cheering prospect was inexpressible, for it convinced me I was in a *civilised country*."

The gibbets, of course, were put up in order to act as warnings to the highwaymen who were the terror of travellers.

The traditional gallantry of these knights of the road is not entirely legendary ; some of them displayed great politeness upon occasion.

In 1796 a young married lady whose coach was stopped on Wimbledon Common was told to hand over her valuables to the robber, who, after having received her purse, politely demanded an elegant ring which he perceived upon her finger.

The lady, however, absolutely refused to give up the trinket in question, declaring that " she would sooner part with her life." The hero of the road rejoined, " Since you value the ring so much, madam, allow me the honour of saluting the fair hand which wears it, and I shall deem it a full equivalent." The hand was instantly stretched through the chariot window, and the kiss being received, the highwayman thanked her for her condescension, and instantly galloped off.

Nevertheless, the vast majority of highwaymen were merely desperate thieves, and anything but the free-handed generous spirits depicted in works of fiction.

At Preston Assizes, on the Northern Circuit, a counsel having been instructed to defend a notorious highwayman, received a fee of five guineas in advance. When the trial came on the judge discovered some flaw in the indictment, which was fatal to the whole proceedings, and the prisoner was in consequence discharged without any of the particulars of the case having been entered into.

The counsel sat until late after the bar dinner in the evening, and the clock struck twelve as he entered his lodgings, which were in a lonely house a short distance from the town. Everyone was in bed, and by this time anchored in the snoring depths of a Lancashire hard sleep. The barrister sat musing over the fire for an hour, visions of future woolsacks figuring to themselves shapes in the burning coals, when a loud knock at the door disturbed his meditations. His clerk, of course, was absent; and supposing some client in a hurry, or some " rascal " of an attorney, had pressing business to transact, he opened it himself, and found himself confronted by a tall, gaunt man, wrapped in a loose horseman's coat, with a handkerchief, from which protruded the tips of a couple of scarlet ears. This very unwelcome visitor was dowered with ferocious whiskers, an obliquity of vision, and a deep scar on his cheek. In a gruff voice he addressed the man of law. "Measter, I a' cum for that five pound."

"What do you mean, my good fellow ? " said the counsel, feeling rather nervous.

"I say I want that five pound that my 'torney, Mr. Stoat, gave you this morning."

"Who are you, sir ? " the counsel enquired, by no means reassured by his mention of Mr. Stoat's name.

" 'Galloping Dick,' that was imprisoned for highway robbery, and they've just let me out, and so I thought I'd come and have back my money, before I was off to London."

"But, my good fellow," replied the counsel, beginning to feel extremely uncomfortable, "you can't claim the money ; your case has been heard, and you are acquitted. What more could you possibly want ? "

"Ah," retorted the highwayman, in a voice something between a growl and a grin, "no thanks to you, measter. It was the old codger above in the wig that got me off. Mr. Stoat handed you over the five pounds to make a speech for me, and you had no speech to make, and you didn't make a speech, so hand me the money, measter. I can't stand here all night."

Just then the wind blowing aside the skirts of the man's coat, the moonlight fell upon the brass mounting of a horse-pistol, no pleasant sight for the counsel. Nevertheless he pulled himself together, and, screwing up a bold face, persisted :

" It is not professional, my good friend, to return money ; for you see if we were once to do so——"

" Oh, I don't understand your trade, measter counsellor ; but I know you have had my money, and done nothing for it ; so hand it back. Come, I can't stop."

With this the highwayman gently insinuated his left hand and foot within the door, and tapped his fingers persuasively on a large blackthorn club in his right hand. The counsel, having looked backwards upon the darkness and loneliness of his room, and forwards towards the unfrequented lane, put his hand in his waistcoat pocket, and taking out the five-pound note, handed it over to the ruffian, who wished him good night, with a knowing leer, and vanished into the darkness, whilst the lawyer, much relieved, crept up to bed.

Those were the days when men were hanged for quite trifling offences, whilst comparatively small value was attached to human life.

A story told of Jack Ketch, the celebrated hangman, illustrates the casual methods which prevailed.

Jack, when on his death-bed, is reported to have sent for the curate of his parish, to whom he said :

# The Merry Past

" Ah, Mr. Parson, I've helped many a poor dog out of this world, and I'm now going out of it myself; and, to tell you the truth, my conscience won't let me alone." " Well, well," replied the curate, " take comfort, you are not to blame; the men who suffered had been condemned by the laws of their country, and you were no more than the instrument in the hand of public justice." " Aye, but I am afeard I once hanged a man a little wrongfully.

" One execution morning, when the men that were going to Tyburn came down into the press-yard, one of them whispers to me, as I passed close by him, 'Master Ketch, could you do a poor wretch a kind service? Twenty good guineas.' ' Are they all weight?' says I to him. ' Aye, that they be,' says he to me, ' not a light guinea among 'em.' My heart was sorry for him, so I bid him to follow my directions, and I would see what could be done for him. ' When you get to the cart,' says I, ' and all the people about it, pop down when I make the sign, and slip under it, and get away among the crowd.' But after he had done so, as ill luck would have it, I happen'd to spy among the mob a journeyman tailor, with a thin white face and a red nightcap on; so I made a dash at him, seized him by the collar, and hoisted him into the cart. 'Tis as true as you sit there. The poor devil lifted up his hands and eyes, and protested his innocence and all that, but I bawled louder than he did, and told the mob he went on at that rate in gaol, and never would confess nothing.

" Now, Mr. Parson, I'm really afeard I hanged this man a little wrongfully."

# The Merry Past

Bull-baiting was a favourite amusement of the people, and it was only when the nineteenth century had begun that any attempt was made to stop it by legislation.

On the introduction of the first Bill to stop this cruel method of torturing an unoffending animal, over one hundred years ago, it was rejected. William Windham himself, a humane man, warmly defended the sport, if it could be called sport, in question, and declared that the proposed prohibition would lead to further legislation against other old English sports and pastimes, which must inevitably result in changing and weakening the character of the people at large. Whilst Windham, a man of great character and the darling of Norfolk, lived, no Bill of the sort passed ; but after his death an Act soon put an end to this form of rank brutality. With regard to the fear which had been expressed that other sports would be attacked, one of the ablest advocates of the Anti-Bull-Baiting Bill distinctly avowed that his enmity was directed to bull-baiting, and to bull-baiting alone. He declared that if he were asked if he deemed it desirable that the other ordinary sports of the day should be put an end to, he should maintain the contrary. He wished not to see the badger-bait or the otter-hunt abolished, the foxhounds left to rot in their kennel, the gun put by in its case, or the rod and line laid up ; he knew better the value of those sports, and declared his conviction that there was no cruelty in them.

Nevertheless, the prediction of William Windham

has in some measure been fulfilled, for cock-fighting has gone, whilst coursing, pigeon-shooting, and stag-hunting are the subject of much invective from humanitarians, who have several times sought their prohibition by Act of Parliament. The English people are now, without any vestige of a doubt, far softer in every way than in the old brutal days when rough sports practically formed the sole amusement of the countryside.

They were anything but humanitarian then.

Pigs were whipped to death, a torture which was supposed to render them more palatable.

Such a dish was in frequent use, and highly praised as a delicacy as late as the reign of George III.

A lady living in 1793 was heard to say that her former husband made a trifling bet (which he afterwards won), that his dog would run at and pin a bull after he had cut off the lower joint of every leg. During the last bull-baiting ever held at Bury St. Edmunds, in 1811, a poor animal not affording much sport, the brutal crowd cut off his hoofs and tortured him to death, whilst he staggered on the bleeding stumps; this rightly aroused great indignation, and sealed the fate of such orgies of cruelty.

Animals and birds would seem to have been believed by the populace generally to be devoid of any feeling.

A particularly cruel sport existed in Scotland, called " Goose-riding." The poor geese were hung up by the legs whilst a number of men rode at them to catch the birds by the neck.

The vast change in popular amusements which has

come over London in the last hundred years is difficult to realise to-day.

At Easter time a pleasure fair was held in Tothill Fields, Westminster, now the more decorous Vincent Square.

From a description of this fair as it existed in 1813, we learn that gambling and dog-fighting were considered as part of the attractions. To these were added a race between three damsels for a shift; jumping in a sack for a cheese, and grinning through horse-collars for a hat, which considerably increased the humour of the evening. The God of Mirth prevailed with undisputed sway, and although a few wrangles did occur, they terminated in the most amicable manner. The swings and roundabouts were almost as numerous here as at Greenwich, and their proprietors, no doubt, reaped an ample harvest, for their vehicles were literally in perpetual motion.

The " Jew's Harp," a petty tavern in the district which is now St. John's Wood and Regent's Park, was a Sunday resort of citizens who were there wont to indulge in the pleasures of tea and hot rolls. As late as the early twenties of the last century this was a wild and dreary tract of land, in which a daisy was a flower of price, and though so close to London, it was the frequent scene of violence and crime. The only houses were a few miserable hovels, the only real house being the tavern mentioned above.

Not very far away were luxurious mansions—about the nearest Langham House, on the site of which now stands the Langham Hotel. One of the chief features here was a number of splendid mahogany doors, whilst there was a large garden with fine trees, which made the end of Langham Place charmingly cool and shady. When Regent Street was formed its line was specially diverted in order to save Langham House, which now, however, has long disappeared.

Primrose Hill, near Chalk Farm, formed another favourite place of resort, and on this were displayed scenes of frolic like those at Greenwich.

Here Londoners had to pay a toll, known as the Halfpenny-hatch.

The Halfpenny-hatch was at Marylebone, and consisted in a halfpenny paid by every foot-passenger for the privilege of passage through some private grounds, which shortened the walk to Primrose Hill, where crowds of both sexes used to repair on a Sunday evening to see Edinburgh, as it was called, which was by stooping down with your back to London, and looking between your legs at that overgrown city. Good sound ale, brewed from good wholesome malt and hops, was sold at fourpence the double mug at the Halfpenny-hatch, and rich cheesecakes four a penny.

On Easter Monday Greenwich was inundated by some thousands of visitors, who, hungry and thirsty after their journey, came prepared to gratify the cravings of their appetites, in compliment to which almost every house was converted into a magazine of provisions. At the fair itself visitors could hardly hear their own voices owing to the din of the gong, the French horn, and the salt-box, all of which instruments charmed or outraged visitors' ears, in addition to which the occasional choruses of Mr. Polito's wild beasts effectually banished all idea of monotony.

Favourites such as Mr. Richardson, Mr. Gyngell, Mr. Moritz, and other Thespians were conspicuous for the gaudy brilliancy of their theatres, which held forth the most flattering promises of the astonishing and astounding excellencies of their respective performances. A number of the minor order of exhibitors added to the fun of the fair. In one booth was shown the miraculous and " flambuginous " sea-monster, known by the name of the Non-Descript. Next to it stood the Musical Rat, which played most divinely on the mouth-organ. Mr. Hobson and his comical family offered other attractions, for, in addition to the ordinary performance of jumping down their own throats, they professed themselves ready to eat a living cat and her kittens for the accommodation of the nobility and gentry. The pig-faced lady, the human skeleton, and many other freaks, including Miss Biffin (who wrote a beautiful hand with her mouth), were familiar features of this fair.

A crowd of bashful maidens were usually posted on the brow of Greenwich Hill, who, in the course of the speedy descent, which was one of the customary amusements, not infrequently exposed, with good-natured generosity, beauties which are easier to be imagined than described. Many who were mere spectators were unwillingly dragged into the vortex, and shared in the universal sport ; at times receiving a species of reward at which modesty would at other seasons be shocked, but which, on this occasion, was regarded merely as the effervescence of good humour. While the lambs and lambkins were thus innocently amusing themselves on the Hill, many groups were seen in the lawn below, occupied in the various diversions of "Threading my Needle, Nan," "Hunt the Slipper," "Kiss in the Ring," "Lug at the Crust," and other old games, the frolic of which was considerably heightened by falls and other humorous accidents.

At such times the gloom of the English character was dissipated, and gaiety of the most free and unrestrained kind was the order of the day.

The tea-gardens in the neighbourhood of the metropolis were crowded with visitors. Among those most numerously attended were Bagnigge Wells, White Conduit House, Canonbury House, Chalk Farm, and Cumberland Gardens, in which the consumption of those delicacies—tea and hot rolls, ale, gin and ginger-bread, and other trifles, was truly surprising. Indeed, so great was the call for grub, as it was poetically termed at White Conduit House, that it sometimes became necessary to send off a man express to London to fetch a new cargo of second-hand hot cross buns.

In 1805 it was calculated that the number of Londoners who spent their Sunday in the inns, tea-houses, tea-gardens, and villages adjacent to town was not less than two hundred thousand.

These, it was said, each spent about half a crown,

which made a total of twenty-five thousand pounds, which, multiplied by the number of Sundays in a year, gave, as the annual consumption of that day of rest, the immense sum of one million three hundred thousand pounds.

Of these two hundred thousand persons, a facetious chronicler calculated that there would be :

| | |
|---|---:|
| Sober .............. | 50,000 |
| In high glee ........ | 90,000 |
| Drunkish ............ | 30,000 |
| Staggering tipsy ...... | 10,000 |
| Muzzy .............. | 15,000 |
| Dead drunk ........ | 5,000 |
| | 200,000 |

The estimate in question was, of course, more or less a joke, but there is no doubt that temperance was at a considerable discount during the holidays of the past.

In those days there was a good deal of rough humour and fun to be observed in the streets of London, which are now so decorous and staid.

On one occasion two men, vendors and buyers of " old clo," both with long beards, passing near Tottenham Court Road, were so much attracted by a couple of jackets which hung on a stable door as not to be able to resist adding them to their stock. Unfortunately, however, for the patriarchs, the owners, two postboys, who were drinking on the other side of the road, observed the transaction. In a moment they were upon the pilferers, whom they seized and locked up in the stable, with the idea of extracting some fun from the incident, rather than invoking the forces of the law. Tying the two old thieves together, they matted their two beards and smeared them with warm shoemakers' wax. As soon as the wax was cooled, and the people around had enjoyed sufficiently the sight of the venerable patriarchs in this fraternal embrace, the postilions applied to each nose at intervals a few pinches of snuff, which occasioned such a concussion of noses, and such sputtering, that the crowd of loungers which had collected vowed the sight to be the most amusing they had ever seen.

Women running in smocks for prizes, or playing matches against each others at various games, was not an uncommon thing. As late as September, 1835, considerable excitement prevailed at Parson's Green, Walham, in consequence of a cricket match for £10 and a hot supper between eleven married women and eleven girls. The married women wore light blue dresses, their waists and heads being decorated with ribbons of the same colour ; the single women were attired in close white dresses, with pink sashes and cap bows. The game commenced about eleven o'clock, the married taking the first innings, and obtaining 47 runs. The single then commenced play, and were not so successful, the whole of them being bowled out after 29 runs. The two next innings were played, and the game was won by the single women, but only by 7 runs. After the match, country dances, accompanied by a band of music, took place on the green, and in the evening a supper was provided at the " White Horse " by the host.

Songs and singing were very popular. From 1759 to 1769 the following were those most in vogue : " Haste away, haste away, to the Marquis of Granby, haste away " ; " Hearts of Oak " ; " Balance a Straw " ; " The Sweeper " ; " Buffler at morning, and Buffler at night " (was the vulgar daily chaunt all over England about 1760) ; " Nancy Dawson " ; " Three Ladies come from France " ; " Charming Kitty Fell " ; " The Brave Captain Death " ; " Paddy Whack " ; " Lango Lee," revived, again then nearly forty years after date ; " Say, Little, Foolish, Fluttering Thing " ; " Stony Batter " ; " Says Yellow Molly, I'm a Maid " ; " As I was walking one morning in May " ; " The Gipsy Laddy O " (then old) ; " Saw you my father, saw you my mother " ; " Tidy Widow and a tidy one " ; " Wilkes' Song."

From 1769 to 1779 : " The Pilgrim blithe and jolly " ; " Little John Alcock " (old Irish tune of the " Grey Mare ") ; " When War's Alarms " ; " British Fair " ; " British Grenadiers " ; " The Dusky Night rides down the Sky," and various hunting-songs ; " Oh, Father, Father, give me my portion."

From 1779 to 1789 : " Peggy Band " ; " Pretty Peggy of Darby, O " ; " Sweet Mog the Brunette " ; " Guardian Angels " ; " There was a Frog lived in a Well " ; " The Jolly Young Waterman " ; " Robin Grey " ; " Gang down the Burne, Davy " ; " Young Colin stole my Heart away " ; " Ye Scamps, ye Pads, ye Divers " ; " Fal de ral tit " ; Le Moine's " Saucy Rolling Blade " ; " My Nancy quits the rural train " ; " Why should the foolish Marriage Vow."

From 1789 to 1799 : " The Little Ploughboy " ; " Cheer up, my lads " ; " The Jew Boy " ; " O, my Billy, my Billy " ; " The Little Dandy " (the author of this song, whoever he may have been, is entitled to the honour of having furnished the public with a substitute for the term *Macaroni*) ; " Ballast Heaving."

From 1799 to 1809 : " Teddy the Grinder " ; " High randy dandy O " ; " A Valiant Soldier I dare not name " ; " O Dear, what can the matter be ? " " Nobody's coming to marry me " ; " The Curly-headed Boy " ; " Jenny's Baubee."

From 1809 to 1822 : " I'll cross the Salt Seas " ; " Pretty blue-eyed Stranger."

After this date popular songs began to approximate in character to the old-fashioned music-hall ditty which still survives in a somewhat bowdlerised form. The music-hall itself did not take its place as a public amusement till a considerably later date, though many informal bacchanalian gatherings were held where songs were sung and enormous quantities of drink were consumed.

The drinking habits of the English in the past were of such a kind as to make the records almost beyond belief. At Harwich, for instance, in 1796, three topers, determined to have a thorough soaking, set to one day and drank fifty-seven quarts of upright, that is to say a quart of beer with a quartern of gin in it, within the space of six hours and a half; on their taking leave of each other for home, one of them declared he was still thirsty, and stopped, smoked a pipe, and drank a pint more to himself.

As late as 1812 an auctioneer having a public-house to dispose of in the metropolis, frankly stated in his advertisement that it was situated near the "Seven Dials," "a noted gin-drinking neighbourhood."

Many of the upper classes drank just as much as the lower, and a number of anecdotes attest their prowess in this direction: a well-known one is that of the Duke who, going to a fancy ball, asked Foote what character he should adopt. "Go sober," was the reply.

Fox-hunters, in particular, prided themselves upon their capacity for swallowing large quantities of port. One of these, not unnaturally indisposed, went to consult a doctor. "There is not much the matter with you," said he; "and if you will only drink three glasses of wine a day, instead of a bottle, which you fox-hunters often do, and take a little of this medicine, you will live to be a hundred." "Your medicine, doctor, I will take," said the toper, "but the other part of the prescription is quite out of the question."

The clergy of that day do not appear to have viewed intemperance as a vice, for they did little to impress their parishioners with principles of sobriety.

A certain country clergyman, noted for his convivial habits, being informed that drunkenness was

# The Merry Past

rife in the parish, did indeed once declare that such a state of affairs must be checked. Accordingly he preached a long and eloquent sermon on the horrors of intemperance, during which he defined exactly what the vice in question was. There were men, said he, who, quarrelsome in their cups, should never drink at all. There were others to whom one bottle was refreshment, but to whom two caused sickness; they were, therefore, intemperate when they drank more than one. Some men enlivened a circle of friends, and were kind to their wives, even after they had drunk four bottles; and it was not right in them to diminish their kindness by drinking less. There were others more highly gifted and favoured, who felt their hearts warm with gratitude to their Maker while the generous juice circulated in their blood, who were friendly with their families, generous to all, and even nobly forgetful of injuries, when they had drunk five bottles; with them, therefore, intemperance only began with the sixth bottle. " But these," he said, " were the peculiar favourites of Heaven, to whom the joys of this world were given as a pledge of a joyful hereafter."

During election times liquor fairly flowed; everyone drank his candidate's or someone else's health, it did not matter much whose.

During the Southwark election in the early part of the nineteenth century, Mr. Illidge, a glass and earthenware dealer, who was a committee-man of one of the candidates (Mr. Calvert, the well-known brewer), called upon that gentleman, and apologising for the liberty he was about to take, said that he should be most happy to drink Mr. Calvert's health in a glass of his own brewing. " I should be most happy to drink yours *too*," replied that gentleman ; " and, therefore," continued the newly returned M.P., " we will walk into the counting-house, and there you shall have a glass of the finest ale in the kingdom ! " " I beg pardon," replied the modest and domestic committee-man, " but my good lady at home has a desire equally with myself to drink health and long life to you, and to taste your October ; so, with your permission," continued Mr. Illidge, " I will send a *mug*, in order to gratify Mrs. I. But, sir, in the event of your not being at the brewery when I send, do me the favour to give me a *written* order that there may be no mistake." " By all means," said Mr. Calvert, " and you shall have a *mug* of the finest ale in the cellar ! " Whereupon the member for Southwark wrote an order, and gave it to the "free and independent elector," to the following effect :

" Fill Mr. Illidge's *mug* with the best ale in the brewery.  (Signed)  " C. CALVERT."

The next day two men entered the premises with a large hamper slung upon a pole, and carried between them upon their shoulders, in which was a *mug* of the extraordinary and appalling size of at least thirteen gallons and a half. The men delivering the above order to the " proper authority," the *mug* was immediately " filled foaming to the brim " with " ale of the right-knock-me-down sort," and the men departed as they came, with the exception of the addition of one hundredweight of ale to their load ! On its arrival at Mr. Illidge's there were all the brother committee-men of that gentleman assembled to do honour to the toast of " Health to Calvert, and long life to him, and may nothing ever *ale* him ! "

Mr. Illidge, being an extensive earthenware dealer, the *mug* in question, " the great, the important *mug*, big with the ale of Southwark's new M.P.," was used by that gentleman for many years as a *show-mug*, being placed over the warehouse door as a " sign, to the passers-by, of the trade therein carried on."

Mr. Calvert afterwards laughed heartily at the joke practised upon him by Mr. Illidge. " I shall be always most happy," said the member for Southwark, " to see the light of the countenance of my worthy and indefatigable committee-man, Illidge ; but, notwithstanding, curse me if ever I desire to see his d—d *ugly mug* again ! "

All classes then were a good deal rougher in their methods of amusement than is now the case—witness the widespread popularity of prize-fighting.

In its palmy days the Fives Court, both as regarded its amateur attendance and the ability of the professors in pugilism, was a regular London institution. At the time that the glories of the "ring" had reached their zenith the Marquis of Worcester was often to be seen strolling arm-in-arm with Crib, whilst many other scions of nobility were thickly sprinkled amongst a very heterogeneous crowd—

carriages out of number were to be seen setting down their aristocratic occupants at the top of the lane on a grand sparring day, and all went "merry as a marriage bell." Pugilism was on the same level as racing, fox-hunting, and other first-rate sports; and the prize-fighters themselves looked happy, sleek, and respectable as they strode about amongst an envying "mobility."

The chief supporters of the "ring" were to be found amongst the sporting aristocracy and the proletariat; the middle classes, whose influence, however, was then inconsiderable, seemingly viewed this form of sport with scant favour. This section of the population, however, had its own amusements, generally of a more decorous kind. Many of the better sort of tradesmen kept their gigs, in which, on Sundays, they drove their wives to one or more of the many pleasure resorts or tea-gardens which then abounded on the outskirts of the metropolis.

The Londoners of other days were very fond of out-of-door amusements, and delighted in flocking to Ranelagh and Vauxhall—evening resorts of a very free kind.

Vauxhall first came into fashion about June, 1732, at which time a *Ridotto al fresco* was the entertainment. On this occasion about four hundred people assembled, in the proportion of ten males to one female ; and no very rigid standard of morality was enforced. Most of the subscribers appeared in dominos and masks, and remained till four o'clock in the morning. Such, however, was the licentious spirit of a period when even gentlemen's servants wore swords, that a hundred soldiers were necessarily stationed at the entrance to preserve order.

Vauxhall, in spite of the efforts of its proprietors, was for many years the occasional scene of wild disorder. Ladies were forced from their parties by drunken bucks into the dark walks, and treated with savage rudeness, a state of affairs which prevented respectable females from remaining in the gardens after midnight.

Nevertheless, Tyers, the proprietor of Vauxhall, pledged himself to the public that the dark walks should be lighted ; no *bad women*, known to be such, should be admitted ; and watchmen were hired to keep the peace.

Tyers had a country house near Leatherhead, and it was his delight to pass his Sunday and part of Monday there, during the Vauxhall season, with artists and wits, many of whom were almost entirely supported by his bounty.

On Saturday nights the gardens were closed at twelve, when such visitors as he had invited got into Tyers' carriage, or a hired coach, and set off for his pleasant retreat. There they ruralised until Monday, when, taking an early dinner, they returned to London in time for the opening of Spring Gardens. These parties were of a very pleasant kind.

Roubilliac found a patron in Mr. Tyers, and Hogarth's talent was also called in to aid the decoration of delightful Vauxhall, a golden ticket of admission in perpetuity being presented to him. Hayman's assistance was also enlisted ; he was then (such was the deplorable state of painting in England) considered the best painter of history. A number of minor artists were also liberally rewarded for their assistance in the decoration of this pleasure resort.

Tyers in his own way was a remarkable man, as seems to have been generally recognised, for he was the friend and patron of many cultivated men of his time.

Like Charles the Second, he combined the fine gentleman with the bon vivant, possessed a warm and generous heart, and was consequently most liberal to those whose talents contributed to his plans. He was esteemed by the composers who wrote for his orchestra, and did abundant kind offices for his vocal and instrumental performers. The ladies, whose sweet notes, as a contemporary chronicler poetically put it, "silenced the nightingales of his illuminated groves," experienced in him an intrepid protector from the freedom of the gay bloods and bucks of those hot-blooded times, until everyone, struck with his gallant manners, emulated the proprietor's courteous ways, and public favourites were treated with becoming attention and respect.

It was once the custom for parties of ladies and gentlemen to go by water to Vauxhall, the proprietor stationing two of the beadles of the Watermen's Company to attend at Vauxhall Stairs from five to eleven o'clock, to prevent imposition and abuse. In 1738, silver tickets were sold at twenty-four shillings each, to admit two for the season. A single admittance was one shilling.

# The Merry Past

Later in the century Carlisle House, in Soho Square, became the favourite rendezvous of the fashionable world. Here Mrs. Cornelis presided as ruling Goddess of Fashion. Her luxurious orgies were the heaven of the dissipated, where the libertine could indulge in ephemeral gratifications to his heart's content, and the thoughtless bacchanalian drown his few intellects in the most costly productions of French vineyards. Here, without apprehension of check or hindrance, the voluptuary might revel away the night amidst the most congenial surroundings.

Mrs. Cornelis was by birth a German, who, at a very early age, had become a public singer. She was the delight of Dresden, and in high estimation at the court. From that city she had gone to Italy, where she had soon acquired, under the best masters, the grace and charm for which that country was then renowned. Eventually she came to England, in the suite of a British nobleman, who had promised her his protection.

Endowed by nature with an enterprising spirit, and possessing a good understanding, great knowledge of mankind, and specious manners, Mrs. Cornelis soon contrived to raise herself into public notice, and obtained the patronage of the fashionable world, who flocked to all the amusements which her taste and fancy could devise.

The foundation of her fortune laid, she determined to complete it, and opened a magnificent temple in Soho Square, calling it after the name of her first benefactor, Carlisle House. This soon became the favourite resort for the nobility and the fashionable world of the metropolis, for she had so diversified and so well contrived her amusements that no public place could pretend to rival their attractions. Her prosperity now seemed to distance the most sanguine expectations ; but she was not contented, like the fool in the fable, with her golden egg every day, and killed her goose to seize at once upon immensity.

In addition to her many other attractions, she introduced Harmonic Meetings, and at once became a competitor against the managers of the Opera, who took alarm, and strove by every means in their power to counteract the successes of so formidable a rival.

A part of her friends presently withdrew themselves ; and those attached to the interests of the opera managers, on the ruins of the old *Savoir Vivre* club in Pall Mall, raised the new coterie ; subscriptions came in from elevated quarters to support this new temple of fashion and pleasure ; and in less than three weeks their fund amounted to four thousand pounds. Chin Hughes was made the croupier, and a well-known man about town placed at the head of the treasury. This was the first shock, and Mrs. Cornelis felt it ; but, like a skilful general forced for a moment to retreat, she soon rallied her forces, and attacking the enemy in the most vulnerable part, gained a complete victory. Her exultation was of short duration ; for the opera manager, enraged at the defeat, lodged an information against her for unlawful proceedings before the Bow Street magistrates ; in consequence of which, notice was privately sent from Sir John Fielding to the lady, acquainting her that an application of a serious nature had been made respecting the impropriety and unlawfulness of her amusements, and advising her to regulate her conduct in future, or she would hear from Bow Street in another way. From this condescension on the side of the magistrate, the lady concluded she might with safety play a card which she deemed to be a trump. A purse was delivered to a trusty friend, with a letter addressed to Sir John Fielding, Knight, requesting his acceptance of the sum within, and that his worship would be pleased not to be too severe in looking into the conduct of a defenceless woman, who only endeavoured to gratify the wealthy, the high, and the fashionable, and from whose amusements the lower orders of society were wholly excluded. Fielding, however, was incorruptible ; and, instead of accepting the purse, sent his myrmidons at a most unfortunate moment. On the evening in question a fête had just begun, the lamps for that night had been doubled, and in the middle of the promenade was raised a capacious bower, composed of vine leaves and artificial roses, in the centre of which stood an altar with a flame thereon. At a signal from the band, a large group of maskers, composed of gentlemen performers from the theatres, and others, entered like Comus and his crew. Mr. Vernon sang an Anacreontic composed for the occasion, the rest the chorus ; thus ended the first scene.

The visitors were fashionable and numerous, the

masks whimsical, and everything in the highest taste. At the top of the walk was a hermitage, from the side of which issued a real cascade ; from this recess the singer Guadani came forth, attired as the hermit of the cave, and sang a charming song. Just, however, as he was in the middle of his quavers, the police officers entered, and bore him off in a manner so theatrical that the company conceived the attack part of the evening's entertainment. Guadani, it should be added, eventually got bail and was liberated, on a promise of never appearing again as a public character in these Soho amusements. Meanwhile the bacchanalian crew had been joined by Lord Lyttleton, Mr. Daisey Walker, and Mr. Fitzgerald, who commenced the third act by approaching the altar where the flame was burning ; each man held a torch in his right hand and a goblet in his left, and on a signal being given for the dance, they suddenly thrust in their torches, which were quickly lighted. The revels then began ; their cups overflowed with wine, and they singing, dancing, and drinking in the most riotous manner. Without the slightest method in their madness, and of a sudden, as if moved by one impulse, they rushed from the bower and flew to the square. It had struck five o'clock, and a long train of Calvert's drays were setting out upon their daily duty. The bacchanalian maskers fell upon the drivers, and attacked them with their lighted flambeaux, till a general engagement ensued, which made a great noise. The inhabitants of the square became alarmed, up went the windows, and, in spite of the earliness of the hour, all was mob, riot, and confusion. Finally, however, victory declared herself in favour of the knights of the bung, who played their parts so well with their horse-whips that Fitzgerald and Walker were completely flogged out of their shoes, for they were seen retreating down Greek Street barefooted, and as fast as their legs could carry them. Lord Lyttleton lost a jewelled repeater worth a hundred guineas, and many young bucks and green sprigs of nobility got a drubbing, which they probably remembered to the last day of their lives.

By this time the company had disappeared from Carlisle House, except a few young men of quality, who had found their way into the cellars, where they continued drinking till nine o'clock. Nothing could shame these inordinate topers. Great scandal was created by the riotous proceedings which have been described, and the glories of Carlisle House rapidly declined, which was further caused by the opening of the Pantheon. The creditors of the proprietress began to grow clamorous, and in 1785 she was at length obliged to relinquish the concern, and seek in concealment a refuge from legal prosecution. For many years she remained in obscurity under an assumed name.

She purchased a house in Knightsbridge for five hundred pounds, furnished it in an elegant manner for the accommodation of the younger branches of the royal family and the nobility, whom she served with milk, calling herself Theresa Smith.

# The Merry Past

Determined to do all she could to ensure success in a less ambitious line, she was very assiduous in pleasing her customers ; musical instruments formed a part of the furniture in her apartments, and to those who delighted in reading, books were supplied for their amusement, while the lovers of recreation might entertain themselves by promenading in a garden tastefully laid out.

The care which she took of the animals which were the means of her subsistence, attending early in the morning and late in the evening to see them fed, gained her great credit with the fashionable patrons who frequented her house. But the exertions of carrying on this business proving too much for her strength, and finding herself drawing near the verge of life, she entrusted her concerns to those who, either not taking sufficient care, or having their own interests in view, suffered her to be arrested for the sum of £60 14s. for the payment of silk, furniture, and the like to adorn her premises.

Her son, who was a very amiable man, and an excellent scholar, had allowed his mother an annuity till his death. Her daughter, who lived under another name, had long been patronised by some noble families, who knew her mother in better days. Lady Cowper had left her an annuity, and her musical talents easily procured her an introduction into the best circles; nevertheless, the unfortunate Mrs. Cornelis herself ended her life in the Fleet Prison.

## IX

THOUGH there is no doubt but that there has been a general advance in civilisation and manners within the last hundred years, it is equally certain—in England at least—that life has become more sedate and uninspiring than was formerly the case. A somewhat dull and uniform level of well-conducted respectability would appear to have become the national ideal of the great majority, whose main excitement outside business hours is the genteel athleticism which fills so many columns of the Press.

Imagination and enterprise of an individualistic kind is not looked upon with any great amount of interest, indeed anything which is a revolt against the monotonous conventionality which is being gradually imposed upon all classes through the medium of numberless laws and regulations is at a decided discount. The English have become a nicely behaved race, but the originality for which they were formerly renowned seems dormant.

France, on the other hand, though her detractors have at times ventured to call her decadent, still produces men of highly original character—all honour to the gallant son of Gaul M. Blériot, who by his suberb flight across the Channel has shown the world that the spirit of invention coupled with fearless élan still lives. One man such as this is worth all the faddists, pseudo-philanthropists, and mealy-mouthed politicians in the world : would that they could all be packed in some huge aeroplane, contrived to deposit its passengers in a congenial sphere where they could set to work reforming one another to their hearts' content !

Originality even of an eccentric kind is a symptom of vitality, whilst a general undeviating adherence to convention shows that the life blood of a nation courses none too quickly through its veins. England in former days abounded in original characters. Besides those whose names are well known, there were numberless individuals in the British Isles who struck out a line for themselves.

Many of the squires of the eighteenth century were unconventional in the extreme, brimming over with vitality, and ready for mad escapades which seem almost inconceivable to-day. The following is a characteristic example of this :

A number of sportsmen were sitting after dinner in a country inn, nearly fifty miles distant from the metropolis, where they had been staying some days for the purpose of hunting with a favourite pack in the neighbourhood. The conversation chanced to turn upon which of the party would arrive first in London, when a certain squire, on whom the wine had made less impression than on the rest, boldly offered to back himself for £50 against any present. Only after this bet was made and increased to a considerable sum did the maker of the bet remember that he had that very evening sent off his horses to town, it having been his intention to go himself by an early coach. The situation seemed desperate, no horse appearing to be available except a blood hack which he beheld a groom saddling for his opponent. A rough pony, however, was standing in the straw-yard, and this he immediately caught. As no reins were to be found, a twisted silk handkerchief took their place to avoid loss of time.

In full dress, with cocked hat and silk stockings, towards the middle of the night and in a drizzling rain, after sundry kickings and other signs of displeasure, the ill-equipped competitor took the road on his bare-backed steed, which scampered through mud and rain at a capital pace towards an inn where, being well known, the squire made sure of getting at least a post-horse. He had, however, not gone far before the clatter of a horse's hoofs was heard behind, and presently his opponent dashed by at full speed, jeeringly asking whether he had any commands for town. For a moment the squire felt depressed with the apparent impossibility of his task ; but confidence in his own courage and vigour soon inspired him to redoubled exertion, which was at length rewarded by finding himself at the much-wished-for tavern.

The ostler was fortunately still up, although the rest of the establishment were snug in bed. Vainly, however, was he told to saddle a horse ; the obstinate fellow seemed resolved no horse should leave the stable ; and the squire was obliged at length to awaken the host, who immediately authorised him to take his choice among the post-horses, and a saddle was placed on a game blood-looking old horse, whose fore-legs showed many a hard day's work. For a length of time the old horse went jarring and shaking along at a most fatiguing pace, his rider nursing him carefully so as to reach Barnet, where he knew he could obtain a horse from the stud of an intimate friend. The old horse did his best, and eventually reached the desired stables.

Here his rider lost no time in making known his urgent want, and having undertaken to indemnify the man in charge, who knew him well and his intimacy with his master, was allowed to select a runaway well-bred horse from the stud under his charge. The squire had no sooner put his horse into a gallop on the road than he found a new difficulty — the utter impossibility of stopping him. Away he went down the steep hill on the London side of Barnet a most terrific pace, which no effort could moderate or control. Perceiving a flock of sheep on the road before him, he vainly redoubled his efforts to pass them with his horse under some control. The brute dashed among and on them, and for a moment was almost on the ground ; nevertheless, he regained his legs without unseating his rider, and went on at a more moderate pace, amidst the oaths of the drovers, the bleating of the frightened sheep, and the barking of the angered sheep-dogs. The mishaps in question proved a most fortunate event, for on arriving at the turnpike the squire found it closed ; had his horse come up to it at its former mad speed, the consequences would in all probability have proved fatal to both. As it was he found some difficulty in pulling up to call out the toll-keeper, who had no sooner opened the gate but he placed his hand on the bridle of his horse and told him in a gruff voice that he must detain him, for a gentleman who had just ridden through had given him strict charge that should a person answering his description come in sight he was to be captured, having committed felony.

The scurvy trick, however, proved unsuccessful ; an explanation of the real circumstances of the case, bound in gold, soon appeased the toll-keeper, who admitted that the gentleman who had previously passed through the gate rode a beaten horse. Victory now for the first time appeared certain, and keeping on a good steady pace, the jubilant squire soon had the pleasure of viewing his opponent, who with difficulty sat on his panting and jaded steed. In the hope of passing him without attracting notice, the squire took to the turf which skirted the road ; but although he might have deceived the man, the acute instinct of the horse prevented him, for the moment it heard the faint sounds of his horse's hoofs stealing up on the soft turf, its spirited nature aroused it to fresh vigour and its rider to renewed consciousness of his danger. Perceiving further disguise useless, the squire rode up to him, and imitating the ironical tone of his previous challenge, asked in his turn, " Well, my buck, any orders for town ? " " You have not won yet," was the reply, and with desperate energy his opponent struggled for the lead, which the squire allowed him to take, feeling confident that his mount could not long live under it. Nor was he mistaken ; for having lost sight of him for a short time, when he again came upon him it was to find him in a changed position. Spread along the middle of the road there lay the gallant steed in the last agonies of death, while, stunned by the fall, his rider lay stretched motionless by his side.

The kind-hearted squire at once thought of nothing but saving his friend, and having dismounted, used every endeavour to restore animation. In this he at length succeeded, for his opponent had sustained no injury beyond some slight contusions and the exhaustion arising from over-exertion.

Thus ended this extraordinary race.

The sportsmen of the past were often confronted with dangers unknown in this more civilised age. Steeple-chasing in Ireland, for instance, at times when "the finest pisantry in the world" were in one of their acute fits of national effervescence, was a highly perilous sport. Mr. George Smith, in his day considered the best steeple-chase jockey in Ireland, once won a race only by the exercise of great shrewdness and courage.

A steeple-chase had been advertised to take place in the county of Limerick, and thither Mr. Smith repaired with Fidler, a nag of no common pretensions, but who, having had a slight touch of spavin, which somewhat affected him, required a good brushing gallop to warm him previous to starting. At these meetings the peasantry assembled in crowds, and generally had a favourite, into whose cause they entered heart and hand; any other competitor proving victorious stood a good chance of being stoned to death in the hour of victory, for these active partisans stuck at nothing, and were no respecters of persons. Mr. Smith and Fidler were strangers, therefore they were not to win, if there was any virtue in stones. But Mr. Smith knew Fidler could win, was determined he should; and he did win cleverly by a very shrewd stratagem. In giving Fidler his brushing gallop immediately previous to starting his rider wore his jockey dress, but contrived, just before the actual start, to slip on a hat and great-coat. From the very start Mr. Smith took a determined and decided lead, and kept it all through. At the various fences, where bands of brutes were stationed, stone in hand, he called out that the favourite was winning, described him by name, and called on them to clear the course. This they did, taking him for some hard-riding partisan : thus did this clever rider save his horse and himself from being maimed or killed, and won his race.

Ireland was the very head-quarters of originality, a conspicuous example having been Mr. Fitzgerald Caldwell, a gentleman who had had a very varied career. Born a younger son of an old family, at a time when education and refinement were less thought of than boisterous conviviality, Mr. Caldwell passed much of his early life at sea ; but by nature attached to horses, on marrying a widow lady of title, with a good fortune, he betook himself to the Irish turf, in the successful practice of which, and an undeviating hospitality, he spent a long life. His habits were so singular as to have attracted attention even at a time when Irishmen were used to every kind of extravagant freak.

Mr. Caldwell was a compound of the old Jack Tar, the old Irish squire, and the turf-man.

His vocabulary was of an amphibious kind, the oaths recorded in "Tristram Shandy" being mere milk and water in comparison.

His good qualities, however, were many, and he was warm-hearted, sincere, honourable, humane, and hospitable. Nothing displeased him more than cant, or anything like it. As for himself, he was overnice about nothing. Having been making some alterations in his pleasure-grounds at Brownstown, near the Curragh, and expecting some great folks in a day or two, he employed four or five hundred good Catholics after Mass on Sunday to finish the damming up of a large sheet of water. The Protestant curate of the parish was evangelical, and thence regarded by the squire (otherwise the kindest of men) much as a professed swindler is by a London tradesman. The curate came to remonstrate, and rebuked him before the multitude. All the answer he got was : "May the Devil's mother nurse you when you are sick, you journeyman soul saver ! It is true your Master stopped on the seventh day, as you tell me, you snivelling fellow, but He had done His work, and when I've done mine I'll stop too. Shut your ugly mug, and make haste out of this, or I'll make an anabaptist of you in the pond there, and keel-haul you, hypocrite that you are." This was said with the growl of a lion and the grin of an ogre, brandishing a crutch which gout alone prevented his applying.

A well-known figure in this part of the country was an old Irish priest, whose quaint phraseology and ready wit made him a welcome guest throughout the district. Dining one day at a squire's, the conversation turned upon a curious old marriage ring which one of the guests had acquired, upon which the priest joined in : "A marriage ring thin is it yer talking about ? Faith thin, it's not so curious as one I used yestherday, anyhow. Sure and there were two poor people, Irish ye could tell by their brogue, who came to be married, and they had never a ring; so I'd well-nigh stopp'd altogether ; when the lady suggested a kay. ' Faith ! that's an illigant notion,' said the bridegroom ; ' but where are we to get a kay, Nancy darlin' ? '—' Ain't there his Riverince's strate-door kay ? ' answered Nancy. ' By the powhers and that's thrue.' So I married them with my Riverince's strate-door kay ! "

"What a good notion ! " said the hostess : " I wonder where Nancy learnt it." " Jist what I asked her, my Lady," replied the good Father, and she answered, "And what thin was I married in last year at Ballyshannon, county Fermoy, by blessed Father O'Phelim, to Teddy O'Flanaghan, him as I wouldn't live with no more for his drunken basteliness, but the top of his Riverince's strate-door kay ? "

# The Merry Past

About 1836 a less sympathetic character of pronounced eccentricity excited much surprise and curiosity in the Emerald Isle. This was a rich old bachelor of Jewish extraction, who took up his abode in a large mansion in Queen's County.

He lived in almost total seclusion, and in all his household expenses observed stern economy. The neighbouring gentry in vain offered him the advantage of their society. He would neither give nor take dinners, nor join in the usual amusements of the country. He did not patronise foxhounds, had little affection for beagles, and entertained a positive antipathy to greyhounds; nevertheless, he was a sportsman, and kept a pack of dogs, but they were all bull-dogs—enormous monsters, which he imported in a caravan, and kept barred up in iron cages like the wild beasts in a menagerie. His main delight consisted in feeding these beautiful pets with meat well cooked and carefully separated from the bones, lest any injury should befall their teeth. He also kept a numerous establishment of game-cocks, betwixt which and the sweet creatures in the kennel all his parental cares and affections were divided. This genius was reputed to be worth half a million of money.

The eighteenth century was essentially an age which produced much originality and eccentricity of character in every grade of life, an especial instance of which was Pope the usurer, who died in the Fleet Prison in 1794, where he had been incarcerated over eleven years. He was originally a tanner in Southwark, and dealt so largely and extensively in this branch that his stock-in-trade was for many years supposed to be worth sixty or seventy thousand pounds.

In the latter part of his time in this trade, and when he was well known to be worth a considerable amount, he took to the lending of money, discounting, and buying annuities, mortgages, and the like. In this branch of business Mr. Pope would appear to have been less successful than in his former trade ; for the name of Pope the usurer every now and then appears in the proceedings of the courts of law, when the judges commonly differed widely from Mr. Pope in their opinion of the sharp practices in which he indulged. The most remarkable and the last instance of this sort was, when he was cast in £10,000 damages for some usurious or illegal practices, in some money transactions with Sir Alexander Leith.

This was generally thought a smart sentence, and probably the notorious character of the man contributed not a little towards it. Mr. Pope himself thought it so oppressive that he never ceased to complain of its injustice, and even printed a pamphlet, setting forth the hardship and great loss he had suffered. Immediately after the trial Pope, to be even with his plaintiff, went abroad to France with all his effects and property, where a man in his advanced years, ample fortune, and without any family but his wife, who was a most respectable woman, might certainly have lived very comfortably. But

# The Merry Past

Mr. Pope abroad was removed from his friends and customers; and his money being idle, which was always considered by him as a great misfortune, he resolved to come home, and to show his resentment against the supposed injustice he submitted to imprisonment rather than pay the money. This he did most heroically, suffering the long imprisonment of eleven years and three months.

Throughout the whole of this time (nearly twelve years) Pope never had a joint of meat on his table. His greatest luxury was a groat plate from the cook's shop, and that served him for two meals generally; but in these points he was not much at a loss, for his family, though living at a great distance, knowing of his penurious disposition, sent to him frequently a very comfortable and proper supply; and on these occasions he was actually known, occasionally, to give some leavings to his errand girl or other distressed person.

To do justice to so eccentric a character as Pope, it is but right to state that, while in trade, he had early begun the benevolent practice of giving away, every week, a stone, and more, of meat among his workmen and poor neighbours. This practice he never abandoned, not even when he was every day weighing his candle or looking after the measure of his small beer.

During his residence in the Fleet Mr. Pope was occasionally the victim of hoaxes played upon him by individuals with whom he had had dealings.

One winter's day he was delighted at receiving

a basket which, from the pheasant's feathers protruding from it, seemed full of game.

The man who brought it told the old usurer that it was a gift from a sympathiser with whom he had had dealings in former days.

Pope was quite touched, and remarking that it was pleasant to find oneself remembered by old clients, paid the bearer the somewhat large amount he asked for having brought the basket. The man left full of delight, a feeling not shared by Pope when he found nothing but bricks and rubbish inside.

Sending presents of this kind was very popular in former days. When the dog tax was passed Mr. Dent, who had introduced it, received no less than two hundred hampers containing dead dogs packed up like game with curious complimentary letters.

Another parsimonious character was Mr. Guy, the founder of the hospital which bears his name in the borough of Southwark—a man as remarkable for his petty private economies as for his public munificence. He invariably dined alone, a soiled proof-sheet, or an old newspaper, being his constant substitute for a table-cloth.

As Mr. Guy was one winter evening sitting in his room meditating over a handful of half-lighted embers, confined within the narrow precincts of a brick stove, and without any candle, a visitor was introduced, and after the usual compliments had been passed, and the new arrival asked to take a seat, Mr. Guy lighted a farthing candle, which lay ready on the table by him, and desired to know the purport of the gentleman's visit. The visitor in question proved to be the famous Vulture Hopkins, immortalised by Pope in the lines :

When Hopkins dies, a thousand lights attend
The wretch, that living, sav'd a candle's end.

" I have been told," said Hopkins, " that you, sir, are better versed in the prudent and necessary art of saving than any man now living, and I therefore wait upon you for a lesson of frugality—an art in which I used to think I excelled, but am told by all who know you, that you are greatly my superior." " And is that all you come about ? " said Guy. " Why, then, we can talk this matter over in the dark." So saying, he with great deliberation extinguished his new-lighted farthing candle. Struck with this instance of economy, Hopkins rose up, acknowledged himself convinced of the other's superior thrift, and took his leave.

Sir Hans Sloane was also excessively parsimonious, his usual dinner being a boiled egg. Sir Hans was once told by Doctor Mortimer, when he complained of being deserted by his friends, that people were probably rather disappointed to go all the way to Chelsea to find such slight refreshment as his house offered.

The old baronet flew into a rage at this, and exclaimed : " Keep a table ! Invite people to dinner ! Would you have me ruin myself ? Public credit totters already, and if, as has been presaged, there should be a national bankruptcy, or a sponge to wipe out the national debt, you may yet see me in a work-house." His landed interest was at that time very considerable, and his museum worth much more than the twenty thousand pounds which was given for it by Parliament.

The economies of " Miser Cooke " were notorious. Once, when his horse had a disease in the eyes, Cooke, who mortally hated to pay any medical man, listened to the quackery of some silly journeyman farrier, who told him to take thirty onions, run a string through them, and then putting them round the horse's neck, like a necklace, let him wear them continually, till, drawing the humour out of the horse's eyes, the onions would get dry and shrivelled, and the eyes get well. Cooke, who had not the heart to purchase thirty onions, bought half the number, and did as he was told with them. But, as usual, determined nothing should be thrown away, at a fortnight's end he took them off the horse's neck, put them into a hand-basket, and brought them into the house, as if just returned from market, desiring his maids to make a dish of onion porridge of them for that day's dinner. The maids, however, knowing well from whence they came, peremptorily refused to cook them, which, as usual, set the old gentleman cursing and swearing that he would not leave them a farden in his will—a threat which did not alarm them, knowing well that to disappoint expectants was his greatest delight.

On another occasion Cooke bargained with a stable-keeper to let his horse have the run of a field at so much per day. When he wanted to ride he always took a very accurate account of the number of hours he had him out, the time of his going and returning, and when he took the horse away finally, he desired the man to bring in his bill. On perusing it he flew into a great passion, asking the man, did he mean to be a robber, to plunder and cheat him of his money? The stable-keeper desired him to count the number of days since the horse had been taken in. " Horse taken in! No, it is me that you want to take in. Had I not my horse eight hours out of your field on Thursday? Well, sir, and did I not ride him to Epsom next day, and had him eleven hours? That is nineteen hours. Then, sir, five hours and a half on Saturday. There, sir, there is two days and half an hour, that you want to cheat me of. And have you the conscience, you swindling rogue, to make me pay for my horse's eating your grass, when he has been miles and miles away from it? "

" Sir, I have not only the conscience to expect payment of my full bill, but shall make you pay a little more for calling me a cheat and a rogue." Mr. Cooke, who was afraid of nothing so much as the law, very prudently made an apology, and paid the full amount of his bill, glad to have escaped any further expense.

Cooke, in spite of his intense parsimony, was not such an unpleasant character as the old miser who lived near Doncaster, and went to a great land sale in his filthy rags with a band of hay round his waist, in order to bid for a large estate. After having made his bid, he much surprised the auctioneer, who showed signs of doubting the bidder's solvency, by holding up a £100,000 bank-note, and saying, " Here's the cock, I've got the old hen at home."

On another occasion this miser, going to receive certain dividends, refused to take notes, his idea being that the time had come for cash settlements alone.

" I'll take no more paper," said he. " I want to see whether there's any meaning in the words, ' I promise to pay.' " The clerk endeavoured to explain to him the sort of bullion payment that was intended, adding, that the moment for that was not yet come. " Pooh ! " said the old gentleman, " it's no such thing. I am to have gold, if I like it, and not paper. Where are all your promises ? "

"How should I know ? " replied the clerk; " we never keep any of them ! " An answer which set the old man thinking.

A more pleasant character, though thoroughly unconventional, was the clergyman called the Reverend Benjamin Smith, known as " Walking Smith," on account of his once having won a large wager by having walked against time between Stamford and Grantham.

Himself the son of a clergyman, " Walking Smith " was rector of North Witham, near Stamford, Lincolnshire, and was a half-nephew to Sir Isaac Newton. He was educated at Peterhouse College, Cambridge, and took the several degrees of bachelor of arts, master of arts, and bachelor of divinity.

# The Merry Past

He was twelve years abroad, and spent most of his fortune before he returned home. He brought with him an Italian servant, who was an excellent classic, and also a dog, named Sereno, from that country. In this creature's last sickness he was attended by a medical man, and a nurse, who sat up with him several nights in the last stage of his illness. The animal had been a faithful companion, was a great favourite, and as such his death was much regretted.

He was fortunate as a lead-mine adventurer, and a share he bought for £80 he sold for an annuity of 120 guineas. He aimed at living long, being keen in the pursuit of longevity, was very regular in the economy of life, rode out or walked out every day in good weather several miles before he dined. He was temperate, and always kept his age a profound secret, for the purpose of making advantageous contracts in life-annuities. He was an adept in calculations of that sort.

Walking Smith liked exercise, and was enamoured of dancing, boasting that he had learned a dance in France which cost him twelve guineas. He had a rural fiddler, who was likewise a tailor, and played to him occasionally when he was disposed to dance. The musician's wages were sixpence, a pint of ale, and bread and cheese. In summer, when he was on a journey to dine, or visit a friend, he would quit his horse, tie him to a gate, and dance a hornpipe or two, to the no small astonishment of the passing traveller, then resume his saddle and ride on.

He was never known to join in field sports, but was

passionately fond of games of chance, and when he met with any poor person who was a good cribbage player, he would maintain him three or four months, only for the sake of playing with him.

When he had accumulated any considerable sum, he always purchased with it a life-annuity; one of these he bought of an alderman of Richmond, in Yorkshire, with whom he had long dealt for wine, but after the contract could never be induced to take a drop of his liquor, from apprehension that his friend might shorten his life.

The annual income of these annuities, and his stipend as rector of Linton, in Yorkshire (which he was near fifty years), amounted to about £700 per annum, which he yearly consumed in eccentricities and fantastic projects. He expended many hundred pounds on the parsonage house and glebe lands, and was fond of placing Greek and Latin inscriptions about the premises. He had his clothes made in London, of the finest cloth that could be procured, and walked with a very long stick, which he called his pastoral staff. He was never married.

Mr. Smith died in 1777, when he must have been about eighty years old.

The character of characters, of course, was Old Q, who in his latter years, after he had ceased to take any interest in sport, amused himself by pedestrian parades and short strolls in front of his mansion in Piccadilly. From time to time he made excursions with his phaeton and ponies from the " White Horse Cellars" to Hyde Park Corner, occasionally varied by the longer and more laborious journey of Park Lane, Hyde Park, and home. These, with occasional elegant entertainments and concerts, attended by much facile beauty, filled the measure of his Grace's sublunary enjoyments, and afforded him daily opportunities of ruminating upon the various pleasures of this life, and the uncertainty of the next.

In order to preserve a life which he would seem to have thoroughly enjoyed, Old Q adhered to a daily régime which was as follows:

At seven in the morning he took a warm milk bath, perfumed with almond powder, where he took his coffee and a buttered muffin, and afterwards retired to bed. He rose about nine, and breakfasted on *café au lait*, with new-laid eggs, just parboiled. At eleven he was presented with two warm jellies and rusks. At one he ate a veal cutlet, *à la Maintenon*. At three, jellies and eggs repeated. At five, a cup of chocolate and rusks. At half-past seven he took a hearty dinner from high-seasoned dishes, and made suitable libations of claret and Madeira. At ten, tea, coffee, and muffins. At twelve, supper off a roasted pullet, with a plentiful dilution of lime punch. At one in the morning he retired to bed in high spirits, and slept till three, when his man cook, to the moment, waited upon him in person with a hot and savoury veal cutlet, which, with a potation of wine and water, prepared him for his further repose that continued generally uninterrupted till the morning summons to his lactean bath.

One of the few griefs of this old nobleman were

his teeth, which made it necessary for him to have frequent recourse to dentists, whose charges became to him what he thought a source of serious expense. March, who was accounted by many to be the best dentist in his day, was frequently employed by him. Notwithstanding, they often disagreed upon the terms he desired to be paid. Upon one occasion of the kind the dentist asked him fifty guineas to do something he wanted. " Fifty guineas ! " exclaimed the Duke. " I will not give it you ; your demand is most exorbitant. I can, for less money, send one of my footmen to Paris, have him educated for a dentist, and when he returns he will do what I want much better than you can." " As you please, my lord Duke," said the dentist. " I hope you will succeed. At any rate, those are my terms, so I wish your Grace a good morning."

Not many days afterwards, however, the Duke felt that he must submit, and returned to the operator. When he entered the room, before he had time to explain himself, March exclaimed, " Well, my lord Duke, is your footman come back from Paris ? Is he become a good dentist ? " " Yes ! Pooh ! pooh ! " said the Duke. " Don't be impertinent. You are a very extravagant extortioner ; but you do your work well, so that I will employ you upon your own terms. There are your fifty guineas ; set about the job immediately." " No, my lord Duke," said the dentist, with much nonchalance. " I will not take your money. Those were my terms when you were here last, but I have since raised them. You have sent your footman to Paris, and as you find you cannot make a dentist of him, you come back to me. My terms are now one hundred guineas, to be paid before you leave this room. If you do not, I know you must and will return, and then the price shall be two hundred, and so on increasing, till you do come, as I know you must come at last." The Duke felt that the dentist was right in his conjecture, and to avoid the consequence paid the money.

This dentist fared better with his Grace of Queensberry than he afterwards did with George the Fourth, who, when he entered into fashionable life, sent for March, as the most eminent dentist of his day, with the intention of employing him. When the dentist was ushered into the presence, he began, in his usual manner, by telling His Royal Highness that he must have fifty guineas before he could see into his mouth. The Prince, irritated by this, ordered him to be turned instantly into the street.

In the early years of the nineteenth century a well-known figure in the West End was Sir John Dinely, a little old man, about seventy, rivalling Old Q in years, and surpassing him in gaiety. He used to wear scarlet small-clothes, a blue waistcoat, and orange coat; over all of which was a large shabby drab greatcoat. A large King Charles's wig, highly powdered, crowned his head, uncovered by any hat. And, as if this dress were not sufficiently attractive, he was wont to hold aloft a large silk umbrella, presumably in order to protect his delicate countenance from the sun, and to put to the blush the petty parasols twinkling around him. No wonder that usually Sir John attracted a crowd in his train !

Of a different nature altogether were the numerous adventurers whose eccentricities took a more dangerous form. At that time the most disreputable characters, when possessed of a good appearance and address, frequently obtained admission into the highest circles without much difficulty. Major Semple, a well-known character in London, finding that city becoming rather uncomfortable for him in 1792, betook himself to Paris, where, calling himself Colonel Lille, and armed with a letter of recommendation from Alderman Macaulay, he got introduced to Pétion, the then mayor, who recommended him to the Minister of War, and introduced him to all the principal political characters in Paris.

Here he offered to raise a regiment of Hussars, into which an Englishman named Dr. Maxwell readily entered, by purchasing the rank of lieutenant-colonel of the soi-disant colonel.

Dr. Maxwell soon discovering that the person of whom he had bought his commission was the famous Major Semple, immediately made it public, by having placards pasted up in the Palais Royal and different parts of Paris, offering a reward for the apprehension of the ingenious major, who, however, made his escape with the doctor's purchase-money.

By some means or other he contrived in the course of the winter to be received in the Austrian lines as a deserter from the French service, and brought with him such perfect information of the state of Dumouriez's army, and the disaffection then prevailing therein, that he was received in full confidence. He styled himself Major Delle. At the battle of Tirlemont he was put at the head of a squadron of Hussars, and performed the memorable service of driving the French from their strong battery, and taking three pieces of cannon. After this singular exploit he was received at head-quarters in a manner most flattering to his wishes. He was afterwards constantly at the table of the hereditary Prince of Orange, at Brussels, and had the honour to hand the Princess to her carriage, in preference to most of the military suite. He was at this time received by Lord Auckland, the British Minister; and on the Stadtholder's arrival at Brussels he was introduced at his court, where he became so great a favourite that a command of a regiment of Dutch Chasseurs was promised him.

He wore a hussar uniform, which set off the elegance of figure to the utmost advantage, and this, with the polished style of his address, gave him no small influence in the female circles of Brussels. Unfortunately, however, the career of his singular glory was blasted by the arrival of a Scotch gentleman of great respectability, who immediately recognised in the fashionable pet the celebrated Major Semple.

Mr. Rose, Chargé d'Affaires at the Hague, then also at Brussels, being informed of the discovery, immediately waited on the Prince of Orange, and made him acquainted with the character who had thus risen so rapidly into military estimation. In consequence thereof the major was informed that he must instantly give in his commission, or his degradation would be made in public quarters at the head of the line. By the humane interference of the gentleman who discovered him, he was rescued, however, from this disgrace, and suffered to retain his rank, on condition of his retiring from the service. After his detection it was discovered that scarcely a person of rank in Brussels but had been induced to supply him with sums of money under various pretexts. Mrs. Semple, meanwhile, had been a resident of Calais; but as a consolation for her absence, the Major lived *en famille* with a Frenchwoman of exquisite beauty.

In the early days of the nineteenth century the army contained not a few officers who indulged in outrageous conduct. Such a one was Captain Maclellan of the Coldstream Guards, who one night at dinner, declining to drink any more wine with a brother officer, Ensign Lloyd, was pressed by the Ensign to give his reason.

" To tell you the truth," replied the captain, " I have an assignation with your wife to-night, and as a man of honour, I am resolved to keep it ! " Ensign Lloyd endeavoured to pass this off as a joke; but the other assuring him that he was in earnest, received a glass of wine in his face, and a manual skirmish ensued. The commanding officer having heard the case, with the addition that no further step had been taken by either party, put them both under arrest, and reported their conduct to the Commander-in-Chief.

At the court-martial which was subsequently held, Captain Maclellan was sentenced to be dismissed the service, and Ensign Lloyd suspended and deprived of pay for six months.

Nevertheless, the majority of officers, if wild spirits, were brave and honourable men.

The bold intrepid spirit which animated so many of them appears from numberless anecdotes which have been preserved. One of the most characteristic of these is of a certain Colonel Johnson, who had served under the Duke of York in the Netherlands.

A fine swordsman, his great height and length of arm rendered him a most formidable opponent.

Colonel Johnson, travelling on the Continent alone with a groom, happened to halt at a small inn, glad to seek anywhere rest and refreshment for himself, his servant, and the jaded steeds. The only decent apartment in the house was occupied by a party of French officers. All the provisions the house afforded they had bespoken ; and the colonel was informed that not a ragout or an omelet was to be had for love or money, and under these circumstances sent a polite request to the party that a British officer might be permitted to share in the rations of their mess. The messenger was sent back with a rude message of an insulting kind. Under this unmerited insult Colonel Johnson showed the greatest coolness and intrepidity imaginable. He commanded that the joint then being dished up should be laid before him.

# The Merry Past

He and his servant fared sumptuously, and, with fear and trembling, "mine host of the Garter" carried the mutilated remains to the impatient and vociferating guests of the parlour. Affrighted and astonished, their disappointment and chagrin were soon converted into impotent railing and breathings of revenge. At that period, the transmission of a watch, a glove, a ring, or any article of which the transmitter stood possessed, was considered the gage of defiance, and the colonel soon found his table in the kitchen glittering with mementos of Gallic daring. He allowed the challengers to finish their abbreviated repast, calmly took his modicum of wine, and then, followed by his servant, strode into the apartment. Drawing his sword, and placing on its blade the first article of defiance, at the same moment raising his fine person to its utmost height, and darting an eye of indignation around, as if singling out his victim, he coolly desired its proprietor to redeem it. The effect was prodigious. There was a pause denoting hesitation—a buzz, but nothing palpable; and after a full minute had elapsed the watch was handed over to his bowing lacquey, and a ring dangled on the still extended weapon; that, too, became the undisputed property of the domestic; and so with the rest. "Men but in appearance—soldiers but in name!" exclaimed Colonel Johnson, as he drew his hand across his blade ere he deposited it in its sheath. "Learn from henceforward how to respect the rights of hospitality. I have been told that cowardice is ever the companion of audacity, and that those who know how to convey an insult have rarely the courage to redeem it. I regret that it should have been my fortune to find beneath the uniform of France a proof of the truth of such a statement."

The French officers of Napoleon's day were by training and disposition of somewhat overbearing habits, which clung to them even in the moment of defeat.

A gallant General of Division, having escaped the horrors of the retreat from Moscow, arrived, half frozen, at Schipenheil, in Prussia, with his division, consisting of "three men and himself." They were accommodated with quarters at the Burgomaster's house, and the General was warming himself at the stove, when a young French officer entered the room, demanding, in a loud and arrogant tone, that lodgings should be provided for a division of cuirassiers of 3500 men. The Burgomaster tremblingly answered that he could not procure accommodation for so numerous a corps. " Make yourself easy, my friend," said the General ; " the young gentleman's division is like mine—you may lodge them all in the next room ! "

It can hardly be conceived that in such a terrible retreat, during which thousands of stalwart men perished, an invalid would have had much chance of survival. Nevertheless, an officer suffering from typhoid fever came safely through the terrible ordeal. Being taken ill shortly after leaving Moscow, he was put in a sledge by his friends, where he lay till the

Beresina was reached, which river he crossed strapped on to the back of a horse. By the time Vilna was reached he was practically well. The only nourishment taken by the sick man during the retreat was coffee, and no doubt the lack of food which caused the death of so many men in rude health, together with the chilling cold, saved him, the modern treatment of typhoid being anticipated by the natural conditions of the retreat. The name of the officer in question, who was in a cavalry regiment, composed of men from Würtemberg, attached to Murat's Division, was the Graf von Bismarck, whose son, a most cultivated and delightful German nobleman— himself a veteran of the Franco-Prussian War—is happily still alive. He it was who described the circumstances of his father's marvellous preservation from death to the writer.

# X

THE women of the past, dimly discerned through the mists of time, acquire in our eyes a charm which is without doubt heightened by the beautiful portraits of Romney, Gainsborough, and Reynolds, whose models would seem to have been very paragons of femininity. Whether such was in sober reality the case may be open to doubt, but beyond all question the beauties of the eighteenth century were essentially real women, and had not the slightest desire to pose as imperfect men—the ideal of some portion of the sex in more modern times.

From a physical point of view the girl of the eighteenth century would seem to have been of a somewhat different type from her sister of to-day, who is generally dowered with a willowy figure not very robustly developed. Woman's height also is said to have increased within the last fifty years, though in connection with this it should not be forgotten that boots are now more scientifically made than in the past, and heels more artfully devised.

The English lass, as pictured by Rowlandson, an artist who knew a good deal about women, would seem to have been rather squat, very well developed, and brimming over with vitality and life, whilst smilingly accepting the casual caress of any gay captain who chanced to cross her path. Indeed, were the damsels of to-day to be treated as those of the eighteenth century are in some of the artist's designs, many an admirer would probably be quickly afforded the option of paying forty shillings or a month for assault. The girls of the past, however, do not appear to have much minded anything, provided it was connected with love-making, though they well knew how to treat suitors who were not to their taste.

About 1780 the West End of London was full of rollicking blades much given to accosting any pretty girl whom they might meet. Such was the danger at this time to which unprotected females were exposed, that the mistresses of boarding-schools found it necessary to advertise " that the young ladies were not permitted to go abroad without proper attendants." Nevertheless, most of them seem to have been well able to take care of themselves.

A young lady walking along with her eyes cast upon the ground, a rude fellow accosted her with, " Pray, madam, what are you looking for ? " " A puppy," was the reply, " and now I have found him."

A young married lady who displayed considerable presence of mind was, however, once placed in a very awkward position by an impudent thief.

Entering her bedroom one evening she found, to her consternation, that a thief was there : she rushed out of the room and returned with help.

# The Merry Past

The thief meanwhile had got into the bed, and on the arrival of the police with the lady at once apostrophised her loudly, saying : " I knew your horrible jealousy would lead you to do something of this sort some day ; that's the worst of being loved by a woman." The lady was very much confused, and during the animated disavowals which ensued, the thief managed to escape.

Singularly devoid of false modesty, a number of these ladies made no secret of the fact that they regarded love-making—the pursuit of man—as the chief aim and object of existence ; they were often quite devoid of any prudery on this point, which was perfectly recognised. " Oh, papa," said a girl in love with a handsome but very stupid youth, " I can't think why you should object to our marrying."

" You can't really want to marry such a man as that," was the reply. " Whatever will you do with him all day ? "

" Never mind about that ; think how pleasant the evenings will be," said the girl.

Another very flighty young lady who presented her husband—a collector of prints—with a bouncing boy some two months after marriage, gaily remarked that it was a first impression, which had come near being a proof before letters.

To get a husband was the principal aim and object of every young lady, and a very natural aim it was too. Ireland, in particular, was the country in which husband-hunting was carried on with the greatest keenness and zest.

# The Merry Past

At one time an eligible bachelor could scarcely say a civil thing to a prolific country gentleman's or apothecary's daughter without being called upon to explain his intentions; and if he prevaricated, or had none at all of a serious and uxorious nature, he might as well make his will on the spot.

A weak-minded subaltern once ran his head into the matrimonial noose in a very strange manner. He was invited by an old half-pay officer (who had three sons and five daughters) to come and shoot snipe in Ireland. The eldest son, an officer in the Militia, was a regular fighting man, who in his village passed for a complete fire-eater. The youthful lieutenant, aware of this, and that the practice of getting off sisters prevailed in this part of the country, was, consequently, very much on his guard. He could not, however, help showing the sisters some little civilities, such as dancing with them, and giving them his arm across the bog facing the old officer's house, services which he performed with fear and trembling. The fateful day, however, arrived when the fire-eating eldest brother came in heated with whisky-punch, and too late for dinner, after having had a bad day's shooting. The subaltern thought that he looked dryly at him, so proposed (for the family had dined) a glass of cold punch made with raspberry whisky; this lit up the eyes of the youth more fiercely than before. Raising his hand to his bumper glass, he proceeded to propose a toast, which he prefaced in a very vehement tone by, " Misther Johnson, I'll tell you what "—the young man realised that the moment he had dreaded was at hand, and seeing nothing for it but to accept his fate, nervously blurted out, "Captain, I understand you : which of your sisters do you wish me to marry ? " And the captain, who was a great diplomatist in such matters, replied : " My sister Onor, because it will be a great honour to you, and because she is the eldest and the plainest ; so, brother, here is towards your good health ! I wish you joy of getting into one of the first families in Ireland ! "

Elopements, followed by marriages at Gretna Green, were common, romantic and well-dowered wards going off with penniless captains, who hoped by matrimony to secure the fortune which neither the hazard-table nor the race-course appeared likely to afford.

Sometimes ladies were carried off by force, more often than not accepting their fate with considerable equanimity.

When the brothers Gordon ran away with Mrs. Lee, a woman of great beauty, it was proved in defence on their trial for abduction, that in the carriage the lady drew a camphor bag from her bosom, which she wore as an amulet to preserve her chastity, and threw it out of the window, saying, " The best friends must part ; now, welcome Pleasure ! "

English girls were rough-and-ready enough in those days, whilst quite devoid of nonsense.

A blooming lass of eighteen, just married to an amorous swain of seventy, leaving the church face-tiously whispered in the parson's ear, " It will not be long, sir, before I bring him again ! "

# The Merry Past

Another couple going to be married were at the church door, when the prospective bridegroom stopped the charming creature who hung on his arm, and said, "Dearest, during our courtship I have told you most of my mind, but I have not told you the whole. When we are married I shall insist upon three things." "What are they?" asked the lady. "In the first place," said the bridegroom, "I shall sleep alone, I shall eat alone, and find fault when there is no occasion. Can you submit to these conditions?" "Oh, yes, sir, very easily," was the reply; "for, if you sleep alone, I shall not; if you eat alone, I shall eat first; and as to your finding fault without occasion, that, I think, may be prevented, for I will take care you shall never want occasion."

Those were not prudish days, and there was a good deal of plain speaking.

A married couple, determined to part, were not able to agree with respect to the disposition of the children; to settle the matter they referred the dispute to an aunt, by whose arbitration they respectively agreed to abide.

"We have *three* children," said the husband. "I insist on keeping *two*; the third shall be left to the care of its mother." "But I," said the latter, "have a right to *two*; the care of one will be more than sufficient for you."

"There is no way of settling this dispute," said the aunt, in a tone of the utmost gravity, "but by increasing the number of your children to four."

This decision produced a laugh, and restored good

humour. The contending parties were reconciled, and the idea of a divorce abandoned.

Though women were more plain-spoken, they were more bound by social rules and customs than in these times of female emancipation. Nevertheless, they had a good deal of amusement and pleasure, which they enjoyed with whole-hearted zest.

Whilst the wives and daughters of the mercantile class did not then as now aspire to entering fashionable society, which was irrevocably closed against them, they had plenty of amusements of their own, which were more or less copies of those in vogue at the West End of the town. This is well expressed in some old lines :

> Ah ! I loves life and all the joys it yields !
> Says Madam Fussock warm from Spitalfields.
> "*Bone Tone's*" the space 'twixt Saturday and Monday ;
> 'Tis riding in a one-horse shay on Sunday ;
> 'Tis drinking tea on Sunday afternoons
> At Bagnigge Wells with china and gilt spoons !
> 'Tis laying by our clogs, red coats, and pattens
> To dance *cow-tillions* all in silks and satins !

The annual ball, given by the dancing-master who taught the rich cit's daughters, was always a great occasion for the display of wonderful and stupendous toilettes. A Frenchman named Le Mercier was a most popular teacher of dancing, and by way of advertising himself once gave his annual ball in the great room at the London Tavern, which was crowded to excess. Many City families who in the ordinary course of events could never have gained admission to the assemblies held eagerly bought tickets. The success of the evening, however, was marred by a lady who, standing by a set in which her daughter was taking part, resented some unfavourable comments passed by a neighbour, who said the dancing was bad. "That's a lie!" shouted the proud mother, in answer to which the gentleman very ungallantly gave her a box on the ears, or rather on her lofty head-dress, a cloud of powder from which covered all who were near. The ladies screamed, the music and dancing stopped, and the harmony of the evening being destroyed, the company separated in very bad humour, as a consequence of which poor Le Mercier did not repeat his experiment.

The regular assemblies at the London Tavern were only frequented by the higher class of citizens, none being admitted even as visitors who were concerned in any kind of trade but banking or exportation. This was a source of great mortification to many ambitious tradesmen's wives, who, in consequence, established a rival "New London Assembly" in Cateaton Street.

When the fashion of diaphanous dress had reached England from France, many fashionable women carried it to an extreme, as they frankly admitted.

"Don't tread upon my muslin gown," said a young lady to her partner in the warmth of her dancing heart at a ball. "You see that I have nothing under it."

Eccentricity of female dress, however, reached its highest pitch in 1803, when three Parisian beauties, who appeared one Sunday with tight petticoats, made a perfect display of muscular motion. They were dressed in the finest muslins, with " curricle" jackets, orange shawls over the arm, the neck fashionably bare, the arms bare to the shoulders ; the hair dressed *à la Grec*, with ringlets *à la Meduse ;* no cap or bonnet on the head, but only a rich white lace veil, covering the head and shoulders also. The moment these ladies entered the Park they created a sensation, and were surrounded. They went out· of the public walk in hopes of avoiding attention ; but by this they created more sensation, for seeing a crowd at a distance, everyone ran to know what was the matter. The throng became a downright mob, consisting mostly of young men of the lower class, in their Sunday clothes, who rudely pressed around the ladies. They were not wilfully insulted ; no one spoke to them, nor did anyone touch them ; but the crowd was so great around, and so closely followed them, that though they bore the dust and uproar with much good humour for a time, they soon discovered the necessity of going home. It was said at the time that two of the ladies were Madame Recamier and Madame Talien, but this was not the case.

As the century grew into maturity woman's dress lost much of the grace which had been such a salient feature in the preceding age.

From about 1835 to a comparatively recent date taste in such matters was at a very low ebb. At various epochs some very curious costumes were popular.

# The Merry Past

At the Derby Hunt Ball, for instance, in 1837, the Marchioness of Hastings appeared in a dress of scarlet velvet ornamented with the brushes of foxes killed by her lord in the chase.

This costume was considered a charming innovation, and at a dinner given to Lord Hastings by the gentlemen of the Donnington Hunt in January, 1838, the following verses were interpolated in a song set to one of Moore's melodies :

> She shone at the ball, the Queen of all,
> Her jewels were smiles and blushes ;
> While the folds of her red robe gracefully fall,
> Festooned by a garland of brushes.

> CHORUS
> Then here's to the sport so renowned and so rare,
> That procures us a garland and grace for the fair.

The leaders of eccentricity in costume were generally Cyprians. One of these—a Mrs. Potter, whose abode was near Fitzroy Square—created quite a sensation at Brighton in 1802 owing to her unconventional dress and equipage. The lady in question, after enlivening Bartholomew Fair, where she opened the ball at a hop in fine feather and golden plumage, betook herself to the Sussex watering-place.

There she dashed about in her light blue chariot, or on horseback, keeping two saddle-horses and a footman, besides her carriage ; now she was seen in simple muslins, her hair lank like a water-nymph ; next in a riding-habit, mounted ; then in silks of yellow, blue, and scarlet ; afterwards in crape, silver, feathers, and diamonds; "laced shoes, pink hose, gartered above the knee." She would appear on the Steyne in half a dozen dresses a day, all made of the best materials, though sometimes of a queer fashion, and most gaudy colours. She lived in all respects in a most dashing style; but there was no appearance of the source from whence she drew her wealth, seemingly she had no particular friend or protector. At last, however, her golden dream of pleasure came to an end, and the frail nymph determined to fly by night. Accordingly, one Wednesday, about midnight, in high and jovial spirits, she mounted the coach-box with coachee, put the child she kept into the chariot, and set off for town full gallop, her footman following with the saddle-horses. Arriving at the turnpike near Cuckfield, the carriage passed through, and the footman, with the horses, was left to pay the toll. Unfortunately he had no money, and said so rather insolently, with the result that the turnpike-man, who was a most resolute dog, ran after the carriage, and insisted on payment. Mrs. Potter, however, appeared inclined to give him " more kicks than halfpence," and poured on him a torrent of abuse, enriched by many flowers of oratory gleaned at Bartholomew Fair, besides which she swore that if she had a pistol she would blow his brains out. The turnpike-man, though stout-hearted, was not a little astonished to see so fair a lady in such a fine equipage beat him in his own slang; and fearing the odds were too much against him in a single-hand contest with such an Amazon, retreated home, whence he immediately saddled a horse and set out to stop the party at Crawley gate. The race between the parties on the road was most desperate, neck and neck all the way ; but the turnpike-man beat the chariot, and got the Crawley gate shut against its further progress. Further, in conformity to an Act of Parliament, which imposed a penalty of five pounds on anyone refusing to pay turnpike, he seized one of the chariot horses, of which, with assistance, he obtained possession. To ride into town with one chariot horse appeared impossible to Mrs. Potter. Meanwhile the noise awakened the people of the inn at Crawley, and the whole village turned out, with the result that the lady was asked who she was. To this she replied that she was the wife of a merchant, a lord, a general, and a baronet, and several other titles. The villagers concluded that she must have seven husbands ; and the landlord, who had heard of a plurality of wives, thought she was a Turk. Whatever she might be, however, he advised her to pay the five pounds, which she eventually settled by leaving her saddle-horses in pawn for the sum.

The fantastic fancies of this sort of ladies were endless. The celebrated Kitty Fisher, for instance, whose bewitching smiles were quite irresistible to the gallants of her day, is said once to have swallowed a thousand-pound note presented to her by an admirer. For some reason or other, she put the note on a piece of bread and butter, which she then ate. History does not record whether the bank sent to thank her.

## The Merry Past

A lady of the same class, who many years later became a well-known figure in the West End, was the celebrated Harriet Wilson, who lived in Berkeley Street. Her somewhat apocryphal Memoirs mention many of the celebrated men of her day, some of whom she certainly knew. Little reliance, however, can be placed upon the truth of most of her statements, the Memoirs in question having been written when she had fallen upon evil days and was desirous of making money by any possible means. Some of the illustrations of this book, though totally devoid of any artistic merit, are quaint—one, for instance, shows the Iron Duke in his cocked hat standing outside Miss Wilson's door in a towering rage, whilst the Duke of Argyle (disguised in a mob cap as an old landlady) informs the gallant but unwelcome visitor that his fair one is not at home.

Much was thought a joke in old days which would be now regarded in a very serious light.

A woman, for instance, who kept a house of doubtful fame at York, being brought before a magistrate, was questioned as to her line of business. "Please, your Worship," said she, "I keep a circulating library, the neatest books in sheets your Worship ever saw!" "Indeed!" observed the worthy magistrate, "then I'll take care to bind you and them over to be of good behaviour."

To-day, when all frolic has fled from England, the unassuming freedom which prevailed at the festivities of the past would be little to the taste of the present generation. Even Bohemian dances are as a rule now very staid affairs, especially those frequented by the minor lights of the chorus who have a reputation for rigid prudery to maintain.

" I don't know what I shall do," said one of these damsels to her partner, " I've lost my latch-key." " Take one of mine," jokingly replied the sprightly spark, and he showed his key-ring on which a couple hung.

A terrific disturbance was the result of this remark, at which the lady chose to take offence. Consulting with her companions—dragons of virtue like herself—it was decided that the monster who had dared to speak in such a way was not worthy of being permitted to remain at a chorus-girls' dance, and as the ladies (who declared their reputations were at stake) continued obdurate, the too dashing blade was eventually requested by friends to retire, this being the only way to save the evening from being entirely spoilt. The whole incident is highly illustrative of the curious and fiery prudery which has of late years overwhelmed the lesser lights of the stage.

Whilst the ladies of the past were anything but prudes, a good many of them were well able to exhibit determination whenever circumstances seemed to call for its display.

Lady Cahir, for instance, being at the theatre in Paris shortly after the destruction of the Bastille, was very free in conversation, which much annoyed some rich contractors, who with their womenfolk were sitting close by.

## The Merry Past

Eventually a police officer was sent for, but her ladyship did not brook his rebuke, and refusing to obey his injunctions, he was proceeding to hand her out, which creating some disturbance in her box attracted general observation. Her ladyship addressed the audience, and complained to them, saying she came from a land of liberty to a country, as she supposed, of freedom, and that the proceedings now against her were worse than if the Bastille still existed. The audience took fire in a moment, loudly applauded her, and espoused her cause so warmly that she took her seat again in triumph.

The idea that the enterprise of women in commerce and speculation is entirely modern is untrue. Women have often been exceedingly shrewd shopkeepers. As far back even as 1807 female money-lenders existed in England, one of whom, Betsy Bell by name, would seem to have been a very sharp customer.

A tradesman being somewhat embarrassed in his circumstances, and in need of some temporary assistance, unfortunately met with one of this lady's money-lending advertisements in a daily paper. He applied to the address given, and there found the business was entirely transacted by ladies. There were the lady clerk, the lady book-keeper, the lady money-lender, everything, indeed, except the lady solicitor. Lured by the terms held out in the public advertisement, he repaired to the house in the neighbourhood of Cavendish Square, where he hoped to obtain an accommodation on advantageous terms. He was introduced to a lady, who proposed that he should draw bills, and she would get them negotiated. He was, however, to take, as part of the consideration, a capital hunter, a horse that had hunted with the King's hounds, and that the son of the Archbishop of York had offered 150 guineas for ; this was to be put in, as a great favour, at 120 guineas. The borrower signed the bills, and as a collateral security, he gave a warrant of attorney, confessing judgment to the amount of the sum to be raised. When the hunter came home, however, a sad disillusion followed. The poor animal was in such a wretched condition that it had to be destroyed, and after his bones had been sent to a sham ivory merchant, his hide to a currier, and his flesh to the dogs, the poor animal's inside and outside value did not amount to more than three pounds.

At the time of the Napoleonic wars many women served as soldiers both in the English and French armies.

In 1794 a fine young girl, not more than seventeen years of age, enlisted in the 32nd Regiment, at Hampton. She attended drill regularly, and was considered a very clever recruit. Though she slept in the same room as the corporal, who enlisted her, a fortnight her sex was never discovered, until she disclosed the circumstance to an officer, of whom she was passionately enamoured. The corporal was so ridiculed by his comrades about this business that he requested and obtained leave to quit the regiment.

A less sympathetic character was a young woman dressed in man's apparel, who in 1797 was charged with defrauding a sergeant of Marines of twelve shillings under pretence of enlisting. It appeared she had served as a private in two different regiments for the space of three years ; the first was the Ayrshire Fencibles, from which when discovered she had been discharged ; the second the Light Dragoons, from which she was also dismissed for the like reason. A number of recruiting-sergeants having been defrauded by her under like pretences, and the charge being made out to the satisfaction of the magistrate, she was committed to New Prison for trial.

A few women even served as sailors.

In 1800 there was in the Middlesex Hospital a young and delicate girl, who called herself Miss Talbot, and who was said to be related to some families of distinction. Her story was very singular. At an early period of her life, having been deprived, by the villainy of a trustee, of a sum of money bequeathed her by a deceased relation of high rank, she followed the fortunes of a young naval officer, to whom she was attached, and personated a common sailor before the mast during a cruise in the North Seas. In consequence of a lovers' quarrel she quitted her ship and assumed for a time male military garb ; but her passion for the sea prevailing, she returned to her favourite element, did good service, and received a severe wound on board Earl St. Vincent's ship on the glorious 14th of February, and again bled in the cause of her country in the engagement off Camperdown, on which occasion her knee was badly shattered. Another woman of the same name

# The Merry Past

(for it does not seem likely that the two were identical) created quite a disturbance in May, 1804, at the time of a presentation of colours at Blackheath. Upon this occasion, Mary Ann Talbot, who had served several years in the Navy, and been in some engagements, under the name of John Taylor, resumed her seaman-dress and went down the river in a boat to see the review. The waterman attempted to impose on her, and on resisting his demand, he used much abusive language and challenged her to fight. The proposal was accepted, and they landed at the Isle of Dogs for the purpose. After a sharp set-to her superior dexterity prevailed, and the fellow declared himself beaten, and gladly consented to carry her to Greenwich without further payment. She, however, paid him his fare, and remitted the small wager which he risked on his battle.

The French Revolution furnished similar instances of singular acts of determination and courage in women. Discarding the delicacy of their sex, they assumed the habits of men; they worked the artillery, and charged at the head of the cavalry, while others fought on foot a-facing the Austrian horse, fearless either of the sabre or of being trodden to death. Amongst others may be instanced the two sisters who fought in the battle of Jemappes, as well as in other actions, in the capacity of aides-de-camp to General Dumouriez. These female warriors were strongly recommended by that general to the President of the National Convention, and to the Minister of War, for their heroism and bravery.

# The Merry Past

With the armies of Napoleon were many women who had followed their husbands or lovers to the wars. Many of these ladies were dressed in men's clothes, and some of them actually served as soldiers in regiments. A notable instance of this was Madame Adelaide Langenois, who in 1792, in love with a young noble who had fallen ill whilst billeted in her father's house, braving the opposition of her parents, put on man's clothes and fled with her lover to join the 9th Regiment of Hussars.

The young girl took part in the campaigns of 1793 and 1794 in the Maritime Alps ; was there wounded, and promoted to a cornetcy, while her lover still continued in the ranks.

Being informed by letters that a relation of his was a colonel of the 15th Regiment of Dragoons, young Langenois wrote to him, and was afterwards advanced to the rank of a sub-lieutenant. Either from inconstancy, or from other causes, he had hitherto neglected his promise of marrying her ; and, notwithstanding her entreaties, left her to join his new regiment, then on the frontiers of Spain. Thus deserted and wretched, in hopes of meeting with death, she rushed into the enemy's ranks in the first engagement, where, after having her horse shot under her, and receiving two cuts on her head from a sabre, she fainted away from loss of blood, and, at her recovery, found herself a prisoner in the Austrian hospital. Her sex being discovered, she was treated by the enemy with great delicacy, and, as soon as convalescent, exchanged. She then resigned her

commission as an officer of Hussars to enlist as a
volunteer in the regiment of Dragoons, then in Spain,
where Lieutenant Langenois served.

Having heard that she had been killed, he was most
agreeably surprised at her arrival; and, in gratitude
for her fidelity and for her sacrifices, not only married
her, but procured her from his relation the same
rank with himself. When the peace with Spain was
concluded, her regiment was ordered to join the Army
of Italy, where, at the battle of Lodi, she was wounded
in three places, and promoted by Bonaparte to a first
lieutenancy, at the same time that her husband, who
had greatly distinguished himself, was made a captain.

During the blockade and siege of Genoa, in the
spring of 1800, her regiment belonged to the corps
under the command of General Rochambeau, who
attempted to throw in succours to Massena, the
Governor of Genoa. In one of the daily skirmishes,
in the vicinity of that city, she again had her horse
killed under her, was wounded, and made a prisoner
by General Haddik; who, in admiration of her
courage, presented to her a splendid Hungarian horse
of his own, and released her without being exchanged.
This horse, the General of Division, Duhem, had the
insolence to put into requisition for himself, during
her illness of a fever that then raged in the French
army; and when, on her recovery, she claimed it,
he refused to restore it. She sent him a challenge;
but, instead of fighting, he ordered her under arrest
for insubordination. Such was, however, the regard
that the officers and men had for her, that in an en-

counter with the enemy next day, her horse, upon which Duhem rode, was killed by them, which terrified him so much that he demanded and obtained the command of another division.

After the peace with Austria, at Luneville, she went with her husband to Paris, and was introduced by General Murat to Bonaparte, who ordered a sabre, as a mark of honour, to be given her, which entitled her to number among newly created members of the Legion of Honour. Her commission, certificates, and numerous other papers, proved the truth of her assertion, and that she minimised, rather than exaggerated, her military exploits. That she was much beloved by the troops was evident during the whole journey. Pickets of the 15th Dragoons were quartered in every place where the diligence changed horses ; they all spoke of her courage, generosity, and humanity with the enthusiasm of sincerity and gratitude. They would have narrated many traits, illustrating what they said, but her modesty prevented them. They never ceased to exclaim, as long as she was in sight, " *Oh, la brave et bonne femme !* "

When at Lyons she went to the play, dressed in her regimentals. General Duhem was then Governor of that city. Owing her a grudge, he sent his aide-de-camp to her box, asking her how she had dared to appear at the theatre without first informing the Governor of her arrival. " Tell your General," said she, " that I am no longer in the service, and that I shall be much obliged to him to settle with me, on the other side of Pont Morant, for the horse he stole from me last year. I have here," continued she, laying her hand on her sabre, " an instrument presented me by the First Consul, which shall cut the affair short." As she spoke very loud, her conversation was heard and applauded by the pit.

Madame Langenois retained some of the stern characteristics of a soldier, even when away from her regiment. Travelling on one occasion in woman's dress in a diligence, something rather strange about her appearance caused some young men to seek to amuse themselves at her expense, upon which she declared they should soon be made to repent of their behaviour. When the diligence stopped at an inn for breakfast, she ordered her valise to be taken upstairs, and in ten minutes returned, fully accoutred in the regimentals of an officer of Dragoons, with her sabre by her side, challenging in rather severe expression the four young men to fight her, one after another. She at the same time threw some papers upon the table, saying : " Read these, you who have never been under fire, and you will see that, though a woman, I have made seven campaigns, received nine wounds, and that at present, after having left the army, I enjoy a pension of eight hundred livres (£34) bestowed on me by the First Consul, as a reward for my services."

Some of the other passengers interfering, and those who had unintentionally offended her having apologised, her good humour returned, and she continued, for the remainder of the journey, a very agreeable companion.

# The Merry Past

In a notebook of observations on life in general, the youthful Bonaparte wrote :

" A people which devotes itself to gallantry must lose that degree of energy necessary even to realise that a patriot can exist."

This opinion, however, later experience and the exploits of his by no means prudish soldiery appear to have modified, for the Emperor Napoleon was generally extremely indifferent as to the morality of the men under his command—when, for instance, the Grenadiers, who accompanied him to Elba, somewhat scandalised local susceptibilities by their attentions to the ladies of Porto Ferrajo, the Emperor refused to interfere, intimating that the admiration of French Grenadiers for the fair sex could not be repressed.

When at the time of the Revolution, France, a very volcano of patriotic frenzy, flew to arms to defend its frontiers, the worship of Venus was carried on with less hindrance or restriction than at any time in the previous history of the country.

The morality of Napoleon's soldiers was indeed of a somewhat peculiar kind ; not a few made a practice of marrying several wives.

A conspicuous example of this was Jacques Nottier, an invalid soldier of twenty-five, who had lost his right leg in the service of the Republic, as he stated on his appearance on the sixteenth Ventose, before the criminal tribunal of the Department of the Seine, accused of having married within the last eight months three different women, Maria Dabaud, Maria Ber-

# The Merry Past

trand, and Louisa Perrani, who were all present, and proved their acts of marriage, before the 2nd, 4th, and 9th municipalities of Paris. During the trial it came out that the prisoner had made it, for years, a regular practice to marry a new wife wherever he went with his regiment; and to the knowledge of his own brother he had already fourteen French wives, besides one Italian, one Swiss, and two Dutch women, who had been married to him in those countries, when in garrison or encamped there. Before he was eighteen he had been divorced, according to the laws of the Republic, from five wives, not included in the above number, by whom he had six children; and the three wives now before the tribunal all declared themselves to be in a state of pregnancy by him. Being asked by the Public Accuser if he had many children by the other women not present, though known to be married to him, he answered very coolly, " I had at least one with each woman, and I believe I have as many children alive as I can count years." He offered to give the name and place of residence of as many wives as he could *remember* to have married, and gave in the names of eleven, in eleven different departments. To gain time to enquire after these women, the Commissary of Government proposed, and the tribunal consented, to put off this trial until the sixth Germinal, on which day eight of those women, each with a child, came before the tribunal, and identified their faithless husband, who had the impudence to declare that if he had been a grand Sultan he should have kept

287

them all in his seraglio, as he loved them all with the same affection. After a trial of three hours, he was found guilty of bigamy, and condemned to be punished with a fortnight's imprisonment, and to regard Anna Varois, whom he had married nine years ago, as his only wife. To this he refused to assent, saying, that instead of punishment he deserved a reward, and that many persons had been made members of the Legion of Honour for less patriotic deeds than his, and that he intended to petition the First Consul for obtaining permission to choose his *own wife* among his *own wives*.

.        .        .        .        .

When all Europe was shaken by the storm of the Revolution the question of female emancipation began to be discussed in France ; some even advocated that woman should receive the same educational advantages as men and be accorded equal political rights.

Female education is now an accomplished fact, or rather admirable facilities exist for women to compete in learning with men, though it is not altogether certain that a vast expenditure of money, time, and effort has produced anything more than discontent amongst beings whose finest qualities would seem to be instinctive. The so-called "reformers" who favour the absolute equality of woman with man generally know little of a sex which hardly understands itself.

The men of less strenuous days, many of whom lived but for women, knew that they defy all calculation, and that as the eighteenth-century poet said, " Woman's at best a contradiction still."

# The Merry Past

Women are of necessity banded together in a species of vast trades union, the objects of which are to dominate man. Every woman tacitly belongs to this secret confederation, which has come into existence owing to the weakness of her sex, which for generations has been obliged to resort to the tactics in question. Nevertheless, though women form a sort of offensive and defensive corporation, they generally have a very poor opinion of each other, and at heart have a far greater contempt for the rest of their sex than any misogynist. This applies more particularly to good-looking women, the vast majority of whom are not at all fond of their sisters.

The main end of womankind in general is admiration, which perfectly naturally they value most when accorded to those physical attractions bestowed by nature, in order to further its own weighty ends. As a matter of fact, it is only when women reach a certain age that most of them attach much importance to the pleasures of cultivated and interesting conversation. When, however, a pretty woman is clever enough to add this powerful weapon to her armoury of charms, she becomes the most delightful and powerful being on God's earth, absolutely dominating every man she comes across. This was the secret charm possessed by beauties of the past such as Madame de Pompadour, Louise de Querouaille, Duchess of Portsmouth, and many others, who swayed the fate of nations through the monarchs whom they ruled.

As a matter of fact, women in general are probably

not as stupid as men. All women, indeed, have a certain amount of cleverness, except those who think they have; but few of them are capable of viewing the affairs of the world in general with justice and toleration. The lessons of history (if they ever take the trouble to investigate them) are meaningless to most of the sex, who, living essentially in the present, care little for what does not affect themselves or those they love. For this reason female education should rightly be directed more towards developing the admirable qualities of woman than cramming her with knowledge which, though it is easily acquired, seems to have little permanent effect.

Such education as was received by girls in old days was directed towards producing a gentle, loving, and companionable wife able to manage a household and well fulfil the high destiny of producing a new generation, and in numbers of instances it was eminently successful.

The ideal woman of the eighteenth century was essentially gentle and intensely feminine, and there are many evidences that the type in question was formerly more easily to be found in the British Islands than is the case to-day. In all probability the best description ever written of a perfect woman is that given by Pope:

> Oh! blest with temper whose unclouded ray
> Can make to-morrow cheerful as to-day;
> She who can love a sister's charms or hear
> Sighs for a daughter with unwounded ear;
> She who ne'er answers till a husband cools

# The Merry Past

Or, if she rules him, never shows she rules;
Charms by accepting, by submitting sways,
Yet has her humour most when she obeys.

The advanced woman of to-day would seem to pride herself on being possessed of qualities exactly opposed to those mentioned in these charming lines. In a number of cases she has received what is known as a "high education," which has too often warped and confused her mind.

A dispassionate survey of feminine character in the past and present must inevitably lead to the conclusion that education, which is so essential for man, effects comparatively little in the case of the majority of women, who at heart probably regard the acquirement of knowledge with indifference.

It is not unnatural that such should be the case, for nature has decreed that woman should play the principal part in what, after all, is the most serious business of the universe—the continuance of the race. The true woman realises this, and in consequence troubles little about matters for which she possesses no special aptitude. Man was made to work and woman to make men.

It is man, not woman, who has created the social condition, perhaps rather boastfully called civilisation, and had it not been for masculine invention and research, woman would have continued to live in perfect contentment under conditions which would seem inconceivable to most European races of to-day.

Many a woman who acquires learning assumes it much as she would assume a new dress—it never becomes part of herself or modifies her natural bent, for in her innermost consciousness she knows that her real mission lies in another sphere. Not unnaturally, perhaps, she feels something akin to contempt for everything unconnected with the supremely important work of producing and tending the next generation.

The Anglo-Saxon campaign in favour of absolute equality between the sexes ignores certain physical disqualifications by which women must ever be handicapped, it also deliberately flouts the lessons of biology which, as regards morality, do nothing to assist such a cause. Woman is different from rather than inferior to man, who can seldom grasp her outlook upon life, generally of a most vague and impracticable kind.

In spite of these considerations it can hardly be said with justice that woman is incapable of serious mental effort, or reasonably urged that she should not be accorded the benefits of a good education which, undoubtedly (if nothing else), renders her a more agreeable companion from a purely hedonistic point of view.

Man, probably more than woman, is the gainer by female education, which is strikingly demonstrated in the case of Orientals, who, as is well known, infinitely prefer the society of European women, when they can get it, to that of their own native wives, who, in most cases, have only their own uncultured wits upon which to rely. It should, however, be clearly understood that feminine education, contrary to the mendacious statements so industriously circulated in England, does not improve morality, which is as little affected by it as are indigestion or toothache. What education does is to render woman more skilled in carrying on intrigues without open scandal, which, considering that the great crime in Anglo-Saxon communities is to " be found out," is perhaps a useful attainment.

The passionate and almost illiterate woman of the eighteenth century was at a great disadvantage in this respect, compared with her more cultured sister of to-day, who, in a certain number of cases, realises the valuable weapon which modern culture has so obligingly placed at her disposal.

That mere learning ever contributes to moral perfection all past experience denies. In the reign of Pericles—the time of Socrates, the time of Aristophanes, the time of Phidias—when Greece was the distinguished seat of literature and fine arts, Athens was the sink of human depravity; the virtues and the liberty of Rome did not long survive the famous Augustan age; and, in the more modern periods of Leo X, Louis XIV, and our second Charles, vice and profligacy kept neck-and-neck with the growth of human learning. Nevertheless, mental cultivation is a most desirable thing. In the case of women, however, and more particularly English women, the acquisition of much knowledge seems to produce a certain amount of unreasoning discontent and a demand for rights which would in all probability be dangerous to the very existence of this country as a great power. In connection with the question of conferring political rights upon women, it may be of interest to examine the views of one of the intellectual giants of the past who certainly knew woman well.

In 1784 Mirabeau wrote to Chamfort :

" As to my personal observations, I take the unanimous testimony of the whole of antiquity, which I think has pushed the science of observation and knowledge of the human heart infinitely further than ourselves. I feel myself very well up in the subject. You know what they thought about women —of that sex which, nevertheless, has produced prodigies in its time for the reason that it is a special property of a mirror to show everything on the surface.

. . . . .

" I would beg you to read what all the moralists of antiquity have said whenever they have deigned to speak (of women), which was rare enough, and, what is much more important to remember, what the institutions created by legislators prove that they thought.

. . . . .

" O my friend, those people were more profound than we are, and yet they did not at all believe, as we pretend to do, that the well-directed education of woman could influence the happiness of society, nor that it could assure the stability of the laws, as we have so much affirmed.

" They looked upon those creatures as machines

for child-bearing and pleasure, which certainly did not arise from any lack of fire in the imagination or of refinement in their mind.

" What did it arise from, if not the firm and absolute conviction that these beings without character eluded all order—all calculation ?

" At this moment such a sane philosophy may very well be too strong meat for you, my friend, or more likely you will laugh at the idea of one of the most feeble men where woman is concerned—one who has idolised them so much, and whose mental, even more than his physical disposition, cannot do without a female companion—daring to write to you in this austere way."

Mirabeau knew women well. His knowledge of them, unlike that of many modern philosophers and reformers, was drawn from a more reliable source than blue books and statistics solemnly perused in sanctuaries of stolid respectability. Herbert Spencer and John Stuart Mill could probably have learnt more about the sex from him in a day than all their recondite researches taught them during the whole of their lives. Men of this sort who have lent their aid to fanning the flame of feminine discontent have no notion of the extravagances into which woman's excited imagination is capable of being led. Of this the suffragette agitation is a striking proof. What, for instance, can be more absurd—setting aside its futile vulgarity—than the assaults by these women on policemen who merely do their duty ? Gifted women of the past have exerted great influence on

politics by unostentatiously utilising their natural
sagacity and feminine charm. To-day a certain number of ladies, by way of showing their fitness for the
franchise, behave in a manner which by no stretch
of imagination can be called consonant with the
dignity of their sex. Mrs. Pankhurst, for instance,
boxes Inspector Jarvis's ears merely, it would seem,
on general grounds, the worthy official in question
having never publicly expressed any opinion as to
the question of giving women votes. Meaningless
" policeman-smacking " appears to be growing in
popularity with the militant suffragettes. It is, therefore, not unconsoling to the lover of fair play to
know that they too have had their " castigations."

In July of the present year a band of these ladies
descended upon the small village of Rhos, in North
Wales, which they hoped to awaken to a burning
sense of feminine wrongs. The female portion of the
population, however, were not in sympathy with
their aims, and on the arrival of the suffragettes they
were quickly surrounded by a number of brawny
matrons, in turn placed across the knees of a powerful
Amazon and, after the simple preparations usually
adopted towards erring children, heartily whipped.
The powerful smacks (which were described in a
Liverpool paper as having sounded like pistol-shots)
struck no sympathetic chords in the hearts of a laugh-
ing crowd, which would appear to have thoroughly
approved of this discipline of the scourge. When
the ordeal was over the subdued suffragettes made
a rush for the station, and left by the next train,

apparently well pleased to see the last of this district of "gallant little Wales."

At the present time the position of woman in England is probably more favourable than at any other period in the world's history, and, as a writer in the "Daily Express" recently pointed out, she is more than secured against injustice.

Woman possesses many legal advantages over men, who are compelled to perform a number of public duties, such as serving upon juries, from which she is exempt. A married woman cannot like a man be imprisoned for debt, the law having decreed that she is not personally liable, and that her creditors' only remedy is to proceed against her separate estate, if she has any.

Since the year 1882 a woman's property on her marriage remains as completely her own as if she were single, and she can enter into any legal contract with her husband, or sue him for money lent; she cannot, however, herself be convicted for stealing from her husband.

A wife can pledge her husband's credit for necessaries, while he can pledge her credit for nothing. If a woman lives with her husband, the law presumes that she has his authority to pledge his credit. If a woman is living apart from her husband, through no fault of her own, and he does not make her a proper allowance, she can pledge his credit for all necessaries, in which are included such things as are reasonably consistent with her husband's position in life. Servants in livery and a visit to a watering-

place for reasons of health have been held to be
" necessaries," for which a husband must pay. A
wife may borrow money for these purposes, and the
lender has the right of action against a husband.

The criminal law is more favourable towards
women than towards men. If a crime is committed by a married woman in the presence of her
husband, the law presumes that she acted under his
immediate coercion, and she receives no punishment.
This principle has been repeatedly applied to such
serious crimes as burglary, larceny, forgery, felonious
assaults, and a woman is allowed by the law to bring
an action against her husband for the protection of
her separate property and, under certain circumstances, may even be able to obtain an injunction to
restrain her husband from entering her house. She
may bring an action against him for trespass to her
separate property and for wrongfully interfering
with her business or libelling her in respect of it.
A husband cannot sue his wife for trespass or any
other legal wrong she may commit against him.

Favoured by law during her husband's life, this
advantageous state of affairs extends even after the
tomb has closed over him. If a husband dies in-
testate and leaves a childless widow, the whole of
his real and personal estate becomes hers, if it does
not exceed £500 in value ; and if it does exceed
that value, she is entitled, first, to £500, and then
to one-half of the residue. The administration of
her husband's estate can also be claimed by her.

When, wayworn by the many cares of a troubled

matrimonial existence, a husband dies, his wife is not liable to pay for the funeral expenses, even if she have a separate estate. When, however, a married woman dies, whether she is living with her husband or apart from him (save, of course, by her own fault), her husband is liable to give her a funeral in all respects suitable and becoming to his own position in life, and to pay the entire cost of it.

The vast majority of Englishwomen realise that they suffer under no oppression, and, quite content in the complete exercise of their mental and bodily faculties, are performing their full share of the duties of life, and doing their best to contribute towards the natural, healthy condition of society. There is, indeed, about many modern women a freedom of action, and reliance on their own powers, which denote that they have attained to the highest pitch of perfection compatible with their sex. Unfortunately their virtues open fairest in the shade and a false and undignified impression of the character and aspirations of Englishwomen is conveyed by a small but noxious minority of discontented sisters

> Who with themselves or others from their birth
> Find all their life one warfare upon earth.

With regard to the physical attractions of woman in the past as compared with to-day, it is generally agreed that she is now better-looking or, at any rate, presents a more agreeable appearance than at any time in the course of history. The beauties of other days had not the resources at their command which even a modest purse can now easily procure—they had little or ho knowledge of the laws of health and were besides hampered by many restrictions and customs which must have impaired the free development of their frame.

How the pirate eyes of the bucks of a more rakish and amorous age would have gleamed at the sight of the fine strapping craft which cruise about our streets, and how crestfallen would such buccaneers have been at the more than probable failure of any adventurous efforts to make them strike their sails ! The girls of to-day are not only prettier, better dressed, and more generally attractive than ever before, but unlike their less sophisticated sisters of the past are experts at taking care of themselves and thoroughly understand " what offers to disdain or love deny." Gone are the days when little hearts were wont to flutter at the sight of a beau—now an extinct type. Nevertheless, the bucks of the past would certainly not have failed to toast beauties the like of which their own age never saw, and following this example, the writer, as he says farewell, raises his glass, in honour of the charming and self-reliant Englishwoman of to-day.

# INDEX

# Index

# Index

WILLIAM BRENDON AND SON, LTD.
PRINTERS, PLYMOUTH

www.ingramcontent.com/pod-product-compliance
Lightning Source LLC
Chambersburg PA
CBHW030341020726
47493CB00003B/624